T0248213

PONDER

PONDER

a novel

DANIEL ROBERTS

Arcade Publishing • New York

Arcade Publishing books may be purchased in bulk at special discounts for sales promotion, corporate gifts, fund-raising, or educational purposes. Special editions can also be created to specifications. For details, contact the Special Sales Department, Arcade Publishing, 307 West 36th Street, 11th Floor, New York, NY 10018 or arcade@skyhorsepublishing.com.

Arcade Publishing® is a registered trademark of Skyhorse Publishing, Inc.®, a Delaware corporation.

Visit our website at www.arcadepub.com.

10 9 8 7 6 5 4 3 2 1

Library of Congress Cataloging-in-Publication Data is available on file.

Cover design by David Ter-Avanesyan
Cover photo by Lisa DiNoto Glassner, Thousand Circles Images

Print ISBN: 978-1-64821-069-3
Ebook ISBN: 978-1-5107-8133-7

Printed in the United States

For my daughter.

AUTHOR'S NOTE

Disney World is quite the real place. It is beloved, for good reason, by the author, his daughter, and millions of others. But the World in *Ponder* as seen through the eyes of our often-inebriated narrator, Murray "Cheese" Marks (an utter Disney World neophyte), is decidedly unreal. The Dole Whip is spiked; the Pixie dust is laced with aphrodisiacs. Mickey and Minnie should read no further; their famous ears should stay pure. Any similarities between the world of *Ponder* and that other world in central Florida are purely coincidental. Or not. To adapt Ernest Hemingway (who had Paris to my Lake Buena Vista): "If the reader has never been to Disney World, I invite them to regard this book as factual. If they have indeed been, it's clearly all made up."

CHAPTER ONE

WE MEET AT THE gloomily exotic Shun Lee bar, a black lacquer holdo-
ver from the 1980s. Above the bar, papier-mâché monkeys with red
eyes. Evil. Adorable. It depends on our moods, and how the Wayz are
going down. My best friend and I got into Cockney rhyming slang in
college. *Wayz*. We can drink for Dayz. Hard Wayz means vodka, rum,
scotch, tequila. Spirits. Soft Wayz means wine. And then there are the
Ponders, that rhyme with wander, another bit of Cockney madness.
Wander off to a city for no more, no less, than a long weekend. Friday
morning through Monday night. Philly, Vegas, Baltimore, DC, Atlantic
City, LA, even London once.

John Apple and I are both twenty-nine. Were it not for the
Ponders, I might look my age. John—I call him Johnny Boy—looks
good. Rugged, handsome. A devil when he smiles. He should sell
canned ham. He once described himself to me as more rugged than
handsome. Perhaps—or maybe he's just an inconsistent shaver, with
great metabolism, and his ass looks good in jeans. I'm Murray Marks.
The most Jewish name ever for a non-Jew. My parents bonded over
Irish Catholic guilt and Camembert cheese at a dairy called Murray's

in Greenwich Village. Murray Camembert Marks. John rarely calls me anything other than *Cheese*.

"Hey Cheese, ready for some pre-Ponder airport drinks?"

"Don't you mean *Wayz*?" I'll ask coquettishly.

"What Wayz are you drinking today?" asked Shun Lee's wizened bartender, Jack, humoring our parlance in return for John's heavy-handed gratuity.

An immigrant from Shanghai, his thirty-years-running dumpling-and-egg-roll spiel landed his youngest son at Harvard. John's alma mater.

"Harvard is the best," Jack will say. "Johnny knows this. Murray Marks doesn't know this."

John hadn't the heart to explain he'd dropped out. And I hadn't the will to defend my school. Good old sprawling, faceless Boston University, where it was always February 12.

It was nine months into 1999. The last Ponder of the millennium was coming up. This was a Hard Wayz meeting. Vodka, splash of cranberry, lime. A pink drink which, multiplied by five, packed a wallop. Last time we met at Shun Lee, I produced two pieces of paper, on which were written *Seattle* and *Vancouver*. John chose Seattle. Tonight, he'd slap the two pieces of paper on the bar, and I would choose the Ponder destination.

"You two are always traveling," said Jack. "No good. It's better to stay home."

My wife Florence might agree but she permits me these trips and allows me to miss work the Tuesday after a Ponder. I need it. We work together as attorneys, Florence and I. Real estate attorneys. Marks & Marks. I was the minority owner of our little law firm; Florence had invested her six-figure inheritance after her father's death while I was the sweat equity guy. Some say real estate law is the bottom of the barrel of the legal profession, but it appeals to our love of dotted i's and crossed t's. Although when I return from a Ponder, after Florence mans the office solo, she resents the hell out of me. But invariably lets me fuck her Monday night, wildly and well; perhaps because my dense exposure to Johnny Boy renders me more dangerous and more interesting. I think I adopt his swagger. It's hard not to.

"You know where I was, right?" asked John. "You know where I was when they disappeared into the sky."

His parents died in a plane crash when he was twelve and he rarely spoke of it.

"Your parents?" I asked.

"Yes, Cheese. Yes."

He'd been drinking before Shun Lee; I could tell.

"The amusement park, right?" I asked.

"Not a fucking amusement park. Disney World. Walt Disney World."

"Oh right, sorry."

"They flew me and Tîa down to Orlando in their jet. They only stayed over one night. Only went on one ride. Of course it had to be the Haunted Mansion. Ghosts in the waiting. Then on the flight home, they became the sky."

Tîa was his nanny. Only last year did John eulogize her amid all her Spanish-speaking friends at a Catholic church on Third Avenue. John paid for everything. Spoke from the heart (in English) about his beloved Tîa who, after the tragedy of the plane crash, dragged his ass over the finish line of life.

"I still don't know how she did it," said John. "Five days with me at Disney World. She knew for five days about what had happened but was instucted by my uncle not to tell. It was her idea, in fact: *let the boy have Mickey the Mouse before everything crumbles around him, pobre chico.*"

There was a big place in his heart for Disney. He read all the guidebooks. There were shelves of them in his bookcase. And while he hadn't returned since he was a kid, he'd become an expert. It was probably the weirdest thing about John Apple, which is saying something. You'd think he'd be obsessed with old cars, or Howard Hughes, or collect crap from NASA. Nope. Disney. He swore to himself he'd return before turning thirty: "The greatest homecoming of my life."

"When did Tîa eventually tell you about your folks?" I asked.

"You know what? I don't remember."

"Drinks too much," said Jack. "Johnny Boy drinks too much and it hurts his memory. You need a good memory in this life. Murray Marks has a good memory but he eats too much and drinks too much."

True. I may be balding, round-faced, and pear-shaped, but I have a damn good recall system and also green eyes. Not hazel. Not blue gray, but truly green eyes. Like jade. It's my best feature, and even Johnny Boy is jealous. I'm also well-endowed, and he's jealous of that too. Florence was my prom date, and I've only ever been with her.

"I love Florence," John had said. "But with your dick, and those eyes, stepping out just once—"

"No."

*

"Murray Marks never has vegetable dumplings, only pork. No good."

Jack doesn't like me. I should mention that Florence, my wife, is Chinese. That did not go over well.

"Why?" Jack asked after meeting her many, many years before. "So many round eyes for you," he snickered while Florence was in the ladies' room.

I'm not sure if it was due to his cultural disdain for females, or because I got one of his, or because of Florence's demeanor. Conservative to the point of being brittle. A quality I happen to respect. She's reliable, elegant, skinny. What's not to like? I think John brings something out in her. A boozy inner life.

"What electric dimples," Florence once drunkenly admitted, but I wasn't jealous. He brings out something in me too.

"You ever been to Disney, Jack?" asked John.

"Of course not."

Good for Jack. A principled if miserable man who misappraises vegetable dumplings.

"Don't you wish you could remember when you first heard about the plane crash?" I asked.

"No, not really. Everything after that seminal Disney trip was a blur. Hey, Jack, another drink, please."

"Don't you mean Wayz?" I asked.

"Your little private language will get you in trouble, Cheese."

"Our little private language, Johnny Boy. *Our* language."

"What the hell are you sniffing?" he asked me.

I have a rather keen sense of smell and can appear canine when, for instance: "Someone in the dining room is wearing lavender, like the lavender that grows near the Hotel Bel-Air. Where, on vacation, Florence got drunk and flirted with a pretty young waitress. It was exhilarating, Johnny Boy."

"You guys should have, you know, had an experience with the pretty young waitress. Hey Jack, make it a double. No, in honor of what could have been, a trio!"

Is John Apple an alcoholic? Probably. Well, yes. But he goes on the wagon many times a year. Our Cockney rhyming slang tried to relegate wagon to "being angry as a dragon" but Florence quashed that one.

"Hell is someone else's inside jokes," she'd warned.

Fair enough. So, no dragoning, just wagoning. I'm not *such* a huge drinker, except leading up to a Ponder, then during the trip, and a ramping down process for a week after.

Actually, I do have about five to ten bottles of wine a week. Although my real poison is rich food. Salt and butter. Were Florence and I to have a child, which we won't, thank goodness, we'd name it Alfredo. Thus, the 263 pounds on my six-foot frame. I'm basically fat, but I know how to wear a suit and keep it all together. Florence doesn't mind. Or she says she doesn't. But I've seen her sneak a peek at John's ass, which as I mentioned looks good in his perennially worn Levi's. He buys a new old pair every year from some used clothing store in Paris. Thirty-two-inch waist. I'm a forty-six. Damn him.

On our trips I wear my slacks and blazer, no tie. John wears his jeans, and usually a black turtleneck or black tee. His uniform of rebellion. Oh, and these yellow suede shoes from Italy. I own half a dozen black Florsheim loafers. Always shiny. Tassels. And recently I started wearing glasses at work, but never on a Ponder. One night, Florence, buzzed after sharing a bottle of wine, asked me to keep them on during sex. Once in a while she can really surprise you.

*

"I do remember Tìa and me crying as the plane took off from Orlando," said John, "but of course that was just because we hated to go back home. I think leaving Disney World is the saddest fucking thing that can happen to a human being."

"Johnny Boy, he curses too much when he drinks the hard drinks," said Jack.

"Sorry, Jack," said John.

The Shun Lee bar was rarely populated with anyone but us. Too dim for civilian Wayzers. The primates with the glowing red eyes. The intolerant bartender. But tonight, two tourists wandered in with their laminated Streetwise maps of New York City. At least they were Streetwise maps—our map of choice on Ponders.

"Can't believe we're getting tourist-balled tonight," I said.

Balled. Another neologism born of Ponders past. It was in Austin while John flirted with a saucy brunette after dinner that I dreamily placed a ball of butter in his espresso.

"Why the hell did you just butter ball my coffee?" he'd asked.

I loved it. *Ball.* What fun! And it was born. Even Florence once said, "Murray, do not inside-joke-ball our place of work."

That saucy Texas brunette ended up in his Four Seasons bed. Soulless sex, he'd reported. One-night Ponder stands (and there were many, probably more than he let on) were never what he was after: "Seeing a stranger's lipstick stain on a hotel pillow in the Harveyed a.m. is not for the faint of heart," he'd said. "People can slug you with what they leave behind."

Harveyed. Nothing to do with Harvard. Instead, Harvey Hanginstein. Rhymes with Frankenstein. God forgive us our little language. There was an actual Harvey named Harvey Harstein who frequented my parents' bookstore. He appeared perpetually hungover, although we didn't really know if he ever actually drank. Regardless, the man looked like an even more tattered version of that famous sepia image of James Joyce that was hung in the bookstore: fedora, wire-rim Coke-bottle glasses, stubby little gray moustache and goatee. According to us, he was the embodiment of hangovers; Harvey, our patron saint in a wrinkly old Burberry trench coat that smelled of pre-war cigars. The day John explained to Harvey his pet moniker: "Hanginstein?" asked Harvey, thickly Yiddish.

"Yes," said John. "And bartenders we call Takensteins, as they take our money and often our dignity."

"Are you anti-Semitic?" asked Harvey. "An awful lot of Steins."

"Of course not. Quite the contrary. I believe that the greatest contributions God has made to life as we know it are, in this order, the Jewish people and non-procreative sex. I might convert, if you'll have me."

We aren't sure what happened to the old man but he lives on in us, that's for certain. On Ponders, his name is spoken every damn morning. But our inside jokes should remain in the family of us two lest we anger-ball the generally non-Harveyed public. All true best friends have a secret language of one type or another. They are wise to keep it close to their chest. Safer that way. At least that's John's advice.

"No one likes to feel like an outsider."

*

Before each and every Ponder, John Apple would forecast finding the love of his life. You'd think he would have her by now. Ten years and seventeen Ponders. I once met a fascinating girl. I, Cheese, in San Francisco, got bought a drink by a realtor with a glorious smile. And a soul. I guess she liked green eyes. Or our shared experience about the neat stacks of checks that pass hands at a closing. Broker's fees, mansion tax, mortgage docs, title search, transfer documents, purchase agreement. My realtor friend understood the artfulness of a closing. The signatures, so many signatures; at these closings I always use Parker pens that I gift to my clients just before the keys are handed over. And then there are all the thick dossiers, once executed, folded shut. I love that sound; it sounds complete. A passport opened, stamped, then closed. John didn't have fun on that night of escrow talk. *He* was the romantic hero of these trips, and I was, happily mind you, the interlocutor, the witness. But witness to exactly what? Three nights and four days of abandon.

"I could really live here. I might live here. This. *This* could be my home," he'd say of every city, then return home empty-handed and empty-hearted.

Could it be that we are too self-sufficient, or too intense, or too drunk? Or ate too many goddamn cheese fries the night before, before passing out at 2:00 a.m. in our respective hotel rooms.

"Girls like healthy men," I'd told him. "And these road trips are admirably toxic, but toxic nonetheless, Johnny Boy. Most women want nothing to do with a Ponder-afflicted man."

"You'll see," he'll say. "One of these days. I can feel it. It will come to pass. She will come to pass."

A kid who loses his mother so early; I guess he's always searching for the womb. Me? I'm comfortable just about everywhere. John says it's my roly-poly form that positively melts into every seat in the world. Although, like John, I might be most at home during our trips. Our wanders, I mean Ponders. Inside our friendship, at a dark bar, in an alien city. Begging time that it should never end.

John pays for the Ponders. We stay at the local Four Seasons. Fly business class. John's parents were wealthy and he inherited it all then invested it all, presciently and perfectly. As a junior at Harvard, he abandoned schooling for private investment. His expertise was tech; he'd worked at the Byte, Harvard's computer repair shop, and had even been recruited by Apple Computer to come out west. Despite his ridiculous fortune, the things money could buy meant little to him. Sure, he owns a loft in Soho, but it has so little furniture, and unpacked suitcases from his move five years ago. It has a dart board (is it a sign of schizophrenia to play darts against yourself?) and a leather chair that belonged to Hemingway's Paris, literally. And a bed. He sits in that chair, reads, divines, then goes to the gym. Then he's at his local, holding court from four 'til he gets laid.

"The tourists just ordered vegetable lo mein, smart," said Jack. "How is Kathy, Johnny Boy? You never should have left her." He wagged his finger.

John had married early and awfully to a five-foot-tall bottle blonde. The wispy-voiced gold-digger hawked her engagement ring for a fake one in order to afford a black sable coat that looked absurd on her diminutive if busty person. Still, Jack thought the world of her ersatz self and was devastated when John and I came to Shun Lee hours after the dissolution was final. "Johnny Boy just divorced Marilyn Monroe. Stupid." I think Jack cried that day.

"As far as I know Kathy's fine, Jack," said John. "Thanks for asking."

Now he was hunched over, on his BlackBerry, typing maniacally quickly. He was an early adopter of the thing, and got one for Florence and me as well, specifically for our Ponders. Communication was key. Where to meet. What to order if one of us was running late, which Wayz to order. We'd decided that the ubiquitous Nokia cellphone was less elegant than the BlackBerry's huge silent screen. Besides, pay phone Wayz still had a big place in our hearts.

"Those typing machines are the devil," said Jack. "They will take over your ghost."

"They're the future," said John.

"Then future will be empty. There will be no ghosts in the future."

*

John Apple can't cry. He didn't cry when he received the news that his parents died in the plane crash and he can't remember the last time he cried since before that day. The only thing he'd said that made him cry was, when he was a child, leaving freaking Disney World.

"After that bout of postpartum despression, I have not shed a single tear," he'd said.

"Girls don't like that. They can sniff out that failure to squirt a few," I'd said. "Perhaps some feminine sixth sense confuses it with not being able to ejaculate."

"Well, one day, and I feel like it's coming soon, a girl will be drawn to my emotional drought. She'll be beautiful, and cry for us both, down her long dark lashes."

He had long lashes too. I watched them as he blinked at the dangling Shun Lee monkeys above.

"You ever been in love, Jack?" he asked.

"Ha!" scoffed Jack.

I liked that Jack had no time for love. Disgruntled pragmatism is the only true religion. Were it not for Florence I would join his cult.

"You know, I've never been to Disney," I said.

Florence and I did not have any children. By design. We've kicked around the idea of rescuing a greyhound but decided that we're both too selfish to commit to the care of another animal, aside from one another.

"If there were better restaurants and bars at Disney, I'd consider taking Florence for a day or something."

"You don't know what you're talking about," said John. "There are actually some incredibly inventive themed bars. You just have to invest in the concepts, drink steadily. The Adventurers Club might be the most lusciously anachronistic bar in the world."

"How do you know?"

"Research. There are books just about the Adventurers Club and its past. The Imagineers are fucking gods."

"Always too much cursing with the hard drinks," said Jack.

"The hard *Wayz*," I corrected.

"Yeah, yeah, Murray Marks," said Jack. "Why do you order twenty-four dumplings? Too much."

"I bring Florence leftovers."

"Chinese girls know enough not to eat cold dumplings."

Life is unbearable by and by, two dozen dumplings and then you die. Soon he'll bring out the tray of pork dumplings. I'll attack while John goes on about the adventure bar. He sure can talk, and I sure can eat Jack's dumplings. Symbiosis.

"So, where the hell are we going this year?" I asked.

John looked up from his BlackBerry, smiled his radiant devil smile. Look at all those white teeth. Perfection. And with that, slammed down a single piece of paper. It made Jack jump.

"Just one?" I asked.

"No choice this year, my friend. Sorry about that."

He kept on beaming; it was a little unnerving.

"Go ahead," he said. "Wait: two more hard ones, Jack."

"A Harvard man should have better manners," said Jack.

"Please," said John.

"Even Murray Marks has better manners."

John pushed the scrap of paper over to me.

"Every great adventure begins at a dark Chinese bar under papery monkeys with red eyes," said John. "Given the truly evil glow of those eyes, you'd think we'd have gotten into some serious trouble during a Ponder. I believe that life has symbols. They're everywhere. Some of them evil."

"Should I flip it over?" I asked.

"Wait. Just wait a second. I want to remember this moment. Okay, go."

There was a circle, and atop, on either side, two small circles.

"What is this?"

"Let me see?" said Jack. "It's just circles. Makes no sense. I'll go get the dumplings. A Harvard man should not draw like a child."

"What does it mean?" I asked, turning it upside down, sideways. "Are they a planet and its moons? Space exploration?"

"Those three circles are the universal symbol for Mickey Mouse. We are going to Walt Disney World, and this time, our lives will change."

"You're crazy," I said.

"One day you'll look at that piece of paper, and it will all come flooding back. Like Proust and his croissant."

"*Madeleine*," I said. "So we're going to go on rides and stuff?"

My parents owned a bookstore in Cambridge called When I Die, after the Emily Dickinson poem. It's where I met John, who would loiter away the afternoons on the couch across from the cash register reading and napping. My folks adored John, took him in, cooked for him. My mom would clean his clothes. Who doesn't like a handsome orphan?

Johnny Boy slapped five twenties on the bar.

"Did you know that my father almost transformed himself into an actual Paladin just before he died?"

"Huh?"

"He would have been the first modern man to do so since the Middle Ages and he almost made it, poor bastard, white suit and all. He had an idea about a new type of man. A true ascetic. Girls love true ascetics. Who fight for causes. Like love. Fight for what you love, Cheese."

He kissed me on the mouth, which he'd only done once before, after my wedding, then left. What the hell is a Paladin? And why are there judgmental monkeys at a Chinese bar that is straight out of a nascent MTV video in which some mulleted band troubadours its way ironically, replacing drum sticks with chopsticks? But I love Shun Lee and its modernistic dimness. They dip their fortune cookies in choclate. An excess that renders the paper message inside moot.

"Where's Johnny Boy?" asked Jack.

"He left."

"What do the circles mean?"

"Disney World."

"A very bad place," said Jack. "A very dangerous place."

I looked up at the monkeys, who were looking down at me.

CHAPTER TWO

"So, WHAT DID YOU two decide?" asked Florence.

"Nothing yet," I lied. I was afraid to tell her. Two grown men at Disney World would not suit her sense of order, human strength, dignity. *The strength of the strong.* She had it written in florid Chinese calligraphy, a sign on the lintel.

"I see," she said, and mindlessly poked a leftover dumpling. "Well, let me know as soon as you can, so I can plan a trip with Mama. God forbid we end up in the same city."

Her mother was her best friend and travel companion. While John and I ate and drank and yapped our way through Santa Fe or Austin, they would do something of cultural value. Or a wellness trip. Or a cooking retreat. And once, a week-long intensive about bird-watching. So while our cells suffered a slow—or sometimes speedy—death from vodka and smoked brisket, my wife's brain cells flourished. She wasn't a snob about it, though. Although she once scolded me: "You're almost thirty. You're too old to be vomiting Stolichnaya, on a Sunday night, in a five-hundred-dollar hotel room in Atlanta. John doesn't vomit, does he?"

"His tolerance is legendary," I'd said. "He has all year to work on it."

It's tricky working with one's wife. Our work life is separate from our weekend life. The former is pretty much mannered and taciturn. We are only really married on the weekends, or on vacations. In our four-person office, it's all business. We are the sort of couple who shower before going to bed. Have breakfast in silence while reading the paper. Walk to work without holding hands. Get to work before the secretary and our mortgage guy. Turn on the lights. Turn on the computers. Press *play* on the answering machine. That's her job, actually. It sounds lonely, or cold, but it's just really . . . orderly. And it makes the work weeks go quickly. We're good at what we do. It's a niche gig, residential real estate attorneys, with small profit margins and no room for error. We probably average two to four closings every week. Two to four times we see keys changing hands. First-time buyers are the best. And Florence permits us to ask them out for a Wayz to celebrate. She has a heart after all, my Florence. Tall and willowy China doll who irons her pants every night. And sometimes irons mine. I have to ask her one day about her decision process. About what compels her to also iron my pants, and why on some nights she just doesn't. Or maybe best left alone? Marriages should have some secrets.

"I think Mama and I are going to go to Philadelphia," said Florence. "Do you think that's where you'll have your road trip?"

"Where we'll have our *Ponder*."

"There's an antiques show in Philly, but Mama has a cold. First of her life."

"Goddamn Mama."

"Be respectful."

We earn a good salary. Travel well. Eat well. Shop well. But we don't save. Nothing. We spend what we make. You'd think it would irk Florence, but it doesn't. She's oddly proud of our seat-of-the-pants *bon vivantism*.

"It's courageous," she'd said. Her father was a radiologist. And her mother a high school biology teacher at a private school for girls. Both were born in China. Mr. Fu died of a heart attack nine years ago. Rail-thin Mr. Fu. What a joyless man. I think his heart got sick of having no fun. And Mama? Strict. Not a big fan of her son-in-law. I think she once said in Cantonese: "I don't like fat people. They are lazy."

But that Mama sure can cook. She cooks with great love and spirit. Without cooking, she might have suffered her husband's fate. I love her for her cooking. Truly. Sitting at the kitchen table watching her prepare a six-course feast? Pure theater.

Dancing woks. Dancing knives. The lacquer of it all. Nothing makes me hungrier. And watching Florence play obedient sous chef? Nothing makes me hotter. After Mama is done cleaning up, we have sex in the kitchen. But it requires such patience. For Mama does not believe in dishwashers but does believe that the chef should do all the dishes. Midnight, one o'clock. Sometimes later. Between the three of us, we'll go through four bottles of wine. Laugh. Well, Florence and I laugh.

"You know who I ran into outside her gym?" asked Florence. "Kathy."

"Kathy who?"

"Kathy Apple, silly."

"Why were you outside her fancy gym? And why the hell is she keeping his last name?"

"Seeing her reminded me of something that happened a long time ago, that I promised myself I'd tell you before the year 2000."

With this, she took my hands in hers. Not good.

"What?" I wanted to liberate my hands. The hand trap preceded bad news, most recently last spring: "*Mama needs to live with us, just for the summer.*"

"Do you remember, Kathy and I rented a home upstate when you and John went to Baltimore that Memorial Day weekend when they were starting to have trouble?"

So much Old Bay seasoning. John fell in love with a bartender at a crab place. Purple-haired, nose ring. Tough girl. We had crab every meal. While I developed a new personal aversion to Old Bay seasoning, he wrote her love notes. She wrote back: *I have a boyfriend.*

He found a jewelry store and bought her a diamond-encrusted Maryland-blue-crab ring. The store's most treasured piece. Blue sapphires for claws. They spent the night at the restaurant after closing, screwing on the sawdust floor. After all that, it turned out that she literally had crabs.

"I remember Baltimore," I said. "I thought you hated Kathy? I thought everyone did?"

"No, only you truly loathed her. Anyway, Murray, listen, she and I thought we'd grow really close over the years, because you and John were so close and when their marriage seemed destined to fail, well, we sort of decided to, well, experiment by having a one-time-only tryst."

She released my hands, sat back, slowly, regally, eyes closed; from this pose I inferred that the tryst had been good.

"What the fuck is a tryst? I mean, you did things? Sexually?"

"It was just a tryst. No more and no less. Aside from David Pang I've only ever been with you, and as you know David turned out to be gay. I just wanted this one experience, Murray."

"With *her*?"

"She was lovely."

"Not to John. Wait—"

"It was one night. Three years ago. Can you forgive me?"

"Make me a hard Wayz."

"Coming right up."

Kathy did have an amazing chest. I suppose that some part of me was turned on and the other part disgusted. Two sides of the same coin, and I imagined that coin flipping in slow motion over a bed where my wife's face was in between that busty little bitch's legs.

"Does John know?"

"I think she told him. After they divorced, but I'm not sure."

"He would have told me."

Wouldn't he have?

She'd made herself a soft Wayz: "Because it was a girl, and an experiment, I compartmentalized it as occurring outside of my life."

She'd always been more sexual than I. Most people think she's on the bloodless side, but she really isn't. I was a little proud of her.

"Whose idea was it, yours or Kathy's?"

"Mine, in fact."

Why did that make it a little better?

"Did you, like, seduce her?"

"It was a tryst."

I wanted to know everything about it. I wanted to take notes. See pictures? But my avid interest might come across as acceptance of her infidelity, and then she'd do it again. The flesh is weak. Even noble Chinese flesh. She can trace her lineage back to the Tang dynasty. Tang. I wondered what Kathy tasted like. Being aroused while being revulsed is hard on the human spirit.

"Jesus, Florence, repeating 'it was a tryst' isn't some antiseptic. You fucked someone else."

"Yes."

"Was she good?"

"Um—"

"I don't want to know."

It was hard to look at her mouth, her hands. Women are stronger than men. Here I am in my own kitchen staring down at my pink drink, unable to look at my wife. She's showered over one thousand times since the tryst. We've had sex hundreds of times since. Can't it be washed away?

"Why did you feel the need to tell me?"

"I didn't want to keep any secrets with the new millennium coming, and I kind of . . . thought it would excite you."

Woman are smarter than men.

"Disney World."

"What?"

"Our next Ponder is to Disney fucking World. Where there are beautiful princesses who work at a bar called the Adventure Club, or something, and have trysts with the guests. Would that turn *you* on?"

She giggled. "Oh, Murray."

She knew I'd never cheat on her. What an advantage.

"Never bring this up again, Florence."

"If you say so."

I imagined a safe time a year, maybe two years from now, when we'd be drunk in bed, and I'd ask for details.

"Are you really going to Disney? If so, I think that's cute."

My surprising wife.

"Make me another hard Wayz."

I figured I'd get well-buzzed and enjoy a one-night exemption from saying please and thank you.

"I love you, Murray."

I love you too, you crazy high-cheek-boned, bisexual, mother—

Her long strong fingers were on either shoulder. Is there anything better than a hard Wayz with a massage?

"I forgive you," I said, and the massage ended.

*

John bought me both the *1999 Official Guide to Walt Disney World* and the more critical and irreverent *1999 Unofficial Guide to Walt Disney World*. He owned every single one of the books dating back to his first trip in 1981, and had all but memorized them, not to mention scores of supporting materials. Titles like *The Vault of Walt, The Monorail Blues, Drinking Your Way Around EPCOT*. You'd think he would have returned but he was a staunch believer in timing.

"It had to be perfect," he'd said. "Momentous. I knew it would have to be before I turned thirty. During this, the last year of the millennium. At the most magical place on earth. *That* is the homecoming I was after. Numbers matter, Cheese. Next year we're thirty. It's 2000 AD. Time to grow up, but not tonight and certainly not this long Ponder weekend."

We met at Shun Lee on a November night a week before Thanksgiving. It was a Thursday night, Ponder Eve, and the bar was full, so we loitered by the service area where Jack sneered and sweated.

"1999 is the year of the rabbit," said Jack. "A very bad sign. Horny people."

"To the last Ponder of the millennium," said John.

We usually never met up the day before the trip, but he wanted to quiz me about Disney. Make certain I was all in. I wasn't. I didn't know how we would manipulate these lands; how we would turn it all into a *real* place. The Kingdom was dry. No Wayz. A huge problem. And aside from the Adventurers place, and a few hotel bars; well, from where would the Ponder magic derive? And how the hell would we dress?

"I'm not going to wear shorts," I told him.

"Your thighs will get all chafed from those oppressively ironed trousers," said John. "Okay, concentrate: what was the only ride where the passenger experiences death?"

"Um, the Haunted House."

"One, it's the Haunted *Mansion*, and two, the correct answer is Mr. Toad's Wild Ride. Tîa and I rode it. She needed to clutch her rosary beads during the scene where Mr. Toad runs us into an oncoming train. Then we see the devil; we're in hell."

Hell? Indeed. I must admit I liked that many of the rides were dimly lit. Air-conditioned for people of my size. Although John had assured me that I'd be one of the more fit guests by virtue of the fact that I did not require an obese person's electric wheelchair.

"Disney Biggunz are fascinating," he'd said. He called the morbidly obese *Biggunz*. Never mocking them; purely out of respect for their unapologetic lifestyle. John was chubby as a child and his mother was cruel about it. Now he was a staunch advocate for larger people, like me. Should he ever see someone tease or bully a Biggunz, God knows he'd have the lout whacked.

"They eat these huge turkey legs that they sell in Adventureland. Rumor has it they are really made of ostrich and contain 5,000 calories.

Tia and I couldn't finish one. Not even close. She always spoke so highly about that tremendous piece of poultry. Its smokiness and succulence. Its fat."

"What the hell are we going to do about Wayz?" I asked.

"My god."

"What?"

"You have no idea: the deeply cloaked network of bars and clubs. Behind the facades are worlds. Rooms. Secrets that so few know about. But I do."

He had that rare look in his dark eyes. Rare, because he wasn't smiling his goofy dimpled smile. He was staring through me, into the bowels of Shun Lee. Accepting a fate.

"You mean like a crew bar or something?"

"In Disney World, the employees are referred to as 'cast members.' Over the years they've created a world behind the World. Veritable dungeons dedicated to Wayz. To sex. To love. To real adventure."

"You're drunk."

Jack was eavesdropping. He was polishing the same wineglass over and over.

"Adventure is not for you, Johnny Boy. And definitely not for Murray Marks," said Jack.

"Sorry, Jack," said John. "But we are being called by Walt himself. What a world-class drinker that man was."

"Hang up the phone on Walt," said Jack. "You want adventure? Meet an American girl at a Chinese bar."

"Hey, what did Kathy think of Florence?" I asked.

"My Kathy?"

"Yeah, of course."

"Why?"

Shit, he knows. Maybe.

"Just never understood their relationship."

Jack arrived with my plate of dumplings. "Miss Apple was very pretty. Big mistake to leave her, John."

It was the best thing he ever did. Just when she was skipping her birth control pills, or so I surmised after snooping around the bathroom trash. Women, I learned, can buy birth control packs composed entirely of sugar pills. There's a code word for them at certain dubious pharmacies downtown: *I'll take the Virginia Woolfs.* No idea why; I'll have to ask my bookstore parents about the reference.

"Kathy was a rounding error," said John. "Plus, she hated Disney World."

I transitively fucked your ex-wife, I told myself. Maybe on some weird ride at Disney, drunk, I'll tell him about the lesbian tryst. Actually, better to hoard the secret and presume he doesn't know.

"Florence runs into her outside that stupid gym."

"Reebok is the best in the city," said John.

"It doesn't even have a bar."

"Exercise is very important, Murray Marks," said Jack. "You should run one mile for each dumpling."

Fuck off, Jack. I actually respected the little shriveled man, and his hands like a baby eagle's talons. Works every day of the week. All ninety stringy pounds of him.

"What time is the car picking me up tomorrow morning?" I asked.

The tradition was that a shiny black limousine would collect me; in the back, Johnny Boy with a bottle of champagne and a pound of fruit slices. The Ponder officially began when he'd slice open the bubbly with a miniature sword. It was something he practiced, mastered in fact.

"Six-thirty a.m., on the dot," said John. With that he patted my shoulder, gave Jack the five twenty-dollar bills, and left. Neither of us wanted to be hungover for that ride to JFK. Although I decided to get a last Wayz or two. Being a little hungover pre-Disney made great sense.

My BlackBerry buzzed: *Don't have a last Wayz. You'll be hungover which will suck.*

"Let me have one more, Jack, Harvey Hanginstein be damned."

"Yeah, yeah, yeah."

"You ever take your kids to Disney, Jack?"

"No, no, no, never." He wagged his finger at me.

"I'll get you in the spirit, Jack. I'll bring you back a souvenir."

"Bring back Johnny."

What a Takenstein, that Jack. Whoops, I mean *bartender*, that Jack. Sometimes I think the Chinese are just stronger than us. I harbor a secret premonition that one day they'll enslave us. That they are waiting very patiently for their moment. Some part of me wants them to do it. Just get it over with. At least I'll lose weight and become stoical. Jack had it in his heart to place me in a miraculously wide high chair near his drink prep world so that I needn't stand. Cheese: a big old baby. Tonight, baby Cheese will study a truly stoical man. Screw it, I'll become like Jack. Easy to plan for a stoical life when there's all the vodka in the world in front of you and an egg roll on the way.

CHAPTER THREE

THE AIRPORT MAMA. SOULFUL, sweet Airport Mama, the patron saint of our Ponders. She presides over Newark airport's Terrace Grille, a simulation of al fresco dining in Terminal C. The simulation: wallpaper depicting green vines. Grease-crippled wallpaper, splattered from a single hotdog grill that's always rolling. In the cash register drawer, she keeps a pack of tarot cards that John gave her years ago. They were designed by Salvador Dali, crazy looking things. Little does the Airport Mama know that they are the originals. Now probably worth at least $10K a card. Johnny Boy won them at auction, out-bidding Bob Dylan. Dylan was pissed. Mumbled something about putting a curse on him.

"Oh boy," said the Airport Mama. "And here they come."

Lest you think us racist Pondering white dicks, the Airport Mama is a middle-aged black woman who *demanded* we call her Airport Mama. *The* Airport Mama. An avocational bartender, Fridays through Mondays, she also works as a private nurse for an old rich dude. Plus she served in the army. Plus she thinks that we're harmless, if ridiculous, one of which rings true.

The ride to the airport had been standard, save for John and his sword play. While beheading the bottle of Veuve Clicquot he some-how cut his thumb. The sight of his blood on a yellow fruit slice? Glorious. And the Airport Mama was already out with her first aid kit.

"What did you do to your hand?" asked the Airport Mama.

"I had a very rare mishap with the saber."

"I told you this would happen eventually, John."

"Yes, but it will mean I'll pick a most auspicious tarot card," he said, not grimacing despite the spray of antiseptic. Brave people shouldn't be so conscious of their bravery. It spoils it.

We'd forgo the luxury of the United Club for the Airport Mama; in fact, John would give her our day passes, and in turn she'd gift them to stressed-out looking families. A saint, this Airport Mama.

After the limousine's champagne Wayz, we'd counter with screw-drivers and of course the Airport Mama's famous hot dogs. Dogs so depravedly neglected that they formed a gourmet crust composed of salt, fat, the Airport Mama's CO_2, and time. These were perfectly aged pork products. We theorized that some of them had been turning on the griddle since 1983. Hot dogs and hard Wayz never go bad, but their patrons? I suppose that at Newark's Terrace Grille the march of time dead on to middle age is halted, for we bask in the jaundiced yellow lighting of the Grille and are returned to our early twenties, where hangovers and guilt do not invade the mornings.

"You got the Prince of Cups," said the Airport Mama to John.

"Amazing," said John.

There was an actual resemblance. The Prince's pallor, his elegant hand splayed over a golden chalice; the controlled blankness of his gaze, as if he'd seen his own ghost and could care less. The mother of all Wayz cards. I got something that looked like the Grim Reaper. We would use our cards as coasters for our final screwdriver, then place them safely in our wallets for the duration of the Ponder; when we landed, they'd be returned to the Airport Mama, and into her cash reg-ister they'd go until next time.

"She's awesome," said John.

"She really is."

Invariably, we'd leave her bar feeling so damn optimistic about the world and its inhabitants. It was a perfect relationship. Thirty-five minutes, once every nine months. Buzzed, the whole trip in front of us. A woman twice our age with twenty-something-year-old kids of her own, laughing at us, with us. Mostly at us.

"I love human beings," said John.

"You think she ever speaks about us to her kids?"

"No," said John. "The Airport Mama would want to protect her sons from us monsters. They should never know that there are people like us, who are their age, who Ponder the country the way we do, marauding innocent cities."

*

After the Airport Mama we would part ways, so to speak. John went to a mysterious venue: Shoeshine? Airport chapel? The warm suffocation of the smoker's glass cube? Whatever it was, he'd come back smelling of shoe polish, cigarettes, and consecrated pews.

"Where the hell do you go?" I'd ask.

"You wouldn't understand."

For John, places had secrets that were revealed only to him. Panels in libraries that accessed catacombs. Trap doors through which one would fall into the arms of a 1930s flapper.

"Where'd you get those beads?" I'll ask. "Just tell me, for fuck's sake!"

I, however, was utterly upfront about the food court. Where I would buy forty-eight chicken wings with hot sauce and a half dozen cinnamon buns. The chicken wings were collateral damage for the hot sauce, which I used as a sort of gravy for the buns. My breakfast and lunch on our flight out. The chicken would be deposited with the Airport Mama, who would turn them into a blood-slaking soup we'd retrieve on our way back, post-Ponder, and consume once home. It most probably saved our lives. God's broth.

Sin Chick.

Cinnamon buns with hot wing sauce.

We brought my hot-sweet concept to the Jacob Javits Convention Center for a specialty food show. A convention reviewer called it "white trash fusion" and said that he "wouldn't feed Sin Chick to a dead squirrel." Ah, well, a short-haired white Caribbean girl loved it, and loved Johnny Boy, too. I guess there's something about a man in an apron. They dated for ten days. She came from wealth and brought the concept back home to her native Curaçao, where it was a hit. We discussed visiting her and the world's only Sin Chick stand but realized the trip would devolve into a sticky mess; John had confessed that the girl believed that the hot sauce–slathered buns were an aphrodisiac and incorporated them into their lovemaking.

"Here's your chicken," I said to the Airport Mama.

"You boys really going to Disney?"

"Afraid so."

"Pick me up a doll or something for the grandchild."

"You're a grandmother? Wow."

Both only children, John and I were bloodline killers. Bloodline killers in their latest twenties going to Disney World to get wasted with Donald. The duck.

"Get him something with Goofy on it," she said.

"Goofy?"

"He's the foolish dog, Murray."

"Am I the only person in America who doesn't know this stuff?"

"Probably, but don't worry, Cheese, John will set you straight. And watch that cut on his hand. You don't want to get an infection in the Haunted Mansion. Worse case, pour vodka on it. I'm sure you boys will be carrying all sorts of flasks."

"I fucking hope so, Airport Mama."

"Language."

"Oh. I'm sorry."

"See you in three days for your soup," said the world-weary Airport Mama who, despite our infrequent interactions, had the world-class sensitivity to remember our post-Ponder salvation.

"I bleeping hope I'll see you," I said to the good woman.

*

Sinéad O'Connor sang "you used to hold my hand when the plane took off." On John Apple's trip home from Disney World, his parents somewhere under the Atlantic Ocean, Tîa clutched the boy's hand. And ever since, he needed it held. By me. We would get some looks. Snickering gray-haired ladies who wore pearls in business class. Most often the stewardess would tilt her head, lovingly smile.

"So cute," one of them had said. John got her phone number, but never called. He didn't want to get to know one romantically. His mother had been a stewardess. It was how she met his father.

"I think that arrangement is cursed," he'd said.

Today we had our most favorite United flight attendant, named Ann, with whom we'd had the great fortune of flying with four, now five times. We called her the Ann Abler, as she was expert at filling our glasses, encouraging the slow IV drip of our onboard Wayz consumption. She'd kneel in the aisle between us and ask us what was in store this time. She'd listen to John's tarot card augury and facilitate my hot sauced cinnamon buns. Ann was in her late thirties, we thought, and clearly had a place in her heart for Wayzers. Such dark blue eyes they looked black in almost every light. And a lightning bolt of gray bisecting her black mane. She was Greek, we surmised. Thick hair. Abundant nose. Ann flirted with me the same as she did John, and my heart welled with gratitude. "How are you this morning, Mr. Marks?"

"Please, Ann, call me Murray."

"Oh, Mr. Marks."

"Hahahahaha," I'd laugh.

"Hahahahaha," she'd laugh.

Then she'd touch my knee and retrieve my preflight mimosa. And of course a stack of Wash'n Dries for my chicken wing sauce.

"I wish Florence was more like the Ann Abler," I told John, while he highlighted a paragraph in *Birnbaum's 1999 Walt Disney World: The Official Vacation Guide*.

"The Country Bears. There's a whiskey still in there. Moonshine, ghosts of the Goldrush. And large bears."

"Real bears?"

"Maybe, Cheese. Maybe."

Our seats were wonderful islands on these Ponder flights out: my aisle seat island; John's aisle seat island; the Ann Abler kneeling between us, both islands' source of every bounty, topping off our soft Wayz and equal-opportunity flirting. Those stockinged legs, the unapologetic streak of gray; she stirred my Day One Ponder loins like nothing else. Plus, she would dip a finger in my wing sauce, then put it in her mouth, and leave it in there for an extra second before drawing it clear. "Mm," she'd say.

Mm, I'd think. I would never cheat on Florence. No one else should see me naked, not even Johnny Boy—although he claimed he did once at some hazy Ponder hour after I'd passed out in his room. As well, actual sex strikes me as less interesting than fantasizing about the Ann Abler over half a dozen soft Wayz, across from my best friend, a whole Ponder ahead of us.

"What brings you men to Orlando?" asked Ann.

Men.

"The boys are hitting Disney World," said John. "And hitting it hard."

"Wow," said Ann. "And whose idea was this? Mr. Marks?"

I pointed across the aisle. John was already barefooted. Ann had commented on his hairless, almost womanly feet and toes. She didn't even offer him the business-class slippers. Florence had lovely feet, too. Not a fetish of mine, although I found it odd that the two most important people in my life were blessed with such gracious append-ages. Who knows, maybe I did have a fetish. My feet? No flip-flops, not ever. No sandals. A yearly pedicure with a brave Korean woman.

"Do you get your toenails polished?" I asked John while he flipped through Birnbaum's *Official Guide*.

"Of course not."

"Then why are they so shiny?"

*

"Have you ever been?" I asked Ann as we flew over the Panhandle, thirty-five minutes from landing. John was passed out. He rarely stayed conscious after takeoff, which meant many more Ann conversations for me. She would remark on the cleanliness of Johnny Boy's slumber: no snoring, no drooling, no sudden movements.

"To Disney? Well, not the one in Florida, but Disneyland in California. It's smaller, classier I'd say. It felt more like the 1950s. The one you're going to is sort of stuck in the 1980s, at least that's what some passengers have said."

Shit, I wish we were going to the 1950s. The 1980s weren't my favorite. At least the Wayzless first half. Bad songs, too many colors, inchoate weekends, and tech adolescence. An epoch like a Clearasil commercial. Oh, and I had had pimples on my forehead. They went away after I lost my virginity to Florence, like the morning after.

"Do you know what the Country Bears are, Ann? Real bears?"

"They're more like lifelike robots. You have to suspend your disbe-lief. Just pretend everything you see is real. Who knows, maybe some of it is."

"I'm a very literal person. It will take many *many* hard—and soft—Wayz to suspend my disbelief. But maybe I will. Maybe the bears will terrify me. Haunt me for all my days."

"Oh, Mr. Marks."

As I looked out the window, she topped off my pinot grigio. What a rhythm we had while John slept. His slumber was part of the rhythm. The gentle rise and fall of his chest somehow fueling our innocent dalliance.

"Dalliance," I said. I was well-buzzed. "Do you find it boring when people say they see things in the clouds? Dragons, jack-o'-lanterns."

"Did you see something, Mr. Marks?"

"Two clouds having sex."

She snickered at me and shook her finger. Had I gone too far? Now she was checking on John. She put a blanket over him. Lovingly.

"By any chance, Ann, do you have a layover tonight in Orlando?"

Wouldn't it be something to do Disney with Ann? Hold her hand when the angry bears approached.

"No, we're turning right around, back to Newark."

"Isn't it weird that some other kids will be in our seats, as if we were never even here?"

"Kids?" asked Ann.

"I mean men, of course."

No I didn't. I still thought of us as kids. Men were the ones who cleaned up after us. Who couldn't afford to be hungover nor indigested. Men made the world turn. Kids got drunk and laughed at their own inside jokes.

Now John was awake. A *Good morning, Mr. Apple* Stoli-splash-a-cran already on his tray. That spry Ann Abler. As well, my cinnamon and chicken wing sauce mess was gone. A dozen Wash'n Dri wrappers? Gone.

"You know," said John, toasting the fornicating clouds, "romanticizing ordinary women is a form of sexism."

"What the fuck does that mean?"

"The Airport Mama, the Ann Abler? They're hard-working, generous with us, but that doesn't mean you can turn them into your personal heroines."

He got self-righteous just before landing. It evaporated once we checked in.

"Hey, look, Johnny Boy. I think I see the shiny silver ball."

"EPCOT isn't visible from near the airport. Nothing is. You know how depressing it would be to see airplanes flying over Disney World? Kids would immediately be reminded that their trips were terminal. There would be tears, fits."

Ann handed him a toothbrush kit. He patted my knee on his way to the lavatory. Perhaps he realized he'd just been a little gruff with me. Maybe I did see the fucking ball? Maybe I did see the sex clouds? I envied that he wasn't nearly as Wayz deep as I was, and that his mouth would be fresh for Orlando International Airport. But he'll envy me when I call Florence from the ride to the hotel. Oh, how he wanted someone to call.

"Well, have fun at Disney, Mr. Marks," said Ann.

I decided to go for it.

"Quit your job and spend the weekend with us!"

"Believe it or not, I'm tempted, but my daughter and husband rely on me."

"You have a husband?"

Meet me at the first bar before baggage, I wrote John.

The plane touched down while he was still brushing his teeth. Ann allowed him to get away with murder. I am fairly certain that they were once in the same lavatory at the same time, but he said I was just being paranoid.

The Ann Abler is married, and I'm too sober for Disney, I wrote.
Fine, he wrote.

God, I love my BlackBerry. What a little miracle. A little world, really. A world to which I'll surely cling these next three days.

*

"Hey," I said to Florence. She was at work. In work mode. Her voice joyless and bitter.

"Where in Florida are you again?"

"At an airport bar."

"No, I mean what city. Christ, you're already drunk?"

"Oh, please. We had a few—"

"Orlando. What is the hotel, again?"

"The Grand Florida Inn?" I asked John.

"The Grand Floridian," he said.

"The Grand Floridian. Maybe *I'm* the grand Floridian?"

"*Grand Floridian.*" She repeated it, presumably writing it down, then hung up.

At least she wrote it down.

"Why does she always ask that?" asked John.

"It's a girl thing. A wife thing."

We were at yet another airport bar that spelled grill with an 'e.' Oh, the dark circles under the eyes of Disneyfied adults whose tours of duty had ended. Their irises lubricated with hard-earned wisdom, they drank double scotches in absolute silence, nodding at one memory or another. Ghost, pirate, bear?

"Does she still put a note in your luggage?" asked John. "So smart of her. That way you'd never be able to stray. That love note is a chastity belt for your impressive package."

"She forgot once. Portland. Didn't make a difference."

"Summer. Maine," said John, nodding at one of the war-torn vets and his crooked mouse ears. "Those brunette girls with blonde arms. Remember that girl who could open a crustacean with her teeth? She was great at oral sex but hadn't much of a personality. Remember?"

I only remembered the buttery lobster rolls. And my incapacity to find it inspiring, the majestic Atlantic making lobster skiffs sway.

"Cheese, your lobster rolls come from fishermen in yellow overalls who haul in traps in the dark of morning," John had said.

It didn't register. John could put himself in other people's shoes; I suppose you could call it *empathy*. A quality I disqualified for, my friend. Moral largesse doesn't count when you are very wealthy. For a working stiff like me to give a shit about a lobster roll's origin story would be a minor miracle. And miracles do not happen to Cheese, but buttered split top rolls do. When I'm Pondering with the Prince.

CHAPTER FOUR

HOLY FUCKING SHIT: THE Grand Floridian. I was expecting a mall atop a Holiday Inn. Instead—holy fucking shit. Red Gabled roofs and white, *white* walls. A Victorian palace by the sea, made for robber barons, their expansive families, and their mistresses. A fleet of gleaming Cadillacs from the 1920s parked right outside the grand entrance.

Bellhops in costumes. The grills on those Cadillacs exploding in the Florida sun.

"Welcome home," they said.

And inside, the smell. Vanilla? Maybe lavender? Something citrus. Something north of merely clean; a smell I associated with the demands of the very rich. The scent wore a robe of completeness. And somewhere in Victorian America, a Morgan or Vanderbilt nodded in gruff approval beneath his top hat.

"Great smell in here," I said.

"A capital smell. If steak were soap," said John.

Weirdo. My eye caught the antique birdcage elevator, and then it caught its inhabitants: adults dressed like children with huge Midwestern shins. Children attached to leashes. Women pregnant with beer bellies. Holy shit, he was right. In Disney World, I'm lithe. To be fair, there were also grandparents; vestiges of the 1950s, thin hand-holding couples touring the lobby. Older men in Hawaiian shirts wearing a Rolex did my heart good. They probably fought the Japanese and had every damn right to enjoy Disney.

"See those old folks?" I asked John.

We were in line to check in, John's platinum card out of the wallet; he held it before him with both hands as if it were a travel visa and he was anxious to prove he belonged. Soon would come the official first Wayz before we were sequestered to our respective rooms for a solid hour of unpacking, meditation, a shower.

"I see them," said John.

"They probably don't even go on any rides, which is sort of awesome."

"They do go on rides, but very early in the morning, pre-dawn, escorted by elite cast members who dress like Captain Hook."

"You gents here on business?" asked Karl from Tampa. We were at his bar off the lobby.

"Yes we are," I told the bartender.

"No," said Johnny Boy.

"A little fun in the parks and then some meetings?" asked Karl.

"We," said John, draping an arm over my shoulder, "are here *only* for the parks, and of course all that lies beneath."

First hotel Wayz was wine. A single wordless clank of stemware that was always just below the threshold of broken glass. We generated such a promising noise.

"Whoa," said Karl. "Well, I guess that's the spirit."

Karl, like every employee at the Grand Floridan, wore period costume. Puffy red knickerbockers and white leggings, newsboy cap, waistcoat with pocket watch chain. I felt bad for Karl, every day having to dress like an extinct child. I suppose it gave the guests a sense of superiority over the staff; that the hotel was *their* mansion, and the man-children, who merely came with the place, were to be tolerated, and occasionally humored.

"There he is," said a huge man in an electric wheelchair.

"I told you," said John. "The Biggunz here are automated. Happiest people on the planet when they're here. They live and feast with absolute impunity. One day maybe I'll join their ranks. Real Americans. Proud and quick to smile."

"Karl makes the meanest margarita this side of Space Mountain," continued the Biggunz.

"Take the usual to go, Mr. Martin?" asked Karl.

"You betya. Do me a favor, young fellow," he said to me, "hand my goblet over to Karl, will ya?"

The goblet was a plastic container the size of a bottle of wine, sans the neck, on which cartoon characters frolicked. Into the goblet a frozen margarita machine snaked red and white ribbons of adult ice cream.

"Topper today, Mr. Martin?" asked Karl.

"Hey, after Space Mountain I'm gonna need it."

With that, uproarious laughter. Karl shook his head in absolute approval of the joke as he pooled ounce after ounce of tequila atop the ten-thousand-calorie hard Wayz.

"How the hell does he get on a ride?" I asked John. "God, this place is Biggunz-balled. I mean full of Biggunz."

"They take great care of their Biggunz. Advanced forklifts take them from their perches into oversized ride vehicles. And then? They experience liberation. Mr. Martin will be a well-buzzed astronaut. Weightless. What could be more joyous in this cruel life?"

*

John's tales (almost certainly tall) did sound rather exhilarating. I thought of fat folks like me floating about the amusement park, of which I had a view from my room. So many moving parts and pointy things.

Space Mountain's spire looked Gothic by way of an anachronistic future. Something Jules Verne might have imagined on his deathbed.

Somewhere in there, Mr. Martin was floating in space. Frankly, I was growing anxious to follow suit. On the television, on a loop, was an adorable girl gushing about all there was to do in this world. *Must-Do's* she encouraged. A petite brunette with white teeth and a Florida tan, Stacey wore short shorts and a tank top. I would be sure to tell John about her. She seemed a buoyant, Disney-obsessed brunette version of blonde Kathy, D cups and all.

"I love you, Stacey," I said from my bed.

I'd made myself a stiff vodka tonic from the bountiful minibar. I'd never seen a minibar that could accommodate a full bundle of cotton candy. A surprisingly winning combo, the pink stuff and the V and T. John encouraged my rapacious minibar Wayzing; after we'd check out, he'd detail for us every last item I'd consumed. My record came in Chicago: $675 of minibar damage, but that included a $250 bottle of gin. Actually, that bottle pissed him off, so I paid him back. He can get cranky at the end of a Ponder.

"Hey." I had called Florence.

"Yes?" she said.

"This place is nuts. Fat drunken astro—"

"Murray. I'm at work. Call me tonight if you want."

Only once did we have phone sex. I missed that. Maybe tonight? She'd already hung up. Her phone manner turned me on. It was how she was in bed: direct, to the point, on her schedule. Her demands. Except after a Ponder; that's when she'd let me take over for one night. I wondered what John's Disney unpacking ritual was like. I know he used the drawers and dressers, while I lived out of the suitcase until Monday morning when my carefully packed belongings were a tangle of clean and dirty, Wayz-inspired souvenirs, and one carefully gift-wrapped item for Florence. I opened my suitcase and found her note:

Have a great Disney trip. Have fun and be careful.

Love,

Florence

It was always placed above my boxer shorts.

Earlier, I'd passed a store in the lobby that had a jewelry case, behind the case a woman of advanced age dressed in the style of Mary Poppins. There was an actually stunning emerald Minnie Mouse necklace. The mouse glittered with semiprecious stones and even some diamonds. Tiny rubies for eyes. Florence had a place in her heart for childish things. A teddy bear lived on her pillow. *Teddy Fu*. Her maiden name.

"How much for that necklace?" I'd asked.

"I've been admiring that piece for eight years," said the shopkeeper (HEDY said her name tag).

I was happy, buzzed. Any answer would elicit: "I'll take it."

And I did. Even though it was close to two grand. On Tuesday night when we made love those rubies would juxtapose so nicely against my wife's pink nipples but I would need to exile this nice old lady from my sexual consciousness lest she pop up in the corner of our bedroom: "I've been admiring that penis for eight years."

What's up? I wrote John. *Great views from my room. Thanks for everything! Hey, how does it feel to be back? I went shopping for Florence. Where are we meeting?*

I was always sure to get him, and me, matching Ponder gifts as a thank you for the wingspan of his generosity. This trip was easy: I'd ordered silver flasks, prefilled with Stolichnaya Gold, engraved *Ponder 1999/Disney World*. The engravers messed up, however, and it read *Ponder 1999/Disney Word*. Johnny Boy will appreciate the mistake. Ponder anomalies darken the roux. Like the time we saw Claire, Kathy's horribly affected mother, in Boston. Claire: bug-eyed sunglasses, Hermes scarves, never without a hat. And all that perfume. And that accent. Stolen from a European country that does not exist. Wispy Claire.

"Well, hello," said breathless Claire. "Hello handsomes."

This was a year after the divorce. She was drunk at the Ritz Carlton's champagne bar. She did something with her black-stockinged skinny-ass legs that revealed garters.

"Well, boys. Fancy meeting *you* here. Handsome, handsome."

We bought her a drink. Lit her cigarette. Stared carefree at the garters. Some people grow old terribly. I'll be sure not to. Johnny Boy? Can't imagine him old. Actually can't imagine me old either. Our generation's true disease.

*

I'd get to the lobby early; enjoy some peaceful solo time before the force of nature, which is a Ponder, launched us into the day. These trips came and went too damn fast. Blink and it's Monday morning— a Bloody Mary party in one of our rooms where we'd fantasize about extending the trip. We never have. Florence would kill me, if a fourth night didn't.

Johnny Boy asked to meet outside the main lobby in the hot Florida air. Wicker chairs shaped like giant swans with a view of the Seven Seas Lagoon. A trout-stocked man-made body of water full, apparently, of alligators and, according to John, a luxury submarine that belonged to the Disney family.

"If you're really lucky, you can spot the sub's periscope," he'd said. "Imagine having physical congress with a woman in that sub. Silk sheets. A pipe organ."

While waiting for John, a honeymooning couple asked if they could sit in the swan chairs, and asked if I could take their picture.

"This is where it all started ten days ago," the groom said. "We waited for our room to be ready in these very chairs."

They wore JUST MARRIED T-shirts; the bride wore Minnie Mouse ears and a veil. Such unapologetically thick legs. Finger-strangling golden wedding rings. A bucket of rainbow-colored popcorn. Breakfast popcorn. It wasn't yet noon; God bless them.

"You've been here ten days?" I asked.

"Yes, sir," said the bride. "Today's our last day, but we've already planned an anniversary trip for 2009."

Southerners. In ten years, they'd have three kids. I'd already taken their picture; still they remained in the chairs.

"It's my very first day, yessiree." I was affecting Southernness and it was falling flat.

"Oh my God, I'm so jealous," said the bride. "How long y'all staying?"

"Only a few but we sure will make 'em count."

"There you go," said the groom.

They held hands and stared idly at the two flasks I'd lined up on the small table. Non-Wayzers cannot see into the world of Wayz. We and our accoutrements are invisible to their innocent eyes. If I just now took a swig, they'd transmute it to lemonade.

"What do y'all have planned for today?" I asked. "Bears? Space maybe?"

I wasn't speaking their language.

Enter John, wearing denim cutoffs. Slim bastard with his vintage Peter Pan T-shirt. I was sure the couple would shield their eyes from his lanky frame; from his sockless yellow suede slipper shoes. Instead, they stirred in their wicker thrones, then rose to greet Peter Pan.

"We were admiring your vintage Pan shirt, there," said the groom. How the hell could they admire it? They just saw it.

"Thank you," said John. "Top five dark ride in the Magic Kingdom."

"Amen," said the bride.

"I won three of these shirts on eBay. They're from 1978. I like that it's just Peter flying. It would be too busy with Tinkerbell and the kids. He's framed in an oval of endless potential. 'To Neverland, and beyond.'"

Androgynous Peter Pan. I wonder if gay couples go to Disney? I say yes. Definitely. Awesomely.

"Your wives at the spa?" asked the bride.

"Yes," I said.

"No," said John. "No wives."

The honeymooners had heard enough. No wives? Blasphemy on

their last day. I prayed they got wasted and had forceful intercourse that tested the structural integrity of the Grand Floridian Hotel.

"Welp, alright then, we're hitting Animal Kingdom one last time. Got a date with the *Carnotaurus*," said the groom, gritting his teeth, growling. He grabbed his new wife by her wrist and galumphed toward the lobby.

"Saurus?" I asked.

"Flasks!" said John. "Amazing, Cheese. Has a really nice heft to it. A really nice fit in the crook of my palm, like a flattened grenade."

He kicked up his feet and took a slug. "What the hell? Disney *Word*?"

"I know. A memorable error, I'd say."

"*Word, word.* I like it. What *is* the word? Hm. By the way, while the Stoli . . . is it Elit?"

"Gold."

"Gold is good, Cheese. But while the Stoli Gold is delicious, we will want to invest in some rum. There's a drink here, a soft-serve pine-apple delicacy called Dole Whip; one tops it with dark rum while the cannibalistic drums of Adventureland sound in the distance."

It was getting hard for me to know whether he was buying in, gearing up, having fun, or getting sloshed. He looked pretty damn happy, proud even. Nodding at the lagoon and gripping his flask. There were all sorts of watercrafts out there: Twainian ferry boats, little speed boats, pontoon boats. People fishing. Even a waterskiing show featuring the puppets.

"What do you call those things?" I asked.

"What things?"

"The animals on the water skis."

"The big five, Cheese. The big five. Mickey, Minnie, Donald, Daisy, and Goofy."

"If a kid sees them waterskiing, then sees them, I don't know, at Space, the Space Mountain?"

"Nice."

"Well, how does the kid assume they got from this lagoon to the Space Mountain? How does he make sense of that?"

"Magic. Now let's go buy some rum at the Sandy Cove. By the time we board a rocket ship and enjoy God's view of our planet, much will be revealed to you, my friend."

I was dressed in khakis, my tasseled loafers, a shirt better suited for an actual safari. It was an adult uniform. Florence liked how I dressed. Like a middle-aged man from a different generation. Post V-J Day? The well-to-do owner of a famous West Coast tiki bar? Perhaps I'd adopt that persona in order to survive this Ponder. A research trip for the walls of my dark bar.

"Maybe I'll open a restaurant," I said as we walked to the rum store.

"I'd invest."

"Really?"

"Of course. I picture you running a place like the gin joint in *Casablanca*."

"Or a tiki bar, like Trader Vic's."

"Even better. That place tickled Walt's fancy."

"Where'd you get those shorts?"

"My guy in Paris."

Strings of denim draped down over his glossy legs. Limbs that appeared fast if fragile. He was on the swim team at Harvard—well, a substitute. He hadn't the chest strength, according to him, so he sat on the bench. But one night in Boston he swam the harbor, also according to him.

"Ah, the Sandy Cove," said Johnny Boy. "A true canteen, where Disney soldiers such as us can re-fortify. Get a little taste of home before the next mission."

The Sandy Cove was where I'd bought that gold and ruby Minnie Mouse necklace. A cool $1995.00. Totally buzzed, irrational purchase. The poor old saleslady. I should probably just march in and gift her the thing, but Florence would hide it underneath her silk work blouse, and my boxers would come alive with expectation. Sometimes Florence didn't wear a bra. Sometimes when especially bloated it was more appropriate for *me* to have support up there.

At the Sandy Cove we scored two fifths of Myer's Dark Rum and two Cokes. The Cokes were poured out; enter the dark rum. We were great at hiding Wayz in plain sight. Oh, and I also bought a Pop-Tart sampler. When in Rome, flirt with diabetes.

CHAPTER FIVE

On Johnny Boy's Key to the World card was a god-awful hologram of a pirate on a ship that reminded me of childhood fevers and the weekday a.m. children's programming of my 1970s youth. The pirate ship was somewhere in between psychedelic LSD cartoons and the string marionettes that populated the treacle gardens of 10:00 a.m., channel 13, the Vaseline smeared anal thermometer reading 105. The pirate ship on John's card struck me as positively evil.

"My room card doesn't have a hologram," I said.

"Of course it doesn't. None do."

We were on the monorail that looped between our hotel and two others: a fake Hawaiian one, and a fake space one. The latter was the future as imagined by a tightly wound depressed retired policeman, who once sat on a lawn chair in early 1950s suburbia, sketching a monorail disappearing into a cavernous concrete lobby.

"This place is so . . . drab," I said.

"There's nothing depressing about the Contemporary, Cheese."

"The Hawaiian one looked a little brooding, all that dark wood. Wait, was that even real wood, or plastic?"

"The Polynesian is lush, but you're right, it can be a little danger-ous. You know the Beatles broke up there?"

"Bullshit."

"No, it's true. Many Disney geeks, including me, suspect that Lennon staged his assassination only to retire to the Poly, be rid of Yoko and the lads, grow a world-class beard, and blend into the woodwork."

The monorail announcer's voice was impossibly optimistic and proud.

"He sounds like a pedophile," I said.

"He's an avuncular prophet. He's bilingual and cares about your safety, Cheese."

The announcer oversold each and every resort, the Seven Seas Lagoon, the monorail itself. *Highway in the sky.* It was a smooth ride, though, and well air-conditioned. Add the occasional flask swig, and it was downright pleasant. Way too many kids though, and as lunch-time was approaching—glucose tantrums. Thank God for the plastic oranges which presumably held bright, sweet OJ. Mental note to buy a couple of the little guys and spike them with Stoli Gold. Tepid vodka has its moments, but they are few.

"I remember those orange juice containers," said John. "Such sal-vation under the sun."

"We should spike them."

"No. Some things from youth should remain pure."

"So, what is our first, you know, thing?"

"Huh?"

"First ride?"

He pointed to his shirt.

"Save some vodka for the darkness over London. Over which we will fly with Peter. And you will breathe in the veritable air of the past, for in that dark ride it is 1911, before the wars. Smell the salty Thames and its bream-crowded currents."

Jesus.

My hope was that these rides were long and winding affairs, long enough for a substantial buzzed daydream. About the time Florence and I bought matching Burberry umbrellas in old London town, then walked the cobblestones to our hotel where we had rarest daylight sex. But it was December in London, and it became evening in the afternoon. Three p.m., and we didn't need to lower the shades.

"How long is the Peter Pan ride?"

"A better question is 'how long does it *seem*'?"

Fuck, that means it's short.

"Also, it depends on how long we have to wait in line," said John. "I include the waiting as part of the ride."

"We have to wait? I thought you said there were special passes."

"They now have something called FastPasses, but we won't use them. The buildup is necessary, Cheese."

I was the only passenger on the monorail not wearing shorts, and for that matter the only person in ironed pants. Florence and I owned two irons and two ironing boards, facts that delighted Johnny Boy. Or repulsed and delighted him. As best friends we didn't really celebrate our differences. We were a Venn diagram conjoined by Wayz. And loyalty. And of course Ponders. I BlackBerry'd Florence:

Monorail.

No response. I planned on writing her from each ride. Just a word or two. She'd take a break from work to answer her vibrating little blue machine. Maybe lick her lips. Generally thin lips, she enhances them with pale pink lipstick that smells of rose petals. What a pleasant-smelling woman.

"I love my wife," I told John.

"I'm going to find my wife on this trip."

He said something like this every Ponder. This one, though, sounded grave; it was more than a wish. That he could embody mettle while seated next to a grown man wearing floppy dog ears singing over and over again *Yo ho, yo ho, a pirate's life for me—*

He'd been clear about finding his one true love both before turning thirty and before the new millennium. Frankly, I worried for him should he wake on January 1 alone in bed.

"I hope you find her, Johnny Boy. Cheers."

The sound of two silver flasks colliding. No one should be alone; with Kathy he was worse than alone. Florence described her as serene. The unearned elegance of low blood pressure. But I knew the truth: hers was a soul with dead batteries. He was never more alone than in her presence, and the dead batteries would tease light, but only when he acceded to her wish for a sports car. A diamond necklace. Fuck her. Shit. Florence did. Sometimes I forgot, but I remembered just now, while watching a teenage boy walk off the monorail duck-toed, arms akimbo, acting the fool. *The Goofy Walk*, John explained.

"You walk like the dim-witted dog. You purposefully humiliate yourself. You make corny jokes about rides, your surroundings. It's cathartic. A means of freebasing the magic. You should try it, Cheese."

No. No Goofy Walk for me. But there was John Apple walking off the monorail like a putz. Making strange noises. A parody of laughter? More like outrageous hiccups, and no one blinked an eye. He lifted his feet as if he wore size 28 shoes. I suppose that during the Roman Empire, citizens of Rome enjoyed a similarly overbearing gait. Wherever they stepped it was Rome. Even if it was Africa. Fuck it's hot out.

*

Main Street USA smelled of fried things. More accurately, fried cotton candy. I kept looking for errantly placed French fries, but the grounds were spotless. A perfect Victorian town. No unemployment. No crime. No news. Perfection can be eerie. I sensed a smirking sardonic God above us, watching us. Nodding as we marveled at the old-timey smell of . . .

"Do they fry cotton candy here?"

"Of course not. Behold the Castle."

John joined the hundreds who were snapping its picture. I had a theory that overly photographed things had a bitter inner life, resenting the flashes, putting curses on the photographers; curses that would come to be decades later when the photo album would be cracked open. A spirit released. Eiffel Tower, Taj Mahal, and Cinderella's freaking Castle.

"What's in the Castle, a ride?"

"No ride. There's a secret room made of ice. Rumor has it, Walt's frozen body lies in rest, and that cast members are lent fur coats when they pay their respects. Obligatorily, they down a frozen vodka shot in a commemorative crystal glass that's etched with a replica of Walt's wildly large brain. A few years ago, one of those shot glasses appeared on a black-market version of eBay. Asking? Five grand. It didn't last one minute. Someone scooped it up before I could. Ah, well."

Cold vodka. My flask's contents were getting warm.

"I like your shirt," a reddish head told John.

Wow, daylight contact with a girl on our very first day. Unprecedented. It usually took John until day two post-dinner to be approached, and usually it would be a dark soul in a dim bar. But this girl shone. She was pretty. A natural beauty in a Southern belle sort of way, wavy auburn hair, porcelain skin. She bathed in milk and then there was the accent. Not a Biggunz Southern accent; instead I heard the lattice work of Charleston. A white lace dress. A summery girl at midnight, barefooted, holding her shoes and laughing under the moon.

"Why thank you," said John, flashing his dimply smile. "What's your name?"

"Virginia."

"I'm John, and this is Murray."

"Peter Pan is my absolute favorite, and I love the vintage tees," said Virginia, touching one of his sleeves. "This is going to sound weird, but you guys seem cool, and my parents are doing the spa today. Mind if I tag along on a few rides?"

A third Ponder wheel? Preposterous. "It's up to Cheese," said John.

"Who's Cheese?" she asked.

"It's my nickname."

"Oh," she said. "How interesting."

"Of course Virginia can ride with us," I said.

Oh, the fine blonde hair that grew on Virginia's freckly arms. Can you fall in love with a name?

"What's that?" she asked John, who was on his BlackBerry.

"It's my phone. It's called a BlackBerry."

"I have one too." I showed her, and she rewarded me with two fingers on my hairy shapeless forearm. A French manicure against clammy flesh.

They held hands on the Peter Pan line. Is this how fate happens, before your very eyes? Under the sun, in the light of day? Who hand-held first, I wondered, or maybe with fate, it's simultaneous? The gods grab wrists and somewhere in the firmament an iron gate rises. I wrote Florence:

He met someone. Already holding hands.

She responded with a question mark and an exclamation mark. Precisely.

I bought a turkey leg. Jesus Christ, what a monstrosity. Twelve bucks. On no planet did this derive from a turkey. Smoky, fatty—actually, it was more like marbled poultry. I could not tell where flesh ended and fat began. Layer after layer of delectable poultry skin. And how it went with my warm vodka. Perfection. Virginia didn't judge me.

"I knew you'd love the turkey leg," said John.

"Cheers," I said.

Virginia was drinking from his flask; she clinked mine. The white teeth of a smiling redhead. I wanted to clink her white teeth, but the gods would not forgive me if I chipped one.

"I like your nails," I said. "I like that pale pink color."

"Thanks, Cheese."

Weird to hear my nickname in such an antebellum voice.

"Doesn't Florence wear her nails the same way?" asked John.

"Who's Florence?" the girl asked.

"His wife."

God damnit.

"We're business partners."

We had a Ponder rule: no mention of wives or girlfriends when speaking with a girl.

"Must be charming to work with your wife," said Virginia.

*

On the line, one of her hands found his jean shorts' back pocket. It just lived in there. Must be a Southern thing. Hand on ass. Not terribly dignified, but innocent enough. I was a happy spectator, working on the turkey leg, though the vodka was getting low. His flask had to serve two, so it was probably even more depleted than mine. Hopefully, after Peter Pan, we'd need to replenish, or hit a hotel bar. Would it be the three of us? If so, for how long, the whole trip? I buzzed his BlackBerry:

What the hell's going on? Also, what are we doing about empty flasks? Also, why is her hand on your ass?

I watched him read the message, but he didn't respond. Instead, his hand found *her* back pocket.

Not very seemly for Disney World, I wrote. *She seems drunk, is she drunk?*

They boarded first. A pirate ship with a sail, and a safety bar. The woman who helped me on—dressed like a Grimm Brothers towns-woman—was less than delicate with my safety bar; it was impressed upon my fat rolls. How in God's name do real Biggunz cope?

I couldn't see John and Virginia in the truly admirable darkness of the ride. Nor could I smell the Britannic brine he'd spoken of. It smelled like the foxing of old books, like sugar-coated asbestos and the half-life of gunpowder. There was one switchback moment when I did get a glimpse of their ship. They were making out, not even watching Hook and Pan swordfight.

They're French kissing on Peter Pan, I wrote Florence.

"Hi, Cheese," she said after the ride. I resented the familiarity. Actually, I didn't.

"Hello, Virginia." I loved saying her name. Virginia, Virginia, Virginia. I suppose I like girls who are named after places. But while there was not an iota of Tuscany to be found in my wife—

"Wait, where are you from?" I asked.

"Savannah," she said. God, I wish she were named *Savannah*. Don't get greedy, Cheese, *Virginia* is beautiful.

I sniffed the air: "Ivory soap."

"How'd you know?" asked Virginia.

"He has a weapons-grade schnoz," said John.

"My first job out of college was working for a Japanese perfume company. I was their smeller."

"He wore a pink lab coat."

"I loved my pink lab coat."

A blessing and a curse to smell so well. Thank God for Florence's personal hygiene. Lily of the valley betwixt her legs.

"So, what did you think of Peter Pan?" asked John. Their faces were both red from kissing.

"I didn't really get it," I told him.

"What the fuck do you mean?" asked John.

"'You can fly, you can fly. You can fly, you can fly,'" sang Virginia.

"It was just—"

"You can fly, you can fly. You can fly, you can fly," she sang.

"It was . . . solid. I mean, there were lots of little plasticky things whirling round. It's for kids."

"Nope," said John.

"He needs pixie dust," said Virginia. She blew in my ear. Warm breath.

"Maybe the next ride will be better," I said.

"Listen, I wanted to talk to you about that."

Holy shit, he's about to ditch me. Perhaps I was too harsh about his beloved *dark ride*.

"I did find the London-y bits charming." (I actually did. I'm old-fashioned when it comes to London.) "And that turkey leg—"

He squeezed Virginia's hand, then took me aside.

"My plan all along was to desert you in between our first and second attractions. Force you to fend for yourself in Disney World for two hours. Sea legs."

"Such bullshit, you just want to be alone with her."

We were next to an exit sign: CAST MEMBERS ONLY. Dumbo elephants cascading above. In the distance, a Tudor-themed popcorn stand.

"You know they really mix up their time periods around here," I said. "Well, have fun with Virginia. BlackBerry me when you're, whatever."

Virginia was by a man selling annoyingly silvery mouse balloons, standing on one leg, flamingo-like. Sometimes girls can be perfect. The litheness of their limbs. It's unfair, actually.

"I think I'm going to have to part ways with Virginia."

"What? Why? That's crazy. She's pretty amaz—"

"She fell into my lap too easily. As well, her breath was weird."

"I saw you two kissing."

"She tasted like an alloy that would be used to make an alien spacecraft. A mineral not found on Earth."

"Buy her some fucking Binaca."

"Haunted Mansion, 3:30. And, hey, see that sign?"

"'Cast Members'? So what."

He grinned his dimpled grin, then collected poor Virginia.

"What about the sign?" I called after them.

"You'll see," he called back.

*

Riding the monorail alone was oddly exciting. My fellow passengers mistook me for an enthusiast, and I ate it up.

"You ride Peter Pan yet?" I asked a family of lollipop lickers. All red-headed like Virginia, but fiery red; her hair was darker. Definitely auburn. Complexly light brown.

"Sure have. How many times now, Bobby?" asked Bobby's father.

"Free," said the little boy. "Free times."

"You?" they asked me.

"Just the once, but sure is a classic."

"You can say that again."

"Sure is a classic," I said.

And with that, thunderous laughter. They exited at the Polynesian.

"Well, time to hit the buffet," said Bobby's father. "Tonga Toast, here we come."

"Yay!" shrieked Bobby.

"They only serve it at breakfast, Bobby," said Bobby's mother. "How many times do I have to tell you?"

What a bitch.

Free times.

Where to drink during my free times? I'm entirely functional John-less but have to put in extra effort not to become sentimental because I think I'm going to miss this crazy place. On the first day of a Ponder, I usually can't help but become stupidly sentimental about the trip, as if it were already over.

"Cheese tries to slow down time, by hugging it, squeezing the life out of it, which only pisses it off," Johnny Boy had said. "Revenge: time slips clean of his embrace, then speeds itself up, and just like that, Friday becomes Monday."

On my third solo monorail loop, I did just that. But this time, more than a figurative hug.

"Oh, to be behind John and Virginia on Peter Pan, the whole trip ahead of us," I said.

No one thought anything of my pronouncement. Amazing oblivious doofuses of the monorail.

"Fare thee well," I told monorail strangers at the Grand Floridian stop. I even tried my hand at a Goofy Walk. I fear, however, that I looked less like an affable fool and more like someone mocking scoliosis. Which, oddly, fit right in; so many with physical challenges here. Nothing democratizes like turkey legs, dark rides, vodka. I bought a fifth of Smirnoff at the Sandy Cove.

"It's for a party tonight," I lied to the shop clerk, who, like the old dear who had sold me my Minnie Mouse jewelry, was dressed as Mary Poppins. The real Mary Poppins liked to tipple, that much was clear. She would understand my daytime flask Wayz, but not this one. When I asked for the vodka she pointed at gin, ultimately wrapping my Smirnoff in all sorts of tissue and tape. No brown bags here.

"Well," she said, "have a magical time at your fireworks party."

I fucking will.

"Thank you, I will. Wait, what fireworks?"

"Oh, I assumed that's what you bought the bottle of spirits for."

"Oh of course it is!"

"Must be nice to have a balcony with a view."

"I can see the spaceship."

"Spaceship Earth or Space Mountain?"

"Yes."

*

I peered down at the lobby of the Grand Floridian; inhaled that square-cornered, healthy carpet scent, and caught a glint. Metal reflected up three stories bothering my eye. Splayed out over a divan was Virginia. And holy shit, he gave her our flask. I tried a more ginger version of the Goofy Walk descending the stairs. This one seemed . . . Ralph Kramden.

"Virginia?"

"Hey, Cheese."

Drunk, her accent was a plantation.

"Nice flask."

"Yeah, he gave it to me. Consolation prize, I guess."

"Sorry about that."

I sat by her feet. Bare feet. She'd kicked off her sandals; her pedicure matched the manicure. Pale pink. God, John's a fickle idiot. And here she was, heartbroken, yet still had the intellectual mettle to be with a book. Albeit Harry Potter.

"I liked him so much," she said, hugging her book. "Things like that never happen to me."

"He can be a weird guy sometimes."

"He told me what happened to his parents. Death by Disney."

She took a slug from the flask. I was surprised there was anything left. She must have refilled it. No: he refilled it for her. Chivalrous. I unwrapped my Smirnoff, threw the tissue paper to the floor, and in the lobby's light of day, refilled mine.

"Disney *Word*," said Virginia. "*Dumped* is the word."

"So sorry."

"Hey, I like your muumuu."

"It's more of an elegant safari shirt."

She put her feet in my lap. Uh oh. I took a healthy swig, hoping to neuter any arousal.

"Heartbroken at Disney. Oh, Cheese, what's a girl to do?"

"Maybe he'll change his mind."

"He doesn't seem that way."

Perceptive Virginia from Savannah.

"God these carpets are healthy-smelling," I said. Like her healthy head of hair. Some girls smell of their shower all day long.

"He's also a straight shooter, which only made me like him even more."

"He can be a little, um, filter-less."

"He told me why we couldn't be anything more than a flight over London."

"What did he say?"

You can destroy a girl's self-confidence with any, *any* talk of questionable make-out breath. No way Johnny Boy would—

"He said he was in love with someone he has yet to meet. Romantic, huh?"

She twirled the now-empty flask from her finger. I'd never seen a girl flirt with a flask, but that's how it seemed. A slow twirl.

"Ginny?"

Looming above us were, presumably, her parents. Berobed in white Grand Floridian Spa robes, water-slicked hair, sunglasses. WASPs in Disney World. Wonderful!

"Hiya, guys," said Virginia. "This is Cheese. Cheese, these are my folks. Aren't they cute?"

No. Intense. Tall, too. Both of them the same height.

"I met a boy on Peter Pan, but he dumped me."

Her father took the flask, smelled it, handed it back.

"A little early, Ginny," he said.

Ginny. I bet if it were gin, he wouldn't protest.

"I'm sorry, dear," said her mother. "And pleased to meet you . . . is it Cheese?"

"It's a nickname. I'm Murray. Murray Marks."

"Pleased to make your acquaintance, Mr. Marks," said the father.

I stood to receive his crushing handshake. Grip of a man who has, in anger, broken tennis rackets. "Washington Wells, and this is my wife, Constance. Won't you join us for a late lunch?"

"Yeah, you should," said Virginia. "You can be my date," she harumphed.

"By all means," said Mrs. Wells.

Surrounded by drawls, my city voice felt naked. *Washington and Constance Wells.* I saw them in the pictorials of *Savannah Magazine*; saw social aspirants pointing at the page: *Oh, my goodness, come look at the Wellses!*

"Why I'd love to, Mrs. Wells." I tried to adorn my voice with the warmth of Georgia peaches.

"You tryin' to sound *country*, Cheese?" asked Virginia.

I turned red.

*

"Four shrimp cocktails." Washington Wells was the only one afforded a menu. "And then four rare roast beef sandwiches on thinly sliced, toasted and buttered rye bread."

"Daddy likes to order for everyone," said Virginia.

"For Ginny and Mr. Marks, two sober-up lemonades, and for Mrs. Wells and myself, two Beefeater martinis, up and with a twist of lemon."

"Washington has a knack for ordering," said Mrs. Wells.

Fucking A, he does. I was ready for a non-Wayz.

"Excuse me if this sounds impertinent, Mr. Wells, but you two don't strike me as normal Disney people."

"We go for Ginny," said Mr. Wells.

"It's a compromise really. A week or so here and then onward to Palm Beach," said Mrs. Wells.

Of course. They hit the spa while Virginia does the rides, kisses boys, etc. Then a gin-soaked afternoon; only in the early evening will Washington and Constance condescend to ride.

"Any rides?" I asked the Wells.

"They go with me on one ride before dinner," said Virginia. "I spend all day figuring out which one."

Lovely girl. Stupid John.

"So, this friend of yours; it seems our Ginny was quite enamored," said Mr. Wells.

"He's a charming guy," I said.

"Cute ass," said Virginia.

"Drink your lemonade, dear," said Mrs. Wells.

We were seated outdoors, the only table dressed for lunch. White tablecloth, silver flatware, crystal stemware. The waiter called the Wellses by name. Surname, of course. They ate in their robes and slippers. Only during dessert ("Four oatmeal cookies") did a tendril of Mr. Wells's hair become sufficiently dry enough to descend across his forehead.

"Murray Marks. Ethnic name?" asked Mr. Wells.

"Sounds that way, but I'm actually not Jewish."

"Such pretty green eyes," said Mrs. Wells. "I knew he wasn't ethnic, Washington."

"Let me see," said Virginia. She'd hijacked the bottom half of her daddy's gin martini. "Wow, they *are* green, like those cute frogs you see in *National Geographic*."

She hadn't noticed before. When they don't notice my best feature, party's over. Well, the party never starts for ol' frog eyes.

"*Washington G. Wells*," said Mr. Wells, signing the bill.

"Thank you so much for lunch, Mr. Wells."

"Think nothing of it, Mr. Marks."

God, I love WASPs. They order for everyone and broadcast their signatures. He stood and tightened his belt, suggesting the meal had no effect on his waistline. Which it hadn't.

"They do a nice job with luncheon," he said.

"A damn fine luncheon," I said. I'd never used that word in my life. My BlackBerry buzzed:

Are you on your way?

"Guess I should get going, I'm supposed to meet my friend in the amusement park at some—"

"John?" asked Virginia.

"Well, yes."

"Oh, please can I come?"

So adorable with her wizardry book under her arm.

"Um, well, we're supposed to meet at the haunted house—"

"Oh, it's my absolute favorite."

Washington Wells slapped my arm with his robe belt.

"You will let Ginny join you, won't you, *Cheese*?"

Had I given him any answer but the one he wanted, I was quite sure he'd remove the belt and flog me into submission.

"And if John is going to be all difficult again, I'll just ride in the Doom Buggy with you."

CHAPTER SIX

"Don't tell him I'm coming," said Virginia.

We were on the monorail. Plump, balding man in elegant safari shirt and ironed slacks, and Southern beauty. Add matching flasks and it could damn well be our honeymoon. I wanted people to assume this was the case, so I made contact with her shoulder, her arm. She didn't mind.

"Why not tell him?" I asked.

"Some boys just need to be bum-rushed with a kiss. It's how Mama got Daddy. You can't give boys too many choices, or they'll fuck everything up."

Curses from her mouth sounded genteel. Florence said *fuck* so quickly. She'd say it twice, rapid fire.

"I wouldn't fuck things up."

"You mean with your wife?"

"With, um, anyone."

"Tell me about her."

"Tall, thin woman with an extraordinary work ethic."

"That's it?"

Guiltily, I BlackBerry'd Florence: *I love you*. She replied with a single exclamation point.

"Well, she has high cheekbones. Long legs. Elegant, I'd say."

"Did she just run up to you, kiss you, and say *you're mine*?"

She'd bought herself an engagement ring before I'd decided to propose. Right in front of me. At Tiffany's.

"What are you doing?" I'd asked her in the store. She didn't respond, just put the little blue box in my pocket.

"Ask tonight," Florence had said.

"I suppose I like it when a woman takes charge," I told Virginia.

"That's refreshing to hear."

But Johnny Boy? Not sure if her forcing a crazy space alien–tasting kiss on him would be the ideal tack. Perhaps I could buy her some mints.

"You're back," he said.

She kissed him, as planned, beneath the Haunted Castle's din of howling wolves and thunder cracks. She took him by the hand, and they joined the line. He looked back at me, hunched his shoulders.

"Told ya, Cheese," said Virginia. "Cheese met my folks. We had luncheon," she told John.

"I don't like that word," said John.

"What?"

"Luncheon."

"Then you, Mr. Picky, can ride alone. I'm hitching my star to Mr. Cheese. See you after the ride, Johnny. Oh, and by the way, *luncheon, luncheon, luncheon*."

Now it was *my* hand she grabbed, and into the darkness we skipped. She skipped. Our shoulders touched during the ride. It was all I could absorb from the seven-minute adventure, the heat of her bare blade. My hope was that John wasn't upset with me about allowing her to tag along; that he wasn't upset with me about our clavicle chemistry. Maybe it was best he rode alone. This was, after all, the last thing he ever did with his parents. They bought him a caramel-dipped apple after the ride, then said goodbye. Forever. The plan today was for me to buy him a caramel-dipped apple after the ride. He was looking for closure.

"If only I had their ashes, I'd sprinkle them on the grounds of the Mansion, and their cold burial at sea would turn terrestrial and warm. I'd find the tears, after all these years."

After the ride I bought us three caramel-dipped apples. How quickly two had become three. But there she was now, shoulder-to-shoulder with us both. John told her about the significance of the snack, and she kissed him once, luxuriously, on the lips. My sense was that her otherworldly breath had in the Haunted Mansion achieved a human Ph.

"I'll never say *luncheon* again," she said.

"Thank you," he said.

"Can I go freshen up before you take a bite of the magic apple?" asked Virginia.

"Sure you can," said John.

She handed me her apple for safekeeping.

"So, what the fuck's going on?" I asked.

"You brought her here."

"You don't seem to mind."

"Neither do you," he said, counting not one, but two apples in my sweaty clutches.

"Of course not, she's not only a girl who has become a stowaway on our Ponder, but she's a *pretty* girl, and she also treats us as if we're normal. Plus, she likes flask Wayz. Plus, she's smart. And that accent. And that hair. And her—"

"I like the light brown freckles on the bridge of her nose, but I'm not at all sure if she's who I came to Disney to meet."

He surveyed the throngs of whatever land this was (the Founding Fathers meet . . . ghosts?) for *the one*. How could he imagine finding a better-suited girl here? I hadn't even told him about her parents. Or her toenails.

"You're so sweaty," said John. "I told you to wear shorts. Now you look like *melted* cheese. I'll buy you a pair."

"No, thank you. Virginia, for one, appreciates my slacks."

"She said that?"

"No, but I saw her staring at the ironed creases."

"Probably staring at your bulge."

She'd put her hair up, splashed her face with water. An Ivory soap girl doesn't stare at bulges. She likes ironed creases.

"You okay, sweetie?" Virginia asked John. He had brought his nose up against the candied fruit, where it stuck. His eyelashes aflutter.

"Sweetie?" she asked.

A tear the size of a champagne grape was birthed from his tear duct. His face became a sculpture. Pained and frozen, his jaw seemed momentarily dislocated. Then there was relief. There's a final exhale after climax when one forgets that one was ever born or will ever die. Here muscles do not matter. There are no bones or tendons. John Apple crumbled in his seat. The tear. It had popped out, seemed to float even, then landed in Virginia's palm. She watched it there, as if a butterfly had landed. And then she ate it.

"You ate my tear."

Weird-ass Greek mythology stuff, consuming someone's tear.

"So salty," said Virginia.

"You okay?" I asked John.

"I don't know. I don't know anything."

For a moment I swear his dark eyes glowed my irises' green.

"I was back," he said. "Like Proust was."

"Who's that?" asked Virginia.

"An old French guy," said John. "An old guy who one day tasted a little cake from his childhood, a madeleine dipped in tea. Then came the flood."

Marcel Proust in Disney. Shit-ton of pastry smells everywhere, why not?

"Is that what just happened to you?" she asked.

"For a split second I saw them again. My parents. I made them wear mouse ears but caught them disposing of them in the trash as they left Tîa and me."

Throwing away mice ears is bad karma. As is wasting a caramel apple. I ate it while she stared at him, who was staring into the ether. She dabbed his caramel-tipped nose with a Wash'n Dri. Florence also kept Wash'n Dries in her purse. The best girls do.

"So, what's the next ride?" I asked. I suppose I was sort of getting it. Or maybe just enjoyed her company in the last one. Some small part of my safari shirt smelled of her shower. And her shower knew the secrets of her body. She was the sort of girl one could get away with staring at, but I didn't abuse the invitation, allowing myself one glance every three apple bites.

Hi, I wrote Florence.

? she wrote back.

Women just know when their man is in the presence of a pretty girl. That was a heavy question mark.

"So, next ride?" I asked.

"We're going to take some time just sitting here, Cheese," said Virginia.

"Yes," said John. "We are."

"You could do the Hall of Presidents while we figure things out," said Virginia. "The Clinton has a good likeness. All that fuss for a blowjob."

God, she had a way with salty language. Spanish moss hanging from every naughty vowel.

*

I didn't go see Bill Clinton. Florence had a crush on him, especially after the scandal. She paid $10,000 to be in the same room with him. There's a picture on the mantel with her two bony hands shaking his big hand; a hand, Florence said, that sparks a girl's imagination.

"My hands are big too," I told my wife.

"Yes, but you're not president."

I took the monorail to the Polynesian hotel. *The Poly*, both Virginia and John knew to call it. I wondered if they'd sleep together. This afternoon. Maybe they'd use the Poly as their motel? As their sewer? Although there was no stink here. It smelled of chlorine and orange groves.

"Excuse me, which way to the Tambu Lounge?" I was asked.

People always thought I worked in places. That I was official. Department stores, hotels, once even a porn shop.

"You have an oval, open, friendly face," John had said. "And dress in the many uniforms of upper middle management. Grays and blues. Khakis on Fridays. Button-downed helper of men in size 44 slacks."

Actually 46.

"Yes, the Tambu Lounge," I said. I'd seen a sign for it, and pointed them in the right direction. "Have a magical day," I said.

"Will do."

Shit, now I can't go to the Tambu Lounge. They'd think I'd been fired or gone rogue. John had mentioned a rum bar somewhere off the main lobby, accessed through an imposing brown door.

"The sort of door meant to turn away most men. A heavy, brooding door the color of dry blood. An ending disguised as a beginning."

I could find no such door and was too embarrassed to ask an employee about a secret apocalyptic bar. Instead, I settled for Captain Cook's Discovery Lounge, which was depressingly situated in full view of the checkout line. I assumed it was there so that adults could nurse their checkout bill pain before getting the hell out of Dodge. In fact, the only other patron was a bearded guy with curly black hair hunched over a printing calculator whose rolls of paper spilled over the bar. He must have lost his shirt, literally, and his shoes. He wore a slim dark suit, but no shirt, no socks, no shoes. Tall and thin, he stood at the bar crunching numbers, making white paper spin.

"Aloha!" said the bartender, an actual Hawaiian; her name tag read

Ray, Lanai, HI. An orchid flower behind her ear. A straw skirt around her wide hips. She was the first truly rotund employee, but she carried it well, like me. In her case, a Don Ho sunset in the eyes sheds thirty pounds, although the hula outfit made a rustling noise when she moved, which was quaint, the first rustle.

"I'm Ray," she said. "Welcome to Captain Cook's Discovery Lounge!"

Such optimism from Ray. Rustling Ray. What a grind to always be happy. In Johnny Boy's various mythological watering holes, the help were serious and dark. I mean the *cast members*. That's what he said we should call them.

"They're part of the story," he said. "They make things happen."

"What's the deal with that bearded guy at the calculator?" I asked Ray.

"Oh, Dimitri? Do you know Dimitri? Everyone seems to have a Dimitri story."

He looked agitated and was drinking a non-Wayz. Perrier with a lemon. Florence would approve of this snickering teetotaler.

"Is he an accountant or something?"

"Not that I know of."

I ordered a piña colada and moved closer to Dimitri. A Russian voice. Probably a Muscovite.

"Four, no five Haunted." He was speaking to no one. "Seven Splash. Three Dino. Five, no six, no *seven* Pirates."

"Having fun, Dimitri?" asked Ray.

"Fun," he scoffed. "Fun. Four Dumbo, three Space, then three more Haunted."

"Is he some sort of ride safety inspector?" I asked Ray.

"He's a very loyal guest. He's been at the Poly for many months now."

"He lives here?"

"Oh, Dimitri," sighed Ray, her moon of a face tilted in admiration.

"Two Carousel, five Aladdin. Six, no seven Jungle."

With each utterance he'd jab at the calculator. When the train of paper got too long, Ray would walk it back to him, fold it neatly on the bar, and Dimitri would raise his soda water in gratitude.

"What you look at?" asked Dimitri.

"I'm Murray Marks," I said.

"Dimitri. Huh, interesting man blouse."

"It's actually an elegant safari shirt. Are you Russian?"

"What's it to you? But yeah, of course I am Russian. Seven Pans, eleven, no was ten Tower."

"Sounds like you've been on a lot of rides."

"*Rides*, give me break. Rides, says mister safari shirt."

He started lecturing me in Russian, ending with *Na Zdorovie* and a collision of his Perrier with my ceramic pineapple. A Ponder-worthy crash of vessels.

"Can I buy you a drink, Dimitri?"

"What you think I am?"

"Sorry, just thought—"

"I don't drink on the job, my friend. Tonight? Maybe yes. You see this?" he asked gesturing to the *USA Today* that was by his calculator.

"What?"

"Yeltsin, if he resign, it's very bad. Bad guy will take over if Yeltsin resign. Very bad for Russia, even worse for you. Five Dumbo."

"Why me?"

It was a rhetorical question. In the twenty-first century everyone will feel as I do: an Atlas. A hapless Atlas. Every war, every stock market crash, every disease will be Atlas's fault and all one can do is march around in circles waiting for the shoulder cargo to drop.

"Because," said Dimitri. "KGB. Oh, and, four Poohs."

Cracked Russian dude at the Poly bar. Truly mad. You'd love him, I BlackBerry'd John. He wrote back in minutes.

Is it someone named Dimitri? Virginia dated him for a split second last year. Says he's a Romanov. We're on Space Mountain, by the way. I now think she's the one. Virginia says he always wears suits without a shirt. Says he's royalty. Here comes blast off.

Dimitri pushed his adding machine over to Ray.

"Put guy's drinks on my tab, Ray," he said.

"That's not necessary," I said.

"Is," he said.

"Dimitri's known for his generosity," said Ray. "Where to now, Dimitri?"

"Bears," he said and left.

"Doesn't he worry he'll step in broken glass?"

"There's no broken glass in Disney World. Want another piña colada? It's on Dimitri."

"Is it possible to get one to go?"

I felt an unreasonable need to amass more rides. John and Virginia were probably up to four, maybe five. I needed to catch up; what an awful deficit.

Riding rides is an accounting addiction, I wrote Florence. *I want to leave this place with a substantial list. I want to frame the list and place it in the kitchen where I can look at it over a hard Wayz.*

I snatched Dimitri's calculator and pounded out my pittance.

"One Pan, one Haunted."

CHAPTER SEVEN

I TURNED TWENTY-NINE LAST year, and John this past month. A Halloween baby, he'd throw one hell of a party that night. Famously (at least famously to me) he would not attend, leaving guests to wonder under which costume was their host. He'd hire body doubles to approximate him; make sure they dressed in legitimately frightening costumes; make sure they never spoke to guests. Two hundred guests in some rented loft, seven fake Johnny Boys lurking, mute. Only Florence and I knew that he was holed up for the night at the Carlyle Hotel celebrating alone. Well, he no longer went solo after one of his surrogates slept with his then girlfriend. After that, he was sure to bring to the hotel whomever he was dating. Oddly, he rehired the lucky body double. It thrilled him, that one of *him* could score.

"He has too much time and money on his hands," my father had said. The Harvard undergrad who had loitered on the cozy couch of their Cambridge bookstore had changed since his successful navigation of the tech explosion. The fortune hadn't corrupted him; if anything, it seemed to piss him off, and he'd do impulsive things that were a distant or close cousin to self-loathing. When his net worth reached a personal milestone of ever so many zeros and commas, he hired a retired professional boxer, the very Irish and somewhat obscure Gerry Cooney, to knock him out. The deal was, if Cooney didn't knock him out, he didn't get paid. He knocked John Apple out. What a grin from John after Cooney's ancient cornerman snapped open smelling salts beneath his fractured nose.

Weirdo.

"He just wants to feel something," Florence posited, a theory John rejected.

"I feel a lot. That's not it. I'm not a teenager cutting himself."

No, but close. Then why pay a 240-pound middle-aged man, with fists the size of melons, fifty thousand dollars to break your nose?

"Too many green lights. Too many green lights in my life."

The fracture gave his face even more character. A bump. More of a fret, suggesting . . . a twist. I couldn't help but wonder if he'd decided that Virginia was another necessary red light. A knuckle sandwich in the land of turkey legs. What part of him might *she* break? In addition to my new urgency to collect rides, I wanted to save my best friend from a broken heart. Maybe Disney had inspired me to have a real-life adventure? An actual wild ride where I spare my best friend a broken heart only to secure my own whole heart. With her. Me, Cheese, the forever ride partner of Virginia Wells's bewitching shower smell. How can girls smell like their a.m. shower for six rides, ten rides?

I'm going to save Johnny Boy, I wrote Florence.

The only one who can save John is John, and maybe me, she wrote back. *He listens to me, but only when we're one on one.*

One on one?

I have to get back to work. Have fun and don't drink too much.

Too fucking late.

Let me guess, too late.

God, I love her feminine intuition.

*

John Apple is right, words do matter. Parks. People here refer to these places as *parks*. I take offense. I do not like parks. Man-made, unfiltered sunlight, baseball diamond dust glittering with fake diamond dust. Parks mock real places like forests, mountains, and jungles. Manicured to a fault and Wayzless, my heart hurts for picnicking kids and their melted ice cream. What vulgarity is a melted Rainbow Pop, dusk Sunday in mid-October; when Central Park is done with a season, she's fucking done. No Indian summer here. Wipe the July Fourth popsicle colors off your face; prepare your flesh for a woolen turtleneck. Tomorrow's school. Itchy school. *Parks*. Please. The Magical Kingdom is in fact a more appropriate name for this place. Heroes, heroines, a Romanov? But many yellow lights. Proceed with caution.

"Hitting the parks?" I was asked on the monorail en route.

"No," I said. "I am going to the Magical Kingdom."

What isn't magical about a girl's white eye teeth in the dark of a dark ride, shoulders touching, mind racing? John and Virginia, however, were nowhere to be found. He hadn't responded to my many messages, so I wrote Florence:

I can't find them.

They're probably having an afternoon tryst, she responded.

Florence, rarely wrong; my viscera filled with dread and desire. A sensation we associated with the last day of a Ponder. Comically hungover Bloody Mary Mondays. Our minds sent a message to our bodies: procreate before you drunks die.

"Stomach-dwelling butterflies with wings like razor blades, and with each flutter, blood stiffens manhood."

That was John's take.

I simply called it "pussy stomach."

Florence was not amused.

*

Radio silence from the tryst, so in the Kingdom I sought out the orange juice stand.

"Excuse me," I asked a female Biggunz in an electric wheelchair who was sipping from the orange I desired. "Might you know where I can find one of those little guys?"

"Adventureland."

She was a rare gruff Biggunz. John said that they got that way during the calorie-less hours. Or did he say *minutes*?

"And where might that be?"

"Just follow the drumbeats."

"Drumbeats?"

"Just look for the bird. The Little Orange Bird."

"An actual bird?"

She'd had enough and whizzed away.

It was mid-afternoon when I found the stand next to something called Jungle Outfitters. The bird was painted on the stand's side. He resembled, well, me. Round-faced, and indeed good-natured. And his juice, which was served in plastic replica oranges, was ambrosia under the fake African sun. Enter vodka, and I was Rudyard Kipling exploring conquered lands. Screw the Jungle Boat; the Screwdriver Express was where it's at. Kipling himself knew that the real reason to colonize exotic lands was the glory of adding liquor to tropical nectars. I made a mental note to add the Little Orange Bird to my list of rides. And maybe the monorail too. Little worlds where one could Wayz? I'd be sure to ask Johnny Boy's opinion whether these counted as rides. I'll ask him whenever the hell his trysting ends, details of which I sorely needed. I also needed to add a more conventional ride to my list.

It's a Small World was one of the only things Disney about which I knew. Boat ride with insipid song and empty-faced puppets. Growing up, my parents played a record that included the title song. Cultural socialism: we are all empty-faced puppets whether from Panama or Paris. In the line, many got a head start on the god-awful singing, with the exception of a barking adult and his reluctant son.

"Sing the song," he barked.

"But I don't want to," said his sullen son.

"Now you listen to me, sonny boy, you'll sing the song, and you'll sing it loudly, or else."

"You're embarrassing me."

"I'll show you *embarrassing* if you don't sing it."

The man had small muddy eyes and a crew cut. Ex-military for sure; he wore his shorts high and tight.

"*It's a small world after all. It's a small world after all.*" The man sang it like a fight song, his fists swinging full biergarten.

"Jesus," I said.

He turned to face me.

"From where do you hail?" he asked.

"Originally, or now?"

"I don't give a rat's ass."

"New York."

"Only two things hail from New York, steers and queers. I don't see any antlers on your head, so you must be a queer."

Fuck, isn't that from a movie with a drill sergeant?? (I have an unreasonable fear of drill sergeants. All fat kids do.)

Sonny Boy pointed at me and cackled. "Ha Ha," he said, then joined his father in song.

"*It's a world of laughter, a world of tears. It's a world of hopes and a world of fears.*"

Fears are right. In twenty years, the kid will hear it played at some Walmart in the Carolinas that sells automatic weapons and snap.

At last, John:

Meet me inside Typhoon Lagoon. At a place called Let's Go Slurpin'. We'll ride Castaway Creek after a couple of drinks. Bought you a one-piece bathing suit. Very 1930s.

Virginia should never see me in this getup.

*

Fit-rite suit for men. Tank top and shorts connected. I liked it. Black-and-white striped, to boot.

"Where the hell did you find this?" I asked.

"Every shop here sells anachronisms. God, Cheese, certainly shows off your prodigious package."

"Where's Virginia?"

"In my room."

"You just left her there? What rides did you go on? You just left her there?"

Slow nod. He shut his eyes and was back in there. What did his mouth know? A gentleman, I refused further enquiry.

"Wow, frozen margarita machines!" I observed.

"I kissed her in a selective way that made her shudder," said John. "Her ear lobes, the nape of her neck, under her arms. Different places, like the length of her downy arms. There's something about a girl's shallow fur."

We both had an appreciation for that.

"The beautiful fuzz that graces her body, especially those arms. It's just . . . *there*. Out there to be seen, in my case, kissed. It's a preview of what's to come."

She did have great arms. Summery sinewy arms. Lucky bastard.

"Can you mix the frozen strawberry with the frozen chocolate?" I asked the bartender.

"She fell asleep trembling, smiling. And then I left. It was almost too much for me."

"Too much? Too much how?"

"We were both spelled. I've never kissed a girl like that, nor did I know how. Until this afternoon. She taught me but didn't need to say a word. Just her breathing instructed me. Magic."

"What about her spaceship breath?"

"An acquired taste. The minerality of a child's chewable vitamin. Like the Flintstones vitamins you and I both had as a kid."

How did he know that? He knows all.

"Can I have a floater of tequila, please?" I asked the bartender, the survivor of an apparent shipwreck, given his tattered costume.

"I wish I could help you, matey, but the typhoon that hit us, it hit the bottles as well. All we were left with were these gizmos."

"Wait, what year is it supposed to be?" I asked.

"I took quite a spill when she went down," he continued. "Hit my head on the sea rocks and lost my memory, matey. But as far as I can tell, the gizmos are powered by the sharks that rule the lagoon."

"The sharks control the frozen margarita machines?"

"Aye."

"Stop it, Cheese," said Johnny Boy. "Just go with the flow."

"Aye," said the bartender.

John's eyes were closed again. He was kissing the soles of her feet. The hairless pores just beneath her navel. I'm sure he'll review it all with me, but not until Bloody Mary Monday, when it would surely be just us. I'm the honorary host of Bloody Mary Monday, even if it's in John's hotel room, so I get to decide who attends. Well, of course Virginia could attend if only to say goodbye, but only after we reviewed the trip, and all the sexy things he did without me. Deal? Deal.

"What do you think of my friend's swimming outfit?" John asked the bartender.

"Never seen anything quite like it. Is he a prisoner? Break free from the Royal Navy gaol?"

"No, I did not."

"The zebra stripes is what caught my attention, mate."

"Cheese is a prisoner of *Wayz*."

"So are you."

"Never said I wasn't."

"Aye, aye," said the bartender. "Too many barrels of rum for ye."

Is there anything worse than a Wayz-critical fake pirate?

*

An inner tube built for two. Larger, I was instructed to sit in the back, my legs almost around John's shoulders. There were two sets of thick, rubber handles we were told to hold dearly.

"Is this a ride?" I asked John. "Also, can the Little Orange bird be a ride?"

"No it cannot. Let the Little Orange Bird be who he is, and this is a lazy river, but with rapids, coves, mist, and animals and Indians dotting the banks."

Our handler pushed us out and over a small waterfall, and we were launched with all the other innertubes. Spinning, colliding. There were a few cute girls, and I wanted to bump into them, so that my thick leg could meet their glistening Coppertone calf. Invariably, at the last moment just before impact, John would intervene, chivalrously preventing the meeting of our limbs. And they'd smile at him. Perhaps they knew my awful plan and counted him as a good Samaritan, one with a virtually hairless chest, just two dusty halos around the nips.

"I could ride this all day," he said. "Do you smell a campfire from Mark Twain's America, where everywhere is home, and it's always summer?"

My more sensitive olfactory register did not pick up on John's Mississippi mists. I smelled sugared air. Besides, I associated mists with the jungle. Disney mixes metaphors, and it's dangerous, like the sinister hologram of a pirate and his pirate ship on his Key to the World card. That demonic galleon from an infant's feverish daymare. Wish I'd never seen it.

"I only smell sugar water, but I wish I could smell something more earthy on this river. So, what rides did you and Virginia do?"

"Just Space Mountain."

"That's it? Huh. That guy Dimitri said *huh* a lot. What a character. What did she say about him?"

"He's deep into this place."

"They really went out?"

"Just for a week or something. This river is romantic, isn't it?"

It made me blush, and then I passed out. Gurgling brooks and aphrodisiacs in the forced air can do that to a man. I dreamt I was a sharp-clawed bear, hugging a boy, so careful not to cut his tender skin, but I wasn't careful enough, and the lazy river ran red.

Exit, pursued by a bear was my high school yearbook quote. Shakespeare.

Fittingly, I was awoken by a thunder crack. The wind had picked up and I was cold. And John Apple-less. The lazy river was empty, and the wind was having its way with the inner tubes. Emptiness knocking into my half emptiness. I had no sense of time, as my wallet, BlackBerry and clothes were in a locker in the changing area, and the coming storm had bruised the sky.

Exit, pursued by a bear. I had no idea what it meant, I just liked the idea of a man in a bear costume on stage. The stuff of farce, I thought. Only recently had my parents, the bookstore owners, explained that it was a most gruesome stage direction.

"Antigonus exits, then a bear follows him and eats him alive. We were worried about you, Murray, that you quoted something so violent."

"Then why didn't you guys say something?"

"We thought you'd learn on your own, and besides you'll never get eaten by a bear. They say it's the worst way to go; bears eat your liver first."

That'll be one drunken bear.

I was the drunken bear in my swimming outfit. I looked down at my striped belly and imagined being shot out of a Civil War cannon during a water show in old Atlantic City.

Surrounded by passenger-less inner tubes, I made myself tumble into the river, then lugged myself, the drunken bear, to shore.

*

Typhoon Lagoon was deserted, except for the pirate bartender who was shuttering Let's Go Slurpin'.

"Where the hell is everyone?" I asked.

"Park closed on account of the storm. Surprised to see you still about. We made all sorts of announcements, matey. Even had my fellow swashbucklers scour the river for any man overboard."

This happens to me all the time. The swashbucklers don't see me; I am merely an empty innertube.

"Was I you, matey, I'd seek cover. This here storm reminds me of the very same typhoon that knocked me overboard and into the sea rocks. Legend has it—"

"You know, you don't have to do the pirate thing, now that it's just us. And is there someone who can open the locker room for me? All my stuff's in there, and it looks closed."

He was emptying the strawberry margarita machine, filling pitcher after pitcher.

"I'll go see if I can use this here skeleton key to get you to your doubloons."

He was certainly going to throw away the strawberry margarita pitchers. They looked so red and inviting, the only things truly alive in this here lagoon. Fuck it, I took one and hid it behind a fake boulder. I'd collect my things, then snatch it on the way out.

"What do you think you're doing, Scallywag?"

"Me? Nothing. I was just, y'know—"

"Skeleton key doesn't seem to be working today. Maybe the storm put Blackbeard's curse on it. I suggest you come back tomorrow."

"Listen, I really *really* need to get my wallet and BlackBerry, not to mention my clothes."

"Not sure what any of that means, but at least you'll have a pitcher of stolen margaritas to get you through the night. Now be gone with you, the lagoon is off limits. A storm's a-brewin'. Reminds me of the very same one that knocked me overboard and into the sea rocks."

"You gotta be shittin' me."

"*Yo ho, yo ho, a pirate's life for me.*"

*

An off-duty Disney bus driver took pity on me just as the skies opened. What fat Florida droplets. Wetter and warmer than any rain I'd known. And the force with which they fired against the ground. Marbles. A summer squall in November? Why not. Ponders have been known to fuck with the skies, like Prospero in *The Tempest*. Magic. (A child of bookstore owners can always lean on literature.) More magical still, the bus driver took me all the way to the Grand Floridian parking lot, but his real motivation for the trip became clear when he held forth an empty plastic cup, his hand on the lever that could liberate me.

"Oh, so you want some of this?" I asked, my pitcher of strawberry margaritas still half full. With that he produced a second plastic cup. No more questions, just pour, which I did, and the door opened.

"Have a magical day," he said.

"You know what? Fuck off."

"*Huck, huck.*" It was the sound of the Goofy Walk, and it shamed me.

He'd won.

*

What a sight I was, fetal position, shivering in my wet bathing attire. I cannot remember a time in my life when I did not welcome abundant and abundantly cold air-conditioning. My birthright as a portly American. Too embarrassed to approach the front desk about a key to my room; as well, too drunk, now, to speak to management. I decided to sober up on the lobby couch and hope Johnny Boy or of course Virginia would pass by. No answer in his room. *Their* room.

"Mr. Marks? Why, it is you," said Mrs. Wells.

"You'll have to excuse me, I got locked out of my locker and then—"

"I do adore your style, Mr. Marks. I haven't seen a bathing outfit like that since, well—"

"John made me wear it. Not made me, but—"

"Your lips are white, poor dear. Here, take Mr. Wells's robe. He's taking a walk—*the* walk—with Mr. Apple."

What a goddamn wonderful robe. Smelling of cigar and musk. Wearing it sobered me. Washington Wells was sobering me from afar.

Come on, Mr. Marks, don't let us down, son.

"The walk?" I asked.

"Well, your friend is clearly enamored with our Ginny. She has that effect, and we like to nip things in the bud."

"Thank you for the robe."

"Keep it. You know, Washington was so impressed by you."

"Really?"

"Don't sound so surprised. You see, you remind him of his grandfather, Colonel Alton P. Wells, which is the highest compliment my husband can give a suitor. The Colonel was substantial like you. Stout. But kindly like you. Reliable. It's what the parents of a girl such as our Ginny needs. Assurances. At this my grandfather-in-law apparently excelled. He passed when Washington was just ten, but not before hundreds of stories about all the Yankees who suffered at the hands of his saber. We have a portrait of him prominently displayed at Fairvue."

They like fat guys who don't say too much. They like fat suitors they can control; I'll be damned. Wait, I'm a suitor?

"Thank you for the compliment, Mrs. Wells. I rarely remind people of anyone."

Fairvue. What an awesomely pretentious plantation name. I want to be on that porch, with lemony gin drinks, dressed in the good colonel's old grays.

"Don't you want to get out of that cold suit, Mr. Marks?"

"My Key to the World, it's with my wallet and BlackBerry; this pirate guy—"

"Room 1809. They upgraded to the club level. Happens all the time with the suitors; trying to impress her right off the bat," she said, snickering. "But that's not what impresses her."

"What does?"

"Virtue. It's written in our family crest, in Latin of course. *Virtus*."

She stole a glance at my maleness. Holy shit.

"Go knock on Suite 1809, Ginny's in there. Take a hot shower, and we'll see about getting your belongings back to you, dear Mr. Marks. Or may I call you Cheese? What a cute nickname."

"Cheese is just fine. My belongings are in—"

"We'll find them. The Wells family excels at finding lost things."

CHAPTER EIGHT

ROOM 1809 WAS NOT a room, but a named suite. *The Roy O. Disney Suite.* John and I were obsessed with named suites, having never scored one. We did, however, seek them out, bringing our disposable Ponder camera to a top floor and snapping the exteriors of *The Duke Ellington Suite, The Gerald Ford Suite, The Rita Hayworth Suite.* I stood before the plaque commemorating Mr. Disney and missed my green carboard disposable Fuji camera; I missed Johnny Boy and me standing together gawking at the signage; missed the melodious structure of a traditional Ponder. This Ponder thus far? Throw out the rule book. While I gawked at the signage and pined for the old order of things, and the modesty of my green Fuji, the door opened. Berobed just like me, Virginia smiled a sleepy little smile.

"Hi," her voice cracked.

This was the first time I had noticed her eyes; eyes I'd filed away as merely light, very light. More than that, they were practically bercft of any color. A palest olive green? Some sort of jungle-cat yellow? An almost colorless color that didn't exist, only in her irises. Let's call it chartreuse.

"Chartreuse," I said.

"Yum," said Virginia.

"The color of your eyes."

"On my driver's license it says green. How dull. Let's order a bottle from room service and compare."

She slid a finger along my robe's angled lapel. "We match."

"Your mom gave me this robe."

I decided not to tell her it belonged to her father. Not romantic.

"Oh, I know. It's Daddy's robe. Come on in, Cheese."

A grand piano in the living room. A dining room table formally set for sixteen. A half bathroom!

"Did John see this place yet?"

"He sure did. He upgraded us. I told him not to, but suitors get anxious around now. He made such a fuss about the powder room over there."

She picked up a baroque-looking rotary phone. Buttonless and golden, it looked glorious next to her cheek.

"He called me Mrs. Apple," she said, cupping the receiver. "We'd like a bottle of Chartreuse, and two slices of lemon meringue pie."

Fucking awesome choice.

"No lemon meringue pie? I hate to sound like a spoiled little girl, but can't someone make it for us? He's checking," she told me. "You go shower, Cheese. Mama said you were cold. Go on, use the master, and be sure to put that wet suit in the hamper."

But then I'll be naked beneath Daddy's robe.

"Go on," she said, and then was back to her call. "Oh, I don't mind waiting if it can mean lemon meringue pie for us."

Us. Pronouns are sexy. The plural ones.

"Which way is the master?" I asked.

"Follow my scent, and you'll find it."

It was a silly question. I was on that trail the moment she opened the front door.

*

The bathroom, which I'd assumed she'd used but once, was a shrine to Virginia Wells. The capped pink razor. The natural sponge that was barely moist; Florence's was always hard and misshapen, and needed its own ablutions to rise back to life. The bar of Ivory soap, a solid scum-less rectangle. Its cursive *Ivory* still scrutable. By the act of cleaning herself, the room and everything in it had become cleaner; with some girls their hygiene rubs off on the claw-footed tub. A tub I lustily filled.

"Men shouldn't take baths," Florence had said. "Warm, still water feminizes the balls."

Maybe for most men, but not Colonel Alton P. Wells. I could see him in a grand old tub after battle. A victory bourbon in his gnarled fist, and his Confederate hat safe and dry on his proud head. Do mutton chops look absurd on balding men? I'd be sure to ask Virginia after my bubble bath. I'd purposefully not locked the bathroom door. Oh, beneficent bubbles, cover me; turn me into a bodiless head. I wore them well, these bubbles, just as I'd worn Mr. Wells's robe. Stout men are unafraid to cinch a belt or form a bubble hillock with their bellies. I pictured Virginia skiing down my stomach. Ski pants illustrate the female form like nothing else. Curves and hollows. I shuddered.

There was a knock at the door.

"Care for some pie?" called Virginia.

Awful timing; the ski resort reverie had the effect of loosening turkey leg flatulence, and now things stunk.

"Maybe after my bath?"

"Don't be silly," she said. "The butler's here right now."

The door opened, and in walked a man in a business suit pushing a room service trolley.

"Where shall I set it up. By the bath?"

"Um, sure."

As he got closer, he couldn't help but wrinkle his nose in disgust. A rule was broken, we both knew; he couldn't finish fussing with wrappers and silver soon enough.

"Yellow Chartreuse, from France, a 1950s bottling from the collection of Roy O. Disney."

He poured it into crystal, keeping his face as far away as possible. His neck would hurt tonight, and that pain would remind him to hate me for my desecration.

When in the tub, Mr. Disney held the gas inside.

He was able to lower the trolley to be level with the tub.

"Wait, before you go, is the trolley made specifically for bathtubs? Never saw one like that."

He paused at the door, forced to explain.

"There are four trolleys that were designed by Mr. Roy O. Disney for his suite. Sadly, he died before he could experience his genius. One trolley becomes taller. One trolley shorter. And the other two, longer and wider. Inspired by *Alice in Wonderland*, sir."

"Holy shit," I said.

What a gorgeous life, designing fucking room service trolleys. Although Johnny Boy would say that God himself would have provocation to end the human experience if he happened to see old Roy spending tens of thousands of dollars on his precious trolleys while eleven million American kids went hungry every night.

"Anything else, sir?

"You're the only character I've seen who doesn't have to wear a name tag."

"The suite butlers are exempt."

"Interesting."

"Anything else, sir?"

"No, that was great. And sorry for, you know, the smell."

"Yes, sir."

He shut the sliding double doors so gently, barely a click. What a pro. We'd have to tip him extra. No suited adult should have to endure turkey leg farts while bending over a naked man in a marble receptacle.

Screw it, I'll send him a gift anonymously. Bath salts? He must have his own tub; it's probably the most expensive thing he owns. It's his sanctuary, and he spends his weekends cleaning it. Yes, bath salts. I'll have to ask Florence what type. But for now, just look at the glint of yellow in that lemon meringue pie. And the pale iris color of the hard Wayz. All of it, just in reach of my arms. God bless Roy Disney's shrinking trolley. As for the eleven million starving kids, I'd have to speak with John about them when the Ponder was over. I let another rip, then drank her eyes.

*

I awoke to a practically drained tub, fossils of the bubble bath capping my extremities. The butler's revenge was to pull the plug, or perhaps Virginia had paid a visit? I could see her, mischievous, removing the stopper, her hand over her own tittering mouth. This was the second time in so many hours I'd awoken alone in Disney water. Ah, it was my own big toe that was the culprit. There it was crammed into the drainage, scraped and bleeding. What dream had made my toe burrow so forcefully into a dark hole?

"You okay in there, Cheese?" asked Virginia.

"I think I fell asleep."

"Old-ass Chartreuse can do that to you. Let's have some more!"

The bedroom was dark. The sun had just set. The only source of light came from the balcony's open doors. The blue light of Cinderella's Castle stopping just before the room. While its source was brazen, this light had the dignity not to intrude. We were two belt knots removed from nudity. This is what the blue light understood.

"So, where's Johnny Boy anyway?" I asked.

A dresser drawer was open, and I could make out his natty pile of boxers, each folded into a smallest rectangle. He'd probably been organizing that drawer when he was called by Mr. Wells. Virginia and I might be berobed Chartreuse buddies, but this sure as shit was *John's* hotel room.

"Beats me," said Virginia, testing the buoyancy of her meringue: tap, tap. "Daddy's been back for a while now. Maybe Daddy gave him some discouraging news and he's building up a lather, trying to figure out the next move."

"He is my best friend, you know."

"Oh, of course I know, Cheese. He spoke so highly of you. We both did."

I shut John's underwear drawer for him. That's what best friends do.

"John always unpacks first thing. I should do that. I should do many new things."

"My mama unpacks for me. And also packs for me. It's a Southern thing. So, tell me more about your wife, she must be very pretty."

"Well, she's Chinese."

"What a fascinating culture. Dragons and chopsticks. What wisdom."

Would Florence be offended? No way, this girl was so earnest.

She opened John's underwear drawer, then shut it. Was she now his best friend?

"A man's boxers should reach his knees," she said.

Mine did. I could tell that John's were barely mid-thigh. Skimpy things for skinny thighs. Girlish thighs, one might say. A red light joined the blue. Fireworks over the Castle; they might as well have been exploding on the terrace itself. It gave her goosebumps. Despite the thick terrycloth, I could see her pertness. She hugged herself. I should hug her.

"Watch out, Cheese, here comes the grand finale. Gets me every time."

Boom, boom, boom, boom. Green light bathed the room, killing off all the other colors. And into the green entered John Apple. His mouth was open, an oval; his mouth was so rarely open. So rarely did he look as if he was asking fate to explain its fickle ways.

"You okay?" I asked.

"Sorry I left you in the lazy river," he said, but his eyes were on her.

"Cheese," Virginia said, concentrating on him, "you'll find your personal belongings and your clothes, cleaned and pressed, atop the piano."

"My BlackBerry?"

"Everything. Now, if you wouldn't mind, dear Cheese, John and I should take a spell."

Spell was again accurate. She led him out to the balcony where the fireworks had ended. There was only smoke now, and the sweet smell of spent gunpowder. Childhood's cap guns.

*

Having drinks with an old friend, Florence had written.

I'd expected a hundred and five messages from her, starting with *That swimsuit looks ridiculous on you* and culminating with *I don't trust that Southern girl.*

But there was just the one. Par for the course during a Ponder that she'd be coy about a date, hoping to score a jealousy pang. Problematically for her, she had only one old friend, David Pang, who'd taken her virginity. Good old David came out of the closet in college. What a victory when your wife's first lover chooses the other side of the buffet.

David Pang? I wrote back, marveling at my warm and dry clothes. My unmolested wallet. My BlackBerry's battery life. On top of everything, Mrs. Wells must've found the time to charge it.

Kathy Apple. She called me out of the blue.

Bullshit. Nice try, I wrote.

I didn't want to tell you during your trip.

It's called a PONDER.

I didn't want to tell you, unless you asked.

Hold on one second, Virginia, a girl, needs me.

You go have fun and write me when you're safe in bed.

Shit. I dressed and lifted the golden phone.

"Yes, Mr. Apple," answered the butler.

"It's actually Mr. Marks."

"Yes sir."

"I was the guy from the bathtub." Silence.

"Could you come here, please?"

"Of course."

I needed someone to speak with, truth be told. At this stage of our Ponder, the first Friday night, we'd be having trip review Wayz before heading out into the night. Now, there was more to review than perhaps any Ponder ever. While John was in there, continuing to make Ponder history, I needed to regroup. I needed to understand what the hell was happening and could not think of a better interlocutor than this butler. Butlers were used to crazy masters. They were trained to mitigate against indulgence, extravagance, gout. They were aspirin. Swiss Army knives. Healers of the rich and confused. A firm hand on your shoulder, they'd steer you to the right room, the right chair, the right drink, and all would make perfect sense. Fuck, Virginia was in possession of the Chartreuse.

*

The butler stood before me, arms crossed behind his back, his black shoes pointing outward. Many triangles to this man. Sharp angles and also square corners. Again, I looked in vain for a name tag.

"So, what's your name?" I asked.

"Christopher."

"Ah, St. Christopher, patron saint of travelers. Perfect."

"Sir?"

"This has been one hell of a Ponder. Between Virginia and John and—"

"Mr. Marks, I take great pride in serving the Disney company, and despite an apparent moment, um, earlier, I would never risk my employ by way of social interactions with a guest."

"Huh?"

He aimed his eyes down the hallway that led to the master bathroom.

"Wait, what?"

Christopher pressed two fingers to his lips, backed away as if I were the King of England. Or maybe the Queen. Butlers are exquisite about removing themselves from rooms. All you hear is the tiniest click from the door's hardware, and then there's an outrageous silence born of their absence. A buzz in the air. And then you miss them. He thought I was gay.

I miss you, I wrote Florence.

?, she wrote back.

Fucking Florence. By now she'd be in the bathroom at work putting on makeup for her date with Kathy. Kurt Cobain sang, "Everyone is gay." I made myself a rum and Coke from the living room's glorious bar cart. Crystal decanters displaying all the colors of the Wayz rainbow: dark brown, brown, light brown, clear, black. Huge ice cubes, to boot. Solid cubes, clear as glass. So much to go over with John. And the ice prongs, clawless. In their place two Mickey heads grabbed the adult cubes. Johnny Boy was obsessed with Cobain and the shotgun to the temple. Hemingway, too, sucking on a barrel.

"It's brave," he'd said. "What a statement. What a moment, just before the trigger pull. Nirvana. No pun intended."

"Rude to leave a bloody mess for someone else to clean up."

"Don't worry, Cheese. You won't find me. Unless I want you to."

*

An hour had passed. In vain did I press an ear to the bedroom door. In vain did I jiggle my second rum and Coke, hoping the sound of ice would stir them. A butler would know just how to knock. I got back on the golden phone.

"Yes, Mr. Apple." The voice on the other end did not sound like Christopher's.

"Christopher?"

"This is Sandeep, sir."

"Where's Christopher."

"I've taken over his post."

"Forever?"

Silence. Had my bathtub flatulence somehow ruined his life? Was it code in the gay community for something unspeakable?

"Sandeep, may I have a triple espresso?"

"Of course, Mr. Apple."

"Make it three of them."

I'd use the caffeine Wayz to gain entry to the bedroom. "Actually, two triple espressos, and one cappuccino."

Foam on her upper lip.

"Anything else, Mr. Apple?"

"Yes actually, and some sambuca for my dear friend Mr. Marks. Did Christopher say anything about Mr. Marks?"

"Sambuca. Yes, sir."

That meant he did. Sandeep and I agreed that the conversation had ended. As only a butler could, he gently replaced his receiver, inspiring me to gently replace mine. Back to the bedroom door. I made my finger into a faraway woodpecker and tapped. A woodpecker from a neighboring plantation. A thousand acres away. Of course, no response.

*

"Thank you, Sandeep," I said to the skinny Indian man. What a head of hair.

"Are you Indian?"

"Yes, sir."

"I adore Indian food."

"Very kind of you to say."

I'd never seen a more beautiful cappuccino. Its foam mocked the lemon meringue pie's static mountain peak.

"What's your favorite ride, Sandeep?"

"Probably the Jungle Cruise. And you?"

"Haunted. I might smoke tonight. I've never really smoked before. That's the thing about this Ponder—actually, please sit, Sandeep."

Just looking at him made me hungry for lamb vindaloo; does that make me racist? He inspected the seat cushion before committing, then sat squarely. He knew not to cross his legs. Way too familiar a pose for a butler.

"Maybe I'll become a butler? John's butler? Who knows? My wife's Asian, too. But to be perfectly honest, I don't feel her presence here in Disney World. I feel . . . I feel limitless. In love. Not only with the two people in that room, but with everything. I love Wayz. I love Wayzing on the monorail and being generous with Ponder strangers, who are themselves so generous and beautifully fat. I love the idea of buying Marlboro Lights at the Sandy Cove, flirting with the old lady behind the counter. Flashing her my green eyes. Green like the frogs that grace *Natural Geographic*."

He stood and smiled, "I need to see to our other suite guests, Mr. Marks, but please feel free to call me if you need anything else. Disney World can be overwhelming the first time. We are here to help."

"Yes, but not Christopher."

"Well, I'm here for you, sir."

"Things usually don't happen to me, Sandeep. I'm a real estate attorney, and not even the top man in a four-person office. I've only been with one woman. In fact, Virginia is probably my only other girl-friend, and I've only sat on one ride with her. Haunted. One Haunted. One Pan. Hell, I've only known her since today. Disney *Word*," I read my empty flask. "Fucking Disney Word."

Sandeep had already left the room. He knew to spare himself my cursing. He knew I was drunk, and that Disney drunks say vile things. I'd lost track of my Wayz count. Twenty? Twenty-two? I wrote John, asking for his tally. What the hell are they doing in there? I'll use the room service cart to ram the door. No, it would vulgarize the cappuccino foam. What would Christopher do? There was a summoning bell in the bathroom.

"Caffeine Wayz," I rang. "Time for caffeine Wayz, Mr. Prince of Cups."

John had mentioned something about a world-class tarot card reader somewhere in this wacky place. EPCOT world? Something. Maybe the three of us could go. I sorely needed to know my future.

"You two awake?"

I sipped my sambuca-spiked espresso while wielding the summoning bell whose clapper was thoughtfully bundled in felt so as not to punish the butler's keen ears.

"Well, ready or not, here comes Cheese."

Titillating, the jouncing foam. Its whiteness was torchlight; the room had turned dark blue, purple even. And it smelled of them. Not them—I knew their individual scents—not them, but a third person born of their proximity. Suffocating, the aroma of another's intimacy. It was literally phlegmatic. Fresh air, please, but the balcony doors were shut.

"Hello?" I asked.

It took my eyes moments to adjust, during which I found wall space against which to balance, then for myself did I claim Virginia's cappuccino.

"Are you two even in here?"

Feet. Four feet. Two facing up and two facing down. Four soles. I could make out the baby soft folds of their soles. He was directly on top of her, but they weren't moving. Were they breathing? My cappuccino and I tiptoed to the other side of the bed, where I sat so carefully. I faced away from them, toward the windows. There were no signs of life, until the bed moved. Once. She let out a little gasp. Get the hell out of there, Cheese. But Cheese did not budge. I couldn't. The thrusts had a pattern. Every minute or so, it seemed. Always singular, followed by her gasp. I should have spiked the cappuccino.

CHAPTER NINE

It was just before midnight when Sandeep, the butler, delivered my cleaned striped bathing suit to my room at the Grand Floridian. I couldn't sleep and was anxious to bend a stranger's ear, a butler's ear, to confess. But Sandeep left the laundry basket just outside the door and, I imagine, ran down the hall after ringing the doorbell. Butlers hate unsavory confessions. They race for the bathtub to cleanse themselves of their master's naughtiness. Florence was not answering my messages. Her date with Kathy Apple had not concluded; my great hope was that we'd have dueling confessions. They would offset, and life as we knew it would continue until death. Had I experienced a tryst? It sure felt that way. I hadn't had a Wayz since the incident but needed a nightcap in order to write a proper apology to John. Apology Wayz? How about a bourbon? I butlered myself a drink from the un-glorious minibar in my nameless room. From the Murray Marks non-suite I wrote him:

Sorry.

For what? We need to talk. Extraordinary night. Now for sleep. Tomorrow's the day, he wrote back.

Day for what?

It had taken me the better part of an hour to slither from my side of that bed to the lovers'. I traveled the edges of the California king-sized bed, moving inches every few minutes. I'd wait for their congress to progress; conceal my slithering with his thrust, her moan until I made it to their angelic feet. There, I formed my mouth so that when he encroached, my lips might brush against all four soles. It was all I wanted. Needed. And then one of their heels kicked me in the nose, and I tumbled off, then scurried like a rodent. In retrospect I had flattened my body like a water bug and slipped under the door and out of the Roy O. Disney Suite. *For what?* he asks.

Goodnight, wrote Florence.

What the hell is wrong with people? Oblivious, non-sentient, blind to the high dramas of life? Fuck it, I'll have another bourbon and re-remember my brush with their sex.

*

Shockingly, I awoke unscathed from Friday's orgiastic mess. No headache, no guilt, I rushed to open the shades and beheld the whirling Kingdom, which had been awake since 7:00 a.m. on the dot. The Magic Kingdom also was not hungover.

Hey, Cheese, guess who got a cute little BlackBerry!

The message was from VWells324852@aol.com. Adorable that she allowed AOL to generate a meaningless email address.

Hi! Welcome to the club, I wrote.

Shit, what a pedestrian message. And how the hell did she get a new BlackBerry so quickly? What a resourceful family, I gulped. The only child gets what she wants, when she wants it.

I also got one for Mama. Breakfast? she asked.

With John?

With you!

*

Last night I kissed your feet while you and he were one, and now, Wayzless and having little charming to offer in terms of conversation, you want to watch me inhale a rasher of bacon. Virginia, much like Johnny Boy, was always *on*. Wayz or not. Silence didn't bother her, while I needed to fill it with something, anything.

"So how did you sleep? What's going on?" I asked.

We'd met in the lobby. She wore short, short terrycloth shorts and a tank top. I'd showered hastily to be on time; didn't even iron my pants. I had the sense that Virginia did not appreciate waiting for a late suitor, not that I was one.

I hadn't even written Florence good morning.

She leaned on me in order to straighten a sandal strap. "So, let's eat, Mr. Cheese."

She led us to a buffet where life-sized puppet princesses visited tables and signed autograph books.

"I love the character breakfasts," she said and ordered tea and melon from the waiter, preferring that more dignified means of procurement. "I'm not such a big buffet girl."

"Me neither," I lied. Who doesn't love a buffet? Especially one where Biggunz graze.

"Double Bacardi and Coke, please. And a rasher of bacon," I told the cheery waiter. "And a prune Danish." (For regularity's sake.)

"Nothing like a man and his bacon," she said.

"Yeah, definitely. So, where's John?"

"In his room, I guess. I slept in my room, of course."

"Of course."

A very pretty brunette Snow White spun about our table. Seeing no cameras and no book to sign, she spun away smiling brightly.

"Shoot, I forgot my autograph book, would you go get it for me? Once I leave the room for a day at Disney, I can't bring myself to return until the day is over. I'm superstitious about that."

What a long, elegant hickey-less neck she had. "Sure, I'll go, Virginia."

She gave me her key card. I needed a drink before entering her room; it would almost certainly stimulate my nose. It was already 10:17 a.m., an unapologetic Ponder Saturday hour for a first Wayz.

"Do you mind if I wait for my Wayz before going up? Hair of the dog."

I hated my unremarkable speech; did she even know what a Wayz was?

"Sure, you can have a Wayz before doing my errand." She sipped her tea. What a posture, and how clever of her to deduce what Wayz meant.

"Great, thanks, Virginia. How's your melon?"

She rewarded my banality with a little nod.

I'm having breakfast with her, I wrote John.

I know. You wayzing?

Waiting for the first.

Is she drinking too?

Tea.

He didn't know her well enough yet to know she was civilized with her morning tea. Why am I surprised? How could he know her so soon, and why did this fill me with promise? Easy, Cheese. You're Sancho, he's Don Quixote.

"I like that you used the word *rasher*, a rasher of bacon. Hm," she said, a sister sound to last night's moaning. I want to be Don Quixote. And here comes my rum and Coke.

*

A housekeeper was in her room. I'd decided to raid her minibar. I'll just say that I'm her husband.

"The wife needs her puppet book," I told her.

"Have magic day," she said in broken English.

In the process of emptying a trash bin by the desk, she spilled a crumpled ball of paper which I stole before she could notice.

"The wife and her puppets," I told her.

"Is okay." She forced a smile. Poor dear. Cleaning up after Biggunz. I should assume her duties for one entire day, would do me good, and she'd hug me, toss me her apron. It's so easy to dream of virtue when buzzed with a morning's first Wayz. Now for a second Wayz. White wine? Why not. No need for a mixer. Sometimes soft Wayz are really the answer. I brought the half bottle of Chardonnay out to the balcony. She had a lagoon view. I bet she chose it over the Kingdom view. More elegant, and she could squint and pretend she was back home at the mossy plantation.

Dear John was all that was written on the crumpled piece of paper. The bin had been full of balled-up paper. I imagined they all read "Dear John."

I'm in her room, getting her autograph book for the puppets, I wrote John.

They're called characters. I'm going for a run. Need to clear my head.

The cleaning supplies obscured much of her scent, but it was like freebasing the Grand Floridian's profound polish. The virtuous smell commanded that I not open her underwear drawer and glean her thongs. Florence wore granny undies, purely for comfort.

Good morning, I wrote Florence.

Weird. I never say good morning, usually *Hey, what's up*. I drank straight from the bottle. Oh, beautiful twist-off caps; I placed the cap on a finger and tapped the iron balustrade; toasted the lagoon, the families boarding a watercraft, the soundtrack that was piped everywhere. What buoyant jingles. The Nazis played classical music while Jews boarded trains. In six weeks, it would be the year 2000. Frightening. I will miss the past, miss being on Virginia Wells's balcony in a year that begins with a one. Two thousand is too big of a number, bad shit's going to happen with such a bloated number, really bad shit but not today, dammit!

*

Shoeless, shirtless, the suited Russian was in my seat. "This guy," he said. "I know this guy."

"That's right," said Virginia. "You two gents met."

She snatched up her autograph book and bounded toward Goofy.

Dimitri sniffed my drink.

"Rum so early? Huh, impressive. You alcoholic?"

"Only at Disney," I said, and motioned that he was in my seat.

"Apologies. Have to go anyway. Four Splash, one Space. Will see you tonight."

"Where?"

"*Where*, he says. Huh."

The surly bastard left, but not before whispering something to the Minnie Mouse puppet who then immediately danced over to me.

"It's okay," I said. "I'm good."

She pointed at my drink and wagged her finger at my apparent naughtiness.

"It's just Coca-Cola," I said.

Then from her frozen smile I heard a gruff male voice boom: "Rum and Coke."

She threw up her hands, bopped away. Fucking Dimitri.

Are the puppets allowed to speak? I asked John.

Of course not.

One just did.

You're mistaken.

"Can the puppets speak?" I asked Virginia who had returned from autographs, beaming.

"I got every single one!"

"I think one spoke to me."

She was about to spear a piece of melon, thought better of it, and waved goodbye to me like an Italian, *Ciao* over the shoulder.

"Is something happening tonight, Dimitri mentioned—"

But she was gone. Minnie, however, was watching. She put her two hands to her heart, rocked back and forth. Sarcastic fucker.

*

Mexico at one, wrote John. *Inky darkness of the ancient Aztec skies under which we eat Chicken Nachos and behold an erupting volcano. There is History here. This is where we discuss the future. Today is the most important of my life. And from the volcano's plume, a hidden Mickey.*

Where is it? I wrote.

EPCOT. World Showcase. I bought a diamond ring.

Why? I mean for who?

Fuck.

*

Mexico did not disappoint, although John Apple had run here, along-side highways so he claimed, and was sweaty. As was I: The World Showcase was endless and at noon it was in excess of an unseason-able 83 degrees. I'd arrived at EPCOT early and sniffed out a pub in England, a digest-sized highlight reel of lowbrow London. A Twinings tea shop, a Beefeater, a red phone booth. But the pub was well done, and the bartender was actually British. She pulled my Guinness like a pro. Shay Hitchcock was her name.

"Any relation to Alfred Hitchcock?" I had asked.

"Oh, yes," she'd said. "Distant, but yes."

She was Indian, or part Indian.

"Do you know Sandeep, the butler?" I'd asked.

Like me, Shay had green eyes. More hazel, but so exotic against her light brown skin. Naturally pink lips. Plump. And a nose ring. What is it about Indian people? Such noble noses. Aquiline and proud of it.

"She had a nose ring," I told sweaty John.

He had run with a little box in his shorts. A red Cartier box.

"Where the hell did you find a Cartier ring?" I asked.

"The butler had someone visit me from the mall."

"Sandeep?"

"Let me show you."

It was magnificent. Ten carats, one stone.

"Jesus! How much?" I asked.

"A lot," he said, sipping tea.

"No Wayz? Why are you affecting tea Wayz?"

Oh, because Virginia had tea this morning.

"It was 197 grand."

"So, you're asking her to marry you after knowing her for one day."

"To call the last twenty-four hours a *day* is inaccurate, Cheese. Might as well call the Big Bang a Chinese New Year firecracker on a wet day for a parade."

His analogy didn't sound like him; he was off his game. We sat at the bar in view of an Aztec temple where it was indeed always midnight. Astounding air-conditioning here, which we both needed, and as advertised, behind the temple a smoldering volcano. My best friend had a perfect sense of bar ambience.

"Will she say yes?" I asked.

"I don't know. I really don't. We were together, you know, in bed, last night. It was a sacred experience, but she didn't say much and left while I slept."

I kissed your feet. And hers. I was drunk, beyond drunk, and have no regrets. Not in the Mexican night. Last night was the most thrilling and liberating moment of my life.

"I met a really cool bartender, I mean Takenstein, named Shay, Shay Hitchcock—"

"Great name," he said.

"She knows Sandeep, the butler."

"I don't think her father liked me. Weird son of a bitch in his robe and sunglasses. Fuck it, I need a vodka."

"Me too. Didn't you say something about chicken nachos? So, what was she like? I mean in—"

"The warmest girl in the world."

"Did you—"

"The warmest girl in the world."

He was staring at the engagement ring, turning it just so, trying to catch some light in the Mexican night. In the distance a mariachi band played.

"When will you propose?"

"Tonight."

I wondered if Dimitri had also bought a ring. How many suitors? How many rings?

He's going to propose, I wrote Florence. *Un-fucking-believable.*

When you know, you know, she wrote.

How was last night?

Life is short, she wrote. *Back to work. Have fun and tell John congratulations.*

If she says yes. Wait was there another tryst?

Don't worry.

What an equivocal jerk.

"Florence saw Kathy last night," I said. "I think something's going on with them. Do you think something's going on with them?"

"You mean like lesbian stuff? Who knows, maybe. Hidden Mickey! Look, Cheese."

From the volcano, his ears and face. And then he vanished. Life *is* short. It lasts precisely as long as a Mickey puff does. I hope Virginia says no.

*

From EPCOT to the next madness is not for the faint of Wayz. So much walking. So much waiting. There's a palpable impatience amongst the waiting class. At the bus stop, we are a mob, angry that it's not our bus. And then resentful that many must stand. And for what? The Tower of Terror was in Movie Land or Hollywood World or whatever forgettable thing John said. The land was a vast 1930s Art Deco film set where

Charlie Chaplins and Marilyn Monroes roamed the shiny streets; guests were encouraged to request their autographs. Fake movie directors yelled *cut*. Fake stars are born. Poor kids who think they're going to be famous because of some shitty souvenir in sepia, their names superimposed on a fake marquee. Maybe one of them *will* make it. It takes work these days not being cynical. I need to work harder.

"Extra, extra, read all about it," shouted newsboys selling caramel corn.

Thank goodness for the decrepit-looking Tower Hotel, overgrown and ominous. Adult. Because in the adult world things go wrong, are left unrepaired; vines, dust, and cobwebs rule old kingdoms. In this case a luxurious Los Angelenos hotel in which *something happened* one New Year's Eve in the distant past during a time, to quote John Cheever, when everyone wore a hat.

"Is there a bar in here? This lobby is awesome," I said to John.

"Shh."

He was rubbing his chin, ruminating over a chess board whose players had picked up and left that fateful night.

"It's a stalemate," said John.

I wished to God that this wonderfully eerie lobby had a bar. I bet it did, and Johnny Boy was hoarding the secret, but while snooping for it, a bellhop from between the great wars scolded me.

"Cast members only, sir, please return to the queue."

"None of the characters point at things, instead they motion with an open palm. Passive aggressive, if you ask me," I observed to John.

"It's a supremely elegant way for cast members to put you back on the right path, Cheese."

Our first ride together, just us, was underwhelming compared to the lobby. They crammed thirty people into seats in a cage, shot us up to the top of the tower, dropped us. Repeated six times. Although I was somehow able to Wayz from my flask in between drops.

"Jesus, man, you couldn't wait?" asked John.

"If you'd have shown me where the hotel bar was."

"She'll love that her ring has seen the gloom of this place. There is no bar, one only needs the terror."

He'd placed the huge diamond on the chess board, backed away too many steps for my tastes. Someone could have easily pilfered it. He let it sit there for minutes, crazy bastard. Had someone stolen it, he would've probably grinned, bought a plastic Disney ring, and proposed regardless. Recently, I spied his ATM receipt. Well, he crumpled it up one drunken night at Shun Lee and threw it at me. I played softball at BU and had quick hands; snatched it out of the air and into my pocket. The balance? $11,792,389.07. Who the fuck has eleven million dollars on their debit card? I wondered what havoc that sort of financial security might wreak on the soul. Living paycheck to paycheck is best for that soul. Florence and I shop like the French, just the ingredients for that day's meals. Things are fresh. Little is wasted. *Tomorrow* is a dirty word. The future be damned. Our currency is this breath, not the next. My ATM receipt says $18,943.67. Florence's? An even more gallant $7,887.54. A wildly sexy sum; just enough for a vacation, a shopping spree, a rare bottle of collectible wine. After which, it's back to work. And should our little firm fail we'd have enough resources to regroup in the kitchen, conjure up a Plan B over aforementioned collectible wine Wayz. The barely upper middle class are resilient lovers of life. We have a few maxed-out credit cards, and so what? Florence mends my socks with thread and needle and keeps a single sock drawer. Is there anything more optimistic than a single sock drawer?

"There's a 1950s diner here that serves booze," said John. "Lunch is on me."

Is it even generosity when the ATM reads eight figures long?

"We need to strategize about tonight," he said.

I wondered what Virginia was doing. Did she see this coming? Like me, she seemed to live in the moment. Smiling on a ride. Floating in a pool. I bet her ATM card was funded by her parents, always a few grand. What the hell did she do when not in Disney? People who don't work might as well be from a different planet; how do they fill up all that time?

"Does Virginia have a job?" I asked John.

"Her mom decorates Southern mansions. I think sometimes she helps with that."

Johnny Boy tells people he's a "currently retired money manager."

"At twenty-nine?" they'll ask.

"'Fraid so," he'll say with a smile.

Gotta admire his honesty.

CHAPTER TEN

GETTING TO ANIMAL LAND is not fun. Just when you think you've arrived, you're met with a twisting and turning maze of thickets—a jungle with which you must contend even before the turnstyle. Once inside, the place was sub-saharan with heat, and my thighs needed Vaseline. As well, there were few dark air-conditioned rides. On the bright side, there were more bars, and the place looked just like my parents' Peace Corp Africa of the 1960s, brimming with color and against-all-odds optimism. But my thighs.

"I fucking told you to wear shorts," said John. "Now you're a piece of chafed Cheese."

"My khakis and safari shirt befit this land like nobody's business. And stop playing with that ring. I swear you'll lose it. Hey, do they like pump hot air in here or something?"

"Of course they do. Air imported straight from Khe San. Actually, the lowlands just ten clicks to the north."

Whatever. Some fools romanticize soldiering.

We went on a fake safari, but with real animals. The plot had to do with poachers, with whom I sympathized; hundreds of times each day their escape vehicle was overturned. They were caught, mangled in Jeep gears, humiliated in front of gawking Biggunz. Plus, we had to wait like five minutes for a peacock to get out of the way of our open-air bus.

Over mango daiquiris, in spitting distance of a snow leopard and his ransacked Buddhist temple, John Apple echoed a most intimate thought of my own.

"I've never felt like myself until I met her, and now I can't imagine going back to being merely me. A hearth inside suddenly became ablaze, and I cannot possibly allow for it to be extinguished. Cheers."

"Cheers. Hey, you think the snow leopard knows he's a snow leopard?"

"Of course it does, just look at it. Probably thinks it's a god."

He grew silent. Probably became the snow leopard for a second, eternally alone in a wrecked place that had been manufactured by strange hands he'd never know.

"What's the name of the people who build all this stuff?" I asked.

"Imagineers."

Poor snow leopard stolen from Nepal by the Imagineers. All gods are cruel bastards laughing at the snow leopard from behind a curtain.

"So, what if she says no?"

"I can't . . . I can't."

"You're really doing this tonight? I think she has plans for us tonight. Did she say anything to you?"

"I made a reservation at the Adventurers Club. She knows about it."

"What's that?"

"It's the last remnants of the elegant past. Think Teddy Roosevelt, Lord Mystic, Henry Hightower, Henry Stanley."

"Dr. Livingstone, I presume?"

"Exactly, Cheese. Exactly. I asked my butler about a tux. Armani makes good ones, right?"

How the hell would I know? I got my wedding one at Macy's. The label said TUXEDO BRANDS.

"I'll get one for you too. You can wear it at the wedding. Armani is slimming like nothing else."

A woman dressed in a safari getup extended a twelve-foot pole into the snow leopard's world. At its tip was what looked to be a serious hunk of raw, beet-red meat. Sinewy and lean. Venison?

"Good, Paula," said the woman to the animal.

"Holy shit, the leopard's a girl," I shouted, distracting Paula for a moment. It graced both John and me with its blue eyes, and the fake fresh kill that had stained her maw.

*

Sandeep oversaw a rack of formal wear. Box upon box of shiny black, patent leather shoes. A case of cufflinks. Pitchers of iced tea and lemonade. Still-warm shortbread cookies.

"My best guess," said Sandeep, "is that Mr. Apple is a 40 regular, and Mr. Marks a 46 long, but one can never be sure, so I have provided an array of sizes."

God bless Sandeep. I'm actually, comfortably a 48 regular, but he knew to skinny me down.

"Johnny Boy, how about cognacs for our tux fitting?"

"Jesus, Cheese."

I knew that he wanted one too but had to make me seem the irrepressible force of Wayz.

"Will you please humor my friend, Sandeep."

"Of course," said Sandeep. "One or two?"

"Two is fine."

I fucking knew it.

"Let's strip down to our skivvies!" I told John. "Butlers such as Sandeep are trained to be agnostic about their masters in their skivvies."

"*Masters?* Sometimes you can be a real asshole."

"Not really. I'm middle class."

"Upper."

"Barely."

"You can be an asshole and also be middle class, Cheese."

"I'm a little selfish, just like you."

"That ends tonight."

I miss Virginia. At least if she says *yes* it means a lifetime of being proximal. Shoulders touching. The occasional *menage a trois* by way of podophilia. Maybe I'll become the Wells family butler? Mental note to consult with Sandeep. As per my suggestion, we stripped to our skivvies. There were an awkward few moments of silence before Sandeep arrived with our cognacs. Skivvied men need Wayz. In such a state of undress, Wayz are their clothes.

"A toast," said John. "I cannot imagine meeting Virginia without you."

I envy men who needn't an undershirt, whose tits aren't girlish. But I do not envy Johnny Boy's undergarments. Boxer briefs have neutered a whole generation of men, perhaps literally. Feminizing things, those boxer briefs. Way too close to lingerie, says I. Sperm-killing heat, all bunched up in there.

"We met her together," I said, while Sandeep tied my bow tie. What legerdemain.

"Sandeep, do you know a girl named Shay Hitchcock? She's Indian as well, well, half- Indian, I think. She works in EPCOT, at England."

"Oh, I do happen to know Shay," said Sandeep; he had moved on to John's bow tie. He'd made mine especially floppy, bunny ears, an effect I enjoyed, and had made John's skinny, rakish.

"There," said Sandeep.

He ushered us to the hallway mirror. There we were: dimpled John smiling his tight, toothless self-assured little smile, and me with my round unblinking face. It's good for a man to be a little unattractive, to merely possess pink flesh and lots of it. I could beat John at arm wrestling. I have a glorious hundred pounds on him.

"Shay has these rich hazel eyes," I told Sandeep's reflection. "Pretty rare, right?"

"If you gentlemen wouldn't mind, I will steam these suits for tonight," said Sandeep.

Everything fit, including our shiny shoes. His seemed so natty compared to my size 15s. John's cufflinks bore reptiles. That medicine symbol with the two entwined snakes, while I'd chosen diamonds. He didn't flinch after I'd asked the price. A cool eight thousand dollars.

"You'll wear them at the wedding, as my best man."

"Sure, why not."

Virginia shouldn't be the only one with diamonds.

"What's the name of the fake pub where Shay works?" I asked Sandeep.

"That would be the Rose & Crown. I can recommend their fish and chips."

"You like this girl, huh?" said John, pulling at his jacket. Thank the lord for jacket vents; my derriere thrives on them.

What are you boys doing? Both of our BlackBerries buzzed with VWells324852@aol.com.

"Don't tell her about the tuxes," said John. "I want everything to be a surprise. No time to think."

"Girls know when a ring box is going to open. They're telepathic about it and it fills them with a little dread that their youth will formally end. Nothing ages a girl like saying *yes*. It's the end of something precious, Johnny Boy. A huge responsibility for a man, a girl's youth."

"What about our youth?"

"Men never grow up, like your buddy Peter Pan. Pathetic, actually."

"Shay Hitchcock, huh? Good for you, Cheese. Good for you."

Yeah, I like Shay Hitchcock, but I *love* Virginia Wells, and you and your big fat Cartier ring are going to suck the pale green light out of her countryside eyes. And then slam the door on girlhood. I daydreamt her long, light-brown eyelashes falling to her painted toes.

*

Virginia wanted to meet us for a ride or two, but John was adamant about not seeing her before tonight.

We're going to have some just us boys time, I was instructed to write.

I love it, she responded.

"Girls like her have a keen respect for masculine friendships," said John. "Nothing makes her feel more feminine than the age-old practice of fraternity. And while we're way more advanced than the pittance of beers at the sports bar, I can just see her stretching like a cat in her bed, smiling in gratitude that boys will be boys. Just look at that drop."

We were on the long line that wrapped around a log flume ride's grand finale: a long, steep plunge into water. The screech of wet Biggunz. Disney is good at teasing what's in store. Glimpses of hells and heavens, fates that will soon be yours. Well not *soon*, fucking long line. The smell of over-chlorinated water. Too, the sweat of large children hung in the air. Mason-Dixon line critters singing songs.

"Splash Mountain," said John. "We go on a journey through the old South, assuming the persona of a persecuted rabbit who is nearly killed in the briar patch where thorns like sharpened steel can penetrate our vital organs. The reality is, the ride is a referendum about slavery, and the drop is reparation for us white bastards."

"Suppose a Black family rides it?"

"They are immune to the horror of the drop."

"Remember our first Ponder?" I asked John. On the log flume line someone just ahead of us was humming an inane jingle that brought me back to Times Square at the very beginning of this decade. Desolate, cold Times Square in 1990. We stayed at the Milford Plaza across from the last great XXX playhouse. There's something glamorous about the end of an era, when the future is closing in on the past but hasn't quite gotten its grips. Like that exact moment just before the Roman Colosseum's last rabid lion falls asleep forever.

"The Lullaby of Broadway," said John.

"And at the center of it all, is the Milford Plaza," I sang.

"And at the center of it all, is Mister Murray Marks," sang John.

I always thought it was generous of John to allow me to be at the center of it all during that seminal Ponder. Eating greasy pizza from a paper plate inside the porn playhouse, brown-bagging Chianti, humming that jingle while grown men slept or masturbated.

"We'd sing the song whenever a guy would moan in the porn house, right?" I asked John.

"Yes, we needed it to mask a stranger's euphoria."

"That was a dirty Ponder," I said.

The porn had inspired John to solicit a lady of the evening. I was shocked. Shocked that he knew exactly what number to call. Shocked that he was so businesslike about it all. The cash, the condom. Shocked that the next morning he didn't even mention it.

"It *was* a dirty Ponder," said John. "Deliciously so."

This is a dirty Ponder, I thought, deliciously so.

*

The log flume drop did not disappoint. When I thought it was over, it found another depth, then when I was certain that its second life was over, it continued. It reminded me of a famous climax I had when I was nineteen. Even Florence marveled at the volume, the sheer length of it all. That feat, however, was not met with mechanical puppets of every shape, size, and species serenading us with "Zip-a-dee-doo-dah."

"This," said John. "This is our reward. We are in heaven, our sins against the Black man all but forgiven. We died in the briar patch. We are reborn, here, in the new South. God, please say yes, girl of my dreams."

He's really going through with it, I wrote Florence.

Good. We should all be happy.

We are, I wrote.

Was I? Certainly ecstatic in "Zip-a-dee-doo-dah" land: buzzed, galvanized by the big drop, obsessed with Virginia, in love with my diamond cuff links, craving a turkey leg. A full day and a half of the Ponder ahead. But as for long-term happiness, the long months in between Ponders when the work of life is work, and alarm clocks rule the mornings? Tolerable only because of weekend Wayz. That's a limited life, Cheese. That's not a life, Cheese.

"Do you think Florence is happy?" I asked John. "She's been really cryptic this trip."

"More than usual? She's a wise woman. That's how wise women are. They don't reveal the full story. They keep their secrets strategically inside. Until the grave."

"Virginia must have secrets. Hey, let's get a turkey leg."

"Frontierland has the best ones. Extra smoky, extra historical. As for Virginia, of course she has secrets, just look at her."

Agreed. Girls who are perfectly contented to stay silent and stare into space between sips of breakfast tea have some weather inside.

Are you happy? I wrote Florence.

Let's talk when you return. Love, Florence.

So weird, she never signs off like that. Trysting mother fucker. Screw everything. I need a stiff drink and a turkey leg.

"How in God's name does one marble poultry?" I asked John.

This turkey leg, sold to me by an ancient purveyor of gold, replete with missing teeth and an incomplete white beard, was a wonderful confusion: layer after layer of that crispy skin yet somehow retaining the texture of dark bird meat.

"Do you know what a farrago is?" asked John.

My mouth was full of—ostrich leg? Dinosaur leg?

"It's when two apparently different things are combined, such as fact and fiction," he continued. "What you are devouring there, Cheese, is part mythological. Born from pixie dust yet raised on a farm."

I wish I could speak with him more elaborately about Florence and Kathy, but I could never live it down that I turned my wife into a lesbian, and it was just plain weird that our wives had *done things*. I wasn't even exactly sure what two women could do; I mean I could use my imagination but I'd rather not. Thank God for turkey legs and flasks brimming with vodka-splash-a-cran.

"Don't you miss your flask?" I asked.

"Virginia has it, so no. Actually, let me have some of yours. She wore my Peter Pan shirt at some point last night, and I'm having a hard time assimilating that image as a reality."

"Is that a *fargo*?"

"A *farrago*, yes. So many of them here."

He took a healthy swig, winced, wiped the top.

"We're just about swapping spit," I said.

"You wish."

"Not really."

Now *I* needed a healthy swig.

CHAPTER ELEVEN

HE WANTED TO RIDE Haunted solo.

"In there, I can speak with my parents."

We made plans to put on our tuxes together in his suite tonight before dinner. A fat two and a half hours for me to kill. During a conventional Ponder we'd be apart for maybe one hour pre-dinner, but never two and a half. Plus, he requested my flask for his séance in the Haunted Manor. How could I refuse him?

"I think I'll go chat up Shay Hitchcock."

"She's all the way in EPCOT," said John.

"I'll take the train."

"Monorail."

"I do well on the train. People like me there. Although I think I feel superior to them as they're all terribly sober."

"Show some respect," said John Apple, who made a military about-face and left me. He could get stoical all of the sudden. I was rarely heavy of spirit. Good old Falstaffian Cheese.

"Carousel songs play on a loop in your head," John had once said, and it hurt my feelings. Was I merely a pleasure seeker? I'll prove him wrong and speak with Shay Hitchcock of important matters. Of Virginia and Florence. Of how this Ponder threatens to fatten my slight soul. I'll confess to her that my lips were on the feet of a man and a woman. When I wear my tuxedo tonight, I'll seem a man of substance. J.S. Bach on a loop in my head. But first the mountain splash, again. There was a catchy tune sung by frogs and critters, and it made me unreasonably happy. John had said it was a song of the south. The critters repeatedly asking *how do you do?* These days I do just fine, critters. As for the south and its songs, they should all be about its fairest girl who, like a cartoon princess, can gather all matters of swamp reptiles in her soft palms and cause them to blush.

*

On the back of my Key to the World card, one of Mickey's ears infringed on the magnetic strip. I pictured the little guy screeching in agony every time I gained entry to my room or bought a fifth of Smirnoff at the Sandy Cove. The monorail is a wonderful incubator for such thoughts. Flaskless, and therefore Wayzless, I endured an ennui en route to EPCOT. Slumped in my seat, I elicited sympathy from a hardy, happy woman.

"Long day?" she asked.

"I ran out of Wayz," I said.

"Well there sure are more where we're headed!"

"Do you even know what Wayz are?"

She wrinkled her nose at me. My new gravitas was not for everyone.

Shay Hitchcock, though, she of the silver nose ring and smoky eyes, will know that Cheese means business. My inner thighs were raw and when I alighted in EPCOT it was still way too humid for my New England blood; I walked a de facto Goofy Walk to avoid further chafing. But it was less cartoon-like than it was a robot possessed by a demon, and parents held their children close. The music in EPCOT trumpeted a digital buoyancy by way of a 1981 video game arcade on

Boylston Street where a young Murray Marks went through his five-dollar Friday allowance in seven inept minutes, then would watch a famous teenage girl with whom he was obsessed set record after record on Ms. PacMan all the while blowing and popping pink Bubble Yum bubbles. Boys would fight over who got to give her the next quarter. Her sexy little sneer flew in the face of the arcade's beeps and bops. Walking toward the fake pub, I wondered where or who she was today. A high priestess of Silicon Valley? Probably. God, was she hot. Pink streak in her dark hair. That ass in ripped jeans. My first love, I think, and I never got her name. *The PacMan chick* was her handle. Though I once gave her a quarter and she said "thanks" in a surprisingly soft voice. Florence has a deep voice for a girl. A pity. Then again, she thinks I have a high-pitched voice for a man. I'd call it more of an accessible pitch. It makes people feel safe. Unthreatened. Unlike Johnny Boy's raspy under-the-bedsheets tone.

"He's a god," Kathy Apple confided in me one time at Shun Lee. They'd just started dating and she'd do things like smooth down his eyebrows or lift up his T-shirt to tighten the belt on his jeans. The breasty little gold-digger sure could act.

I'm a god, I wrote Florence.

God of Wayz, she shot back.

The joke was on her; I hadn't had a Wayz in forty-two minutes and now stood outside the Rose & Crown in full view of Shay Hitchcock, who wore a corset outside her frilly, rural pub-peasant dress. How the ribs of a woman turn into her breasts.

Miraculous, I wrote Florence.

The day the PacMan chick removed her signature hoodie to reveal ample womanly braless breasts, a hush came over the arcade. I remember my hand involuntarily reaching out to touch them. And now that very same hand, now a man's hand, passed through the open window of the pub and pointed at the half-Indian bartender.

*

"Sandeep sends his regards," I told her. She'd pulled me a black and tan. The pub was nearly empty because outside Mary Poppins had appeared.

"Sandeep? Oh, yes, from VIP services."

"Yes, a damn fine butler, Shay."

"No Mary Poppins for you?"

I was her only bar customer. Perhaps she wanted an empty bar so she could play with her nose ring or feel her corseted ribs. At least that's what I would do were I her.

"I'm in love, Shay."

Saying a girl's exotic name is a placeholder for kissing them. Over and over again.

"Oh, my," said Shay. "Well, congratulations."

"But, of course, there are many complications, and no complications. It's my best friend's new girlfriend and he resembles James Dean. That said, I resemble her hallowed great-grandfather and all indications are that Colonel Alton P. Wells was a roly-poly racist. Screw it, let me have a shot of Jameson's, Shay. Not that I'm a racist. On the contrary, my wife is Chinese."

"I see, how interesting."

"What color would you say your eyes are?"

"It depends on the time of day."

Lilting English accent. I pictured a sarong'd leg thrown over a bejeweled elephant during London's Great Exhibition of 1851 while men in monocles gawked.

"Do you have a boyfriend, Shay? Sorry to be so personal. Shay."

"Like you say, it's complicated."

Mary Poppins ended, and the bar was very unfortunately no longer just ours.

"What's England really like?" a Biggunz asked Shay. "I mean is it like this?"

"This is an excellent replica of a countryside pub," said Shay.

"Well, hell," he said. "Wife and I once had plans to take a tour over there in Europe, but why go all the way there, when it's all right here? Got the Eiffel Tower, got the Leaning Tower of Pisa—"

"Travel is fatal to prejudice, bigotry, and narrow-mindedness. Mark Twain," I interrupted.

"Mind your own beeswax, fatso."

"Holy shit, you're calling me a fatso?"

"You have the prettiest green eyes," said his tipsy wife. "I hope your momma tells you so."

She hadn't, in fact. Both of my parents had similarly bright eyes that had been fashioned into their doughy faces. A dime a dozen, our eyes, in County Kerry from where our ancestors had worked in husbandry. "Even the chickens here have emerald eyes, so what of it?"

However, I imagine that the real reason they never owned up to my ethereal irises was because they'd also given me their squishy faces. Heredity is not a la carte, it's a buffet. We three look like hardy farmers. Trenchermen built to cohabitate with oxen.

"You like pro wrestling?" the Biggunz asked me.

"No," I said.

"Everyone likes pro wrestling."

"John used to be a pro wrestler," said his wife. "Ever hear of the Wombat?"

"Another John," I said.

"John's my best friend; the one whose girlfriend I love," I told Shay Hitchcock. She smiled politely.

"I'm the Wombat," the Biggunz growled. "Here, hit me in the stomach hard as you can."

"No way," I said.

"Pussy poo," said his wife.

"Yeah, come on, pussy poo," said the Biggunz. "I used to charge kids five bucks to get to hit me Saturday mornings at the mall. Tell you what, I'll even buy you a drink if you do it."

"Why?" I asked.

"It makes me feel alive. Brings me back to the good old days in the ring."

"I'd do it," said his wife, "but I'm too petite, just like the cutie behind the bar."

Shay Hitchcock raised her well-formed eyebrows.

"He wants me to hit him," I told Shay.

"Then do it," she said.

"There you go," said the Biggunz.

"Aren't there Disney rules against that sort of behavior?" I asked.

"I won't tell Mr. Eisner," said Shay.

Some girls like to watch men arm wrestle, fight in the alley outside the bar; they keep tissues in their purse to dab at the blood of a stranger. Sleep through the night with a knowing smile on their face, while their silver nose ring collects moonlight. I love women and will do as they say.

"Fine then . . . Wombat," I said.

We both pushed back our stools and stood. This was no ordinary Biggunz. Six foot seven, maybe six foot eight? Solid: I could not discern whether it was fat or meat that composed him. Were a Disney World turkey leg turned into a mortal giant.

"Now put some hip into it, chubby," said the Biggunz.

I'd never really hit anyone and had only vague memories of the time Johnny Boy hired that Irish boxer to knock him out. Something about lead with the right foot? Or maybe the left. Swing your hips? God, that boxer's breath. Dentyne and Scotch, the smell of the ring.

"You really want me to do this?" I asked.

"Hell yeah. Then afterward we'll do a shot. On me like I promised."

"Hit him good," said the wife. "That way he'll be all feisty tonight." She winked at Shay, wiggled in her seat.

"Okay, here goes nothing," I said.

I took the Biggunz's advice and swung my hip in conjunction with my fist; it made a very satisfying popping noise upon impact with his abdomen, which quavered the slightest and he doubled over and howled with laughter. Like I said, hardy stock from County Kerry.

"That wasn't bad," said the Biggunz. "Come here."

He put me in a playful half-nelson and gave me a noogie.

"Okay, now it's my turn," said the Biggunz. "Look at your face. I'm just kidding, chubby wubby."

"You should let him," said Shay.

"What?"

"Let him hit you," she said.

*

I remember steeling myself; trying to identify and activate whatever abdominal muscles I might have picked up over the years. When I came to on the floor of the Rose & Crown, I saw Shay Hitchcock's serene face. A sly smile just like on those ancient paintings of the Buddha. She made a satisfied little noise, then returned to work while one of the Biggunz's meat hooks retrieved me from the floor.

"You okay, Chubbs?"

"Um, yeah, I think."

"Listen, come here."

He brought us over to the window ledge and handed me a shot of whiskey.

"Just between us, I didn't lay a finger on you. See, us wrestlers know how to slam the boot down on the canvas so that the punch sounds real. Now sometimes it is real, trust me, but it wasn't today. You just spazzed out is all; slipped on some spilled beer and hit your head. Don't worry, you can still tell all your friends that you survived being struck by the Wombat. And I won't tell your girlfriend over there either. Bottoms up."

"She's not my girlfriend. I'm in love with someone else."

"Well go get her, then."

"Thanks, Wombat."

"Can we please go to France now, John?" said the wife. "I want a real French kwa-saint."

"Happy wife, happy life. Good luck, Hubba Bubba."

What an ultimately kindly Biggunz. His heart must weigh as much as a horse's. Ten pounds. And as for Ms. Hitchcock's heart? Ounces, mere ounces. Some girls are sadistic. They can't help it; their mothers had pregnancy Wayz. Mine smoked pot in that mother of all marijuana years, 1969. John's took sleeping pills and nightly champagne, or so he says. It could also be that Shay's mom ate too much spicy Indian food, that can do it too. All that fiery lamb conjures the devil in the womb. Florence would have a religiously healthy pregnancy, which was one of hundreds of reasons we'd never procreate. She'd insist I'd join her in her Wayzlessness.

"What a character," I said to Shay.

"Maybe you're the character," she said, and I beamed with protagonistic light.

CHAPTER TWELVE

HE WAS ALREADY IN his tux, pacing the halls of the Roy O. Disney suite, Sandeep standing by with a tray of sparkling wine.

"How was Haunted?" I asked. "Hey, where's my flask?"

"The timing had to be impeccable," said John, still pacing. "I deduced that only in the company of Madame Leota could I commune with my parents. My desperate hope was that the ride would stall in that very room and I could tell them about Virginia, but no dice."

"I'm going to get down to my skivvies," I warned Sandeep, who knew to hand me a champagne flute. "I saw our friend Shay this afternoon."

"Ah, at the Rose & Crown," said Sandeep.

"She's quite a character."

I harbored a hope that Sandeep would come to Shay's very same conclusion and remark in front of jittery Johnny Boy, "It is you who are the character, Mr. Marks."

"I don't know her very well," said Sandeep.

Slipping on my tuxedo pants, I remembered those summer mornings in Cambridge opening up my parents' bookstore. My college summer job. The sound of the automatic gate rising. The sound of my key chain. I'd be the first in, would turn on the AC. Put Brahms or Strauss on the record player before my parents' scourge of Peter, Paul, and Mary. An hour to myself with my Dunkin Donuts mocha smoothie. There, over my breakfast milkshake, I'd wonder if my life would contain nights when I'd feel the cool luxe of Armani slacks. At the time I had Florence and a burgeoning love of Wayz, but only knew John as a frequent customer in the store. I distinctly remember concluding: No. Murray Marks's nights will not be infused with *magic*, or "pixie dust," as the human puppets like to say here. But I will always find an hour alone with my smoothie when I can dream of living an extraordinary life.

Frankly, these visions usually entailed dressing up formally for an unpredictable night when the world would not only be my oyster, but my pearl cuff links. Tonight, they were diamonds, and the crispness I foretold was felt along the length of my legs. Thick legs that now felt long and lean.

"Let's go on a ride in our tuxedos," I said.

"You know what? That's a great fucking idea."

The first time John and I really spoke was also on a Saturday night, this at the bookstore.

I was closing up, and John was lounging on one of our reading couches. It had been a memorable day at the store; John Apple's hands were bandaged. Earlier a man had tried to shoplift *Catcher in the Rye*. It wasn't even a first edition; in fact, it was in our discount bin due to wear and tear. John went fucking crazy. It took both of my parents, and me, to pry him off the poor bastard. The poor bastard who gathered his face in his hands and ran out of the store. We were shocked. This glamorous if cerebral regular became a monster. Just like that. My mom bandaged him up as he panted. All he said after was, "So sorry, but no one should steal from you fine people. Holden Caufield wouldn't have it and neither would I."

That Saturday night I looked over at him. Head on a pillow, hand on a hip. Reading. I forget which book, but I remember him saying out loud: "*Muscular.*"

He said it well, muscularly. Each syllable, as if the muscularity of the prose was so admirable as to anger him.

"It's been a really long day," I said to him. "Let's go get a drink."

I surprised myself. I'd never spoken to a mere acquaintance that way and was quite certain that after my utterance was alive in the air, he'd shoot it down, scoff, leave. Or beat the shit out of me. Him and Holden. Instead, he tossed the book aside and said, "You know what? That's a great fucking idea."

*

You'd think two men in Armani tuxedos would turn heads at Disney World; we only got one comment from a rather fey couple of man-boys who seemed themselves knee-deep in Wayz.

"Congratulations, ladies," they said, and skipped in sync past us.

"In the future, men will marry men," said John.

"No fucking way."

Why should I doubt him? He was actually incredibly good at predicting things. It was the true basis of his fortune. He'd sit all morning in his Parisian club chair holding on tight to the side arms, imagining the future. Then he'd call his broker. Then he'd go to the gym. Then he'd start Wayzing, lucky fucker. Four in the afternoon on some nameless weekday in the middle of the decade, 75,000 shares of Amazon snug in his portfolio. At his local bar he'd attempt to read the *New York Times* cover to cover, but would ultimately get interrupted by a curious girl, or boy, who found his repose ineluctable.

"I need a favor, Cheese."

We were in front of the Haunted House.

"I need some time with Madame Leota. I need to commune with my parents and she's the only ticket out."

"Is she the ugly lady in the crystal ball?"

"Far from ugly. Admirably angular."

"You know that she's, well, not exactly a real—"

"The only way to stop the Doom Buggies is to lift the safety bar. I confirmed this today; the whole ride will stop for at least two minutes. You're strong as an ox, you can do it."

"I'm not that strong . . . Well, I did make the Wombat double over."

"When she says, 'Serpents and spiders, tail of a rat; call in the spirits, wherever they're at. Rap on a table; it's time to respond. Send us a message from somewhere beyond,' that's the signal to *heave*."

He rarely asked after my obscure references, like just now with the Wombat. Neither did Florence. In fact, no one did. The misadventures of a Falstaffian fellow have a low ceiling in terms of outcomes. Little suspense. Falstaff will merely drink and stuff his face, observe things but not touch them. But the tide was starting to turn.

"The Wombat is a pro wrestler I met at Shay Hitchcock's fake bar. He challenged me to punch him in his gut, as it arouses him. Sexually, I think."

"Did you even hear what I said about the safety bar?" asked John.

"I walloped him, then he punched me back, sort of, but we parted on good terms, friends even. He gave me sound advice about going after what I want. I love Virginia."

"I don't blame you, who wouldn't?"

Of course, he assumed it was mere admiration. Yeah, I'll lift the bar of the haunted car. It'll give me some solo flask Wayz time while he speaks to the ugly witch.

I love Virginia, I wrote Florence.

! She wrote back.

Freeing to get the word out, even if these two condescending bastards wrapped my confession in benignly brown butcher paper.

"Cheese's heartstrings are scraps," the butchers will say. "Feed them to the dogs."

Liberation is admitting you're in love. Free am I. A bird on a castle ledge. Icarus without a sun. I pictured myself flapping huge wax wings from atop Cinderella's Castle, everyone pointing, amazed. Maybe someone would throw me a turkey leg; I'd catch it in my beak before takeoff. Still, there was one person I needed to tell in order to take flight over the skies of Walt Disney's World.

*

"Heave, Cheese, heave."

The bar was all but unbudgeable.

"Heave ho!"

Heave ho summoned my most primal rural origins. Just as the witch was babbling about the great beyond, the safety bar budged, and the Doom Buggy came to a halt. Out popped Johnny Boy; stunning to see him in the ride scene, leaning over to whisper into the crystal ball where the high-cheekboned crone who was stuck inside seemed to bend her ear to hear him.

"Get back in your car, you maniac," screamed a fellow rider.

The ride's baritone narrator blamed the stoppage on mischievous spirits; I sank into my Doom Buggy and toasted the inky darkness. I bookmarked the scene: two men in tuxedos amid ghosts. If my maker happened to focus on me this very moment, he would anoint my life a wild success, and perhaps add a wink and a nod at my diamond cufflinks. John's blood-red Cartier box bulged in his coat pocket as he finished whispering to the crone. Virginia will know at once. Girls know their bulges.

Satisfied he'd sent his message, Johnny Boy returned to the Doom Buggy.

"Now what?" I asked, the safety bar still raised.

"The Ghost Host," said John.

"Who's that?"

What an imagination on this guy.

"He's the majordomo of this house. Hung himself outside on the cupola. That was *his* way out. You hear him during the ride, Cheese. He'll lower the bar for us, just watch."

Sure enough, the suicidal narrator came back on the radio. "Do not pull down on the safety bar, please. I will lower it for you." And with that our buggy lurched forward.

"He does have a cool voice," I said.

"Ghosts have amazing bellowing voices. When all the guests leave at night, this house becomes a wild opera of anguished bellows. A human ear would spout blood upon hearing the cries."

"You really believe this shit?"

"Some things are best left misunderstood."

We stopped in the fake town at a cookie store to watch candy-striped bakers pour vats of batter into molds.

"What are you making?" asked John.

"Gingerbread cookies," they said. "Then we dip them in vanilla or chocolate frosting. Our best-sellers during the holidays."

Holy shit, next week's Thanksgiving. Which means Florence's mother begins her feast prep Monday night. It's always just Florence, me, Mama, and a glistening duck. The last Thanksgiving of the 1990s, which will be followed by more Thanksgivings in different decades. How many more glazed ducks for me? It sunk me: the table in the kitchen. Mama's silence and chopsticks skills. Revolting are the sounds of the same people eating duck together, year after year.

"We'll take two," said John. "But unfrosted. Plain as the good lord intended."

He handed them his Key to the World card.

"Haven't seen this design in quite some time," said a baker.

He was referring to that overbright if not outright menacing pirate and his pirate ship that lived on the piece of plastic. I suffered two dangerous fevers in my childhood; they affected my hearing, which in turn heightened my other senses, particularly my sense of smell. The nightmares a child experiences at 105.8 degrees. Death, madness, hell. A grinning pirate captain (I believe mine was of the Claymation variety), one with a very real cutlass cutting off my limbs, only for them to grow back; then he'd cut them off again.

"Why do you say things like 'plain as the good lord intended'?"

"The citizens of Main Street USA are very religious. They like it when guests honor their faith. Did you know that there's a bar just for the citizens of Main Street?"

"Bullshit."

"Sawdust strewn, with a fireplace where it's always Christmas Eve. Even though the citizens of Main Street USA receive minimum wage, they are the happiest people in the world. Pouring batter for Biggunz to feast on, tapping their feet to the Dapper Dans. They also have their own chapel, of course, where every day is Sunday."

"Tomorrow is Sunday."

On most Ponders—well, every single one, except this—there would be such urgency about the coming of Sunday. *Last day.* Dreadful words. And Saturday dusk was terrifyingly close to Last Day. But here we were in real tuxes in the fake town listening to a barbershop quartet, eating freshly baked cookies, neither of us able to imagine leaving this place, this trip. That girl.

"Days are no longer relevant to me," said John.

"Me neither."

"Dapper Dans?" I asked, gesturing to the barbershop quartet.

"That's them."

He threw his arm around my shoulder.

Mr. Sandman, bring me a dream (bung, bung, bung, bung). Make him the cutest that I've ever seen. Give him two lips like roses and clover. Then tell him that his lonesome nights are over.

*

We retired to our respective rooms, a common Ponder practice before Saturday's dinner, the main event. The beating heart of the Ponder. Sunday was always a blur, a desperate day. Us against the brunching world. Those who have to wrap things up in the afternoon lest they start the work week hungover. Those who dine with other couples and their dogs in sweaters. Every mammal at the table in sweaters. Every mammal with hollandaise sauce on their mug. What's so fucking funny about a second mimosa? And why not a third, a fifth, a tenth? Being half-drunk is a sin against nature. Fuck Sundays and their cheery inhabitants. Florence loves Sundays. Women and their errands. She totes a wicker bag from store to store, the bag a gift from Mama who also owns a wicker bag, like every strong and righteous Chinese woman in the world. On Sundays, I follow Florence like an old leash-less bulldog, counting the moments until the only errand left is lapping up hard Wayz from the bowl that is clumsily placed at my master's feet.

Are you going shopping tomorrow? I wrote Florence. *I'm in a tuxedo.*

I'm at the gym.

What gym? You don't belong to a gym.

Kathy Apple belonged to the blasted Reebok Club, working out next to Regis Philbin and drinking $12 smoothies for lunch.

Kathy's gym? I asked.

Florence had admirably skinny legs, way more bone than muscle, and I liked it that way. Virginia's legs though. Her calves. No gyms there. Seven teenage summers on the plantation, bending over to smell a yellow rose. They looked stone-washed, such smooth, round muscles. Seven summers versus a stone you'd see on the banks of a wild river. Seven summers versus four billion years of flowing water, and the same luscious result. I wish my hand could hold such a stone, in lieu of it feeling the lean length of her calves.

The sun had set on the Majestic Kingdom; all the whirly rides lit up in pinks and blues. From my balcony I toasted them once again with a minibar-sourced vodka and pineapple juice. I wished I had a pineapple wedge for garnish. It bothered me that I did not. In Virginia's world, in John's world, they were availed of fresh details like a pineapple wedge, cut just now, and cool. Right there on the side of your glass. Sweating. Would you eat it first? Last? The choice is all yours.

Reebok, wrote Florence.

Pineapple wedge.

Two can play at coyness, you Chinese genius.

At precisely 6:00 p.m., a knock at the door. Johnny Boy was nothing if not punctual. Eerily on time, in fact. Our solo-time hour was over and here comes the Floridian night.

"What's up?" he asked. Nervous, pacing. "Let's play catch with the ring box."

"I fucking hate sports."

"Maybe we'll get married at Disney World," said John, passing the ring box from hand to hand. "Get officiated by the real Mickey Mouse, who only marries members of the Disney family, but if you give enough to one of their charities, you get the real McCoy."

"I thought you said they couldn't talk, the human puppets."

"This one can, and he's not human. Take off his headdress, well, you can't. Also, he marries people using sign language. Of course he doesn't speak, Cheese."

Jesus. I dreamt of snatching the Cartier box from the air and running to Virginia's room and proposing to her first. I dreamt of ripping the head off the signing Mickey, the guts of its neck spilling out onto the Main Street, or wherever the hell people get married here.

"Where do people get married here?" I asked

"With the real Mickey Mouse? In front of Cinderella's Castle, as the clock strikes midnight. It's highly symbolic and impossibly dramatic. Some brides don't make it to the I do's, they are proven unworthy, and their gown turns into jeans and a T-shirt, but that won't happen to Virginia."

"She looks good in everything."

"She looks best in nothing."

With that we both shut our eyes. I wish he'd taken pictures.

"I wish our BlackBerries had a camera," I said.

"They will one day, pervert. Let's get out of here."

"Where to? Virginia's room?"

"Of course not. The fortune teller who lives in Morocco above the bazaar. She knows we're coming."

CHAPTER THIRTEEN

I'D NEVER WALKED SO much in my life. Could Disney World be slimming? I think I'd gone down an entire belt buckle hole. EPCOT required the most aerobic stamina. From the huge golf ball to the phony bazaar seemed to me like Harlem to the East Village, which I'd only walked once, crankily following Florence's historical audio tour of our fair city. The faux bazaar. Piped-in conversations of merchants haggling in Moroccan. Music of the oud and sintir. The heat of the darrabu-kka. Exotic enough, but for the life of us, we could not find a means of accessing the second story of the mini medina where, according to Johnny Boy, the famous fortune teller resided.

"You do realize that these are all fake storefronts," I told John.

"Can't you see the flickering amber lights? Can't you smell the incense? Do not step in camel dung."

"Let's have a Wayz."

"Ah, Restaurant Marrakesh. Belly dancers. Whiskey. And we're dressed like Rick Blaine, except that he wore a white tux."

"Rick Blaine?"

"Bogart. And doesn't that very movie capture the essence of this exotic land?"

Not really.

"If you say so," I said.

"Those are real date palms, Cheese. Let's each pick a date. Their sweetness goes so well with brown liquor."

"Now you're talking."

But when we gazed up the length of the palm, it was barren. And even if it had been fecund with the sweet fruit, we'd need a sixty-foot ladder. Two tuxedoed men up a palm tree is more Abbott and Costello than *Casablanca*.

"They've already been picked this morning," said John. It was night now in this Morocco world.

Are you guys okay? wrote Virginia. John's BlackBerry had buzzed as well.

She considered us a unit. If she says "yes," would that make me her husband as well? Polygamy must be awesome. What variety.

"How did you respond?" I asked John.

"I told her eight o'clock, Adventurers Club. 'Virginia Apple'. What a name."

Virginia Apple-Marks.

*

"How do you know when a Ponder is over?" I asked from the bar of Restaurant Marrakesh, awash in blue tiles and a singular belly dancer by the empty bar.

"How do you know when sex is over?" asked John. "How do you know when brushing your teeth is over?"

It has been my experience that belly dancers have pedestrian bellies. Too round. And the navel too gaping. In fact, belly dancing might be the most overrated genre in all the world.

"I don't really get belly dancers," I said. "I don't think they like me."

"They don't. They don't like it when you stare at their abdomen with a mouthful of couscous."

The belly dancer caught us looking and approached.

"Care for a private dance?" she asked.

Her name tag said Fatima, from Rabat. At least they're all from real places. Like how Shay Hitchcock is from England.

"We'd be delighted," said John.

We stood to follow her, but she motioned that we should stay where we were.

"By any chance do you read fortunes?" asked John.

"My mother is the senior belly dancer, she reads fortunes. Shall I get her?"

"Yes," said John. "Please."

"Very well," she said, and clapped together her finger cymbals.

"Men confuse belly dancers with strippers," said John. "Big mistake. There's a guy with a scimitar in the kitchen. Plus, belly dancers are extremely sensitive, thus the fortune telling skills. In essence, they are mystical humans, but you don't want to date one."

"True. The little hand bells would get annoying."

Fatima's mother moved slowly, and with each long ceremonial step, she would ring her finger symbols, a hint of a smile on her overly-made-up face. Belly dancers overdo it with the makeup, but that's because they're acne-scarred, at least all the ones I've seen. After Virginia's complexion, hard not to be such a judgmental asshole.

"My mother's English is not so good, so I will translate," said Fatima.

"*Antum 'ayuha alssadat yartadun mulabis jayidatin*," said the mother.

"She says that you are so well dressed."

"Thank you," said John. "It's an important night."

"So, who will be first?" asked Fatima.

I pointed to John. I'm accustomed to being a slave to his fortune anyway. Although it dawned on me that if Virginia shot him down, that did not necessarily mean she would choose Cheese instead.

Hi, I wrote Florence, in a panic.

During Ponders I forget I'm married to her, then on Monday night I come home a wounded and wild animal when we have the only truly meaningful sex of the year.

Would I ever dare leave her? Assuming she's not planning on leaving me for Kathy Apple? In this crazy place, the prescription is living in the moment. Disney presses pause on one's harsh realities like nothing else. I give Johnny Boy that; what a wonderfully impractical place. Mortgages, marriages, morality, all to the wayside. While a decrepit belly dancer in clownish makeup closed her eyes and held John's hand.

"Wait," said John and reached into his breast pocket. The Prince of Cups. "I chose this card yesterday morning. I thought you should know."

Fatima did not need to translate; her mother's eyes became so wide.

"Yanqul," she said. "Yanqul!" she pronounced. She bent down to kiss John Apple's shiny shoes then bowed herself away from him, Fatima chasing after her:

"Mother? Mother!"

"Jesus," I said.

"What did she say?" asked John

"It sounded like, I don't know, Yank-u-la, or something."

"Excuse me, sir?" John asked the bartender. "Did you happen to hear what she just said?"

"Yanqul," he said. Fez and parachute pants, "Yanqul, um, it's like, hold on. It's not easy." From behind the bar, he produced a dictionary, *Arabic to English*. "Here," he said, and pointed to an entry.

Transmogrify.

"Transmogrify?" I asked. "What does that even mean?"

"Change," said John.

What does transmogrify mean? I wrote Florence. Her response was immediate.

Magical transformation.

The lucky prince, I guess. Fatima's mother was a fan of his magic, or perhaps, like me, found my friend's blessings a little overwhelming.

*

Unsure how he arranged it, but outside of Morocco, in a canal, a shiny Venetian water taxi waited for us. A tired-looking older man in captain's whites held a sign: APPLE.

"We're arriving at the club in style, Cheese."

"Mr. Apple?" asked the captain.

"That's us," said John. "We have you for the night, right?"

"As long as you want," said the boat captain.

To me, he looked hungover; then again, all defeated-looking adults seemed hungover to me. Although I considered it a badge of honor. A courageous foray. You played with poison, then you won, then you lost. No shame in these battles. Wayz are really the only means by which mortals can dabble in godliness. What else is a great buzz but a glimpse of immortality? And a God-awful hangover? A preview of death itself. The good captain must surely understand.

"Long day?" I asked the captain.

"No," he said, "you two are my first cruise."

"A little hungover, huh?" I asked.

"Jesus, Cheese. You'll have to excuse my ethanol-obsessed friend," said John to the captain.

"There are life vests in the compartment beneath you," said the captain. "And this boat still has some zip left in her so feel free to use the seatbelts."

"What's her name?" asked John.

"*Lealena*. She's all varnished mahogany. Twenty-five years young. She needs a new inboard though, maybe I'll be able to convince the mouse to pony up."

"*Lealana*," said John. "She should have anything she needs. Beautiful name by the way. Maybe we'll name our daughter Lealana, Lea for short. You have any kids?"

"You're sitting in her. Been caring for this boat since we got her in 1974. But like I said, she needs a new four stroke."

"Ever propose to a girl?" asked John.

Dimpled bastard always gets away with the blunt inquiries of strangers. I ask a simple question about hangovers and it's as if the words never even existed.

"Once and got burnt," said the captain.

"As a captain of a water vessel, are you able to marry people?" asked John.

"Disney made me a legal officiant for that very reason, one of the best perks of this job. You have something special in mind?"

"After tonight, this will hopefully belong to Virginia Wells."

He showed him the ring box, opened it. I'd forgotten just how impressive it was. "Oh, I know the Wellses," said the captain. "Been driving them for many years. They like to take a sunset cruise every trip. I think I've known Virginia since she was this high. Wonderful girl. So, the Wellses are here, huh? They haven't booked me yet, but they never fail to."

"Wow," said John. "What's your name?"

"Everyone calls me Cap," he said, pointing to his name tag.

"Cap, of course. This is Cheese, I mean Murray, and I'm John."

"You and Virginia Wells would make a handsome couple," said Cap.

Fucking Cap.

"Hey, can we get going?" I asked, and the engine purred. "Hey, are we going to have a pre-Wayz before the Explorers Club?"

"Adventurers Club, and of course."

A handsome couple. I'd never been part of one, although when I was in line with Virginia for the Haunted Home a lady smiled at us, and I took the smile to mean a handsome couple or at least half of a handsome couple or *she must be a moral girl to accept him as he is.* With Florence all we got was *Looking sharp* or *Your wife is so tall.*

At least Cap said *would* make a handsome couple, not *will.*

Going to the movies with Kathy, wrote Florence. *Goodnight.*

I wonder if Cap can divorce people, too?

*

We sat on a small arched bridge in one hell of a limbo called the International Gateway; looming in the distance were two convention hotels. Real things threatening the fake villages here. We sipped prosecco and peach cocktails that we'd bought in Italy world while Cap waited beneath us, moored the bridge.

"Swan and Dolphin," said John.

"The hotels out there? I don't like looking at them."

"Good," said John. "That's the correct response to them. Married men cheat on their wives there. The lobby teems with ladies of the evening. They serve miniature turkey legs at the cheesy neon-lit bar and there are no characters. No Mickey. No Minnie. Nothing. There, the quasi-Biggunz wear cheap suits and curse liberally from morning to night. All they worship are golf and whores. They curse the rides. *Fuck Space Mountain,* they say, while their neon-lit fat faces get stuffed with inadequate turkey legs."

"Then why did you choose to sit here in full view of these monstrosities?"

"It's good to get a glimpse of the other world. It will only force us to immerse ourselves even deeper in this one."

"You do know we have to go home on Monday, right? I mean, at least I do."

"Nonsense, Cheese."

He sat so lightly, holding his stemware with just two fingers, his legs crossed at a feminine angle. Repose. While I sat hunched over, dreading Monday. Florence had now written twice that we *needed to talk.* She couldn't possibly mean Monday night, though, could she? That was reserved for sexual abandon. Tuesday, I stayed in bed drinking the Airport Mama's miraculously restorative chicken soup. I owned the complete *I Love Lucy* on DVD and would watch and nap, absorbing Florence's resentment all the way from our office, where I'd join her Wednesday morning. Reborn, or at least a little un-destroyed.

"Hey, do you think I look like Fred Mertz?" I asked Johnny Boy.

"Now? No way. But in twenty-five years, a dead ringer."

Shit.

*

The club was in a place called Pleasure Island where it was always New Year's Eve.

"Why does every place here have to be stuck on a day?" I asked.

"Time is virtually stagnant here. It's been studied. It's the opposite of astronauts who age exponentially in space. In fact, astronauts secretly come to Disney World after their missions in order to even the score."

"Wait, isn't Pleasure Island from *Pinocchio*?"

"No, Cheese. It was founded in the 1920s by a man named Merriweather Pleasure. Sadly, he was lost at sea, but as you can see, his dream is alive and well."

Every place here looked like those massive two-story Floridian bars created for the young and sunburnt who were too lazy to visit New Orleans, a real place. Although they nailed the Creole style here, just like those balconies in the French Quarter. From them, the teenaged children of Biggunz celebrated the effectiveness of their fake IDs by shouting inanities from above. A more sinister version of the Goofy laugh. It was a decadent scene. These kids' faces stained with one-hundred-proof reddest punch. It was reassuring that Cap waited for us near the entrance, the *Lealana* docked in the still, dark waters; these kids were angry with sugar.

"Pleasure Island *is* from fucking *Pinocchio*," I said.

"Always cursing, Cheese."

"Children are lured there with the promise of limitless fun, only to be turned into donkeys then sold as livestock. *Transmogrified*."

"I'm not going to be turned into an ass, Murray Marks."

"Hey," they shouted from above.

"Hey you," they shouted.

"Hey you. You two waiters?"

"Hey," they shouted.

"Tuxes," they howled.

We couldn't get to the club soon enough. Their reddest punch was raining down on us two waiters. We started running, our tuxedo jackets over our heads, but their aim was uncanny.

*

When I was fifteen, my parents sent me to a fat camp thinly disguised as a tennis camp. It happened to be near Orlando, and our one field trip was to an entertainment complex called Church Street Station, a place so similar to this Pleasure Island. It was a suppressed memory. Rosie O'Grady's. An endless pub where a thin girl with bright blue eyes feigned interest in me, only to douse my person with warm beer. A memory I didn't care to dwell on but now, drenched in evening-warm punch, I was back in that difficult time. How that girl's rightful boyfriend grabbed my tits with such force that they remained discolored all summer. The bus ride back to camp. In the back of the bus, I contemplated suicide. My fellow fatsos did not console me. They were just happy that it was me and not them. Accused of underaged Wayzing, I was sent home early. I hadn't the resolve to change my beer-fouled clothing and stunk up the back of an Eastern Airlines flight back to Logan where my parents received me. Me, sobbing. The next day, instead of hitting the red bottle of Drano under the sink—death Wayz, I'd come to call it—instead, in my parents' store I read Jack London stories, then joined a gym. The local Y, where I found some muscles.

"Fucking animals," I yelled as we ran for cover.

"Always cursing, Cheese."

"Many things are curse-able."

We arrived beneath a stone archway; an artifact, a giant Balinese head marking the entrance to the Adventurers Club.

"Remember, it's New Year's Eve 1937. Kungaloosh."

"Huh?"

"Kungaloosh. It's the club's creed. It's also a Wayz. A tropical drink."

"What the fuck does it mean?"

"It's like aloha or shalom. Various meanings."

"Tropical drink?"

"Yes, blackberry brandy, spiced rum, exotic juices. You'll lap it up. Ceramic coconut and all."

Well, at least there's that.

Just inside the club was a puppet embedded in the wall. An absurd mutton-chopped British officer who came to life as we passed.

"Welcome, welcome, gents," it said.

"Kungaloosh, Colonel," said John.

"Kungaloosh," said the Colonel, who then turned its head to me.

"Say it, Cheese."

"No fucking way."

"Apologies, Colonel," said John. "It's his first time."

"It's your first time too," I said.

"I've been a member in absentia since 1988."

The puppet was no longer animated; its eyes were closed. It was sleeping, snoring, its chest rising.

"Decent effect," I said.

"The Colonel suffers narcolepsy. He was poisoned in Papua New Guinea. A malicious shaman's handiwork."

"It's a Muppet."

"It has a soul. We have a table in the Mask Room."

He approached a human puppet dressed as a butler.

"Hello, Graves," said John.

I missed Sandeep, a real butler. A great butler. This Graves in his morning coat was overacting. Over-arching his wooly gray eyebrows.

"We have a table for three in the Mask Room. Under John Apple."

"Yes," said Graves, "but the table is now for six, sir. I took the order from Ms. Wells."

"She's here already?" asked John. "Six?"

"Yes, sir."

On cue, the lights flickered. A thunderclap. The sound of pouring rain; Graves opened a large black umbrella. I held forth my palm. Nary a drop.

"I need a drink," said John. "You go to the table."

"Alone?"

"I will accompany you and announce you," said Graves.

"Don't say anything about the ring," said John. "Just say I'm running late."

John Apple disappeared into a wall panel beneath a taxidermized rhino head.

"How the hell does he know where everything is?" I asked no one in particular.

"Sir," said Graves, "before we can proceed, you must invoke the password."

"Password? Um, Kangaroo?"

He shook his head.

"Candle juice?"

He shook his head.

"Kungaloosh. Kungaloosh!"

He nodded. Under his umbrella, in the fake rain we walked down a dark corridor lit by flickering torches. Those were real.

Somewhere in the wacky gloom waited Virginia. I could use a Kungaloosh. Or five.

CHAPTER FOURTEEN

THE WALLS OF THE dining room were covered with masks, all of them scowling, baring teeth. Tribal curses from every corner of the ancient world. And at the center of it all, Virginia Wells, Mr. and Mrs. Wells. Dimitri.

And at the center of it all, I sang in my head, *the Wellses and Dimitri.*

"Huh," said Dimitri. "Look at this guy. "*Kak pingvin*. He looks like a penguin."

"Be nice, Dimitri," said Virginia.

Mr. Wells stood to shake my hand. To crush my hand.

"Mr. Marks."

"Oh my lamb," said Mrs. Wells. "Evening dress at Disney."

"Where's John?" asked Virginia. "You smell like punch."

"Yeah well, these kids—"

"So, is he here at the club?" she asked, leaning into my eyes for him.

"He um, I don't know. I think he's getting ready somewhere. He dressed up too."

He's Wayzing behind a wall. Behind the rhino. Playing with your future ring.

Playing with your future.

"Daddy ordered for us, Cheese."

To a person they wore polo shirts and Bermuda shorts. Mr. Wells's pink collar starch stiff and flipped up.

"You sit next to me, Cheese," said Mrs. Wells.

"Cheese, huh," said Dimitri. "In my country, we call the boss the Cheese, I guess different meaning here."

"Dimitri's heading home tomorrow," said Virginia.

"My work here is done," said Dimitri. "At least for now."

"Care for a Manhattan, Mr. Marks?" asked Mr. Wells. "I bring my own jar of Luxardo maraschino cherries, straight from Italy. And Graves is good enough to provide the Angostura bitters."

"Graves," I said. "Oh, we were taken here by Cap, the boat captain."

"Oh, we love Cap," said Virginia. "Daddy, can we go tomorrow? John and Cheese too?"

"Just look at the rich amber color in your coupe, Mr. Marks. I am sure you already know this, but a Manhattan must always be served in a coupe."

So fucking amazing. Oh, to be his son-in-law.

"Did Cap take John here too?" asked Virginia. She'd curled her hair and the locks cascaded over her white polo, her collar starched upright as well.

"Umm, sort of," I said.

"So, he's here?" she asked.

"Well, he's somewhere."

I'm a horrible liar. Face turns red. Nervous laughter. Awful.

"Do you know about the Kungaloosh drink?" I asked the table, hoping for a diversion.

"Of course," said Dimitri. "But Washington Wells, he likes his Manhattans, huh."

"Dimitri lives in St. Petersburg," said Mrs. Wells. "In a real palace."

"Is what is," said Dimitri.

"Do you enjoy caviar, Mr. Marks?" asked Mr. Wells.

"Well—"

"It's the only commie food I'll eat," he said. "No offense, Dimitri."

"None taken," said Dimitri.

"He's one of the last Romanovs," said Mrs. Wells. "You do know, Cheese, that he asked for Ginny's hand."

"*Mom*," said Virginia.

I saw John standing at the entrance to the Mask Room, watching us.

"*Hand*," said Dimitri, then mumbled something coarse in Russian.

Virginia Wells leapt from the table, tossed her lap napkin into the air. It landed on my head. Only for a moment was I spared John and Virginia's desperate embrace. It was Washington Wells who reached over to grab the covering from my head. With unmistakable force. They hugged and kissed violently. It took her no time to pat down the ring box. After which she pulled away from him and held him by his shiny black lapels.

"Mr. Apple," said Mr. Wells.

He didn't rise from the table to shake his hand as he had with me.

"Huh," said Dimitri. "*Odin pingvin*. Another penguin."

"Beluga," said Mr. Wells. "I only eat Beluga caviar."

"Of course," said Dimitri. "Is best."

"I only want the best for my family," said Mr. Wells, his gazed fixed on the young couple in the flickering torch light.

Virginia whispered something in John's ear, and he shook his head.

"No," said John Apple.

Disappointed by his answer, Virginia returned to her seat. To her Manhattan in its precious coupe.

"Very handsome, Mr. Apple," said Mrs. Wells.

"Pass the bread, Constance," said Mr. Wells.

"So, you are the new Dimitri," said Dimitri. "Huh."

"I like to think of myself as the new John Apple," said John Apple. "Magically transformed."

"I took the liberty of ordering for the table, Mr. Apple," said Mr. Wells. "The Mongolian beef is not on the menu, you have to know to ask for it. World-class and spicy as Satan's ass."

While he went on about the apparently blistering dish, I heard Virginia tell John, "You have to ask Daddy for permission."

Of course.

"But not tonight, John."

"Why the hell not?" he asked.

"I just know Daddy, is all."

Light left John's face so rapidly I thought his cast would join the death masks on the wall.

*

A second Kungaloosh had loosened John Apple's tongue.

"Did Mr. Wells say yes to you?" he asked Dimitri.

"Of course did, but she did not. So . . . one Splash."

The Wells family had left the table to watch some sort of show in the main room.

"What happened to that shirt-free suit and the no shoes and no socks?" I asked Dimitri.

"Was work uniform. Like I say, my work here is done for now "

"Exactly how long have you been here?" asked John.

"Hard to say, but I need vacation."

We'd played musical chairs all night and now I sat between the two gloomy men.

Both sullen drunks, although Dimitri seemed genuinely spent. With the Wells family absent, John sat hunched over, opening and closing his ring box.

"Mine was bigger," said Dimitri. "Was family heirloom and now is back in Kremlin museum. Maybe she say yes to you. I wish you luck."

A woman dressed as an English maid came in and dusted our heads.

"Will miss Disney," Dimitri said, then rose and left.

The walls have eyes, I wrote Florence.

I actually thought some of them did and signaled a particularly suspicious dragon mask with a wink in the hopes that whatever spirit possessed it would find Mr. Wells in another room and whisper, "Just say no."

Not a very good best friend, I suppose, but if I can't have her, neither should John. Unless we make some sort of agreement to share her, which would never happen, and then there's Florence. Fuck it all. I slurped down the remnants of my Kungaloosh. Sat back and further took in the kooky place. Families laughing for no apparent reason. Everywhere an homage to a past that never really existed. The 1920s? The 1930s? Definitely between the wars when people raided the tombs of pharaohs and were cursed for their trouble. And here comes Virginia Wells who walks like a ballerina; it puts another half inch on her bountiful head of auburn hair. I'd like to fuck her posture.

"Gentlemen," she said.

We rose to greet her; she was used to men rising for her. She knew to pause, smirk, wait for us to do the right thing.

"Where's your dad?" asked John.

"My parents are taking Dimitri back to the hotel. He's exhausted, poor thing. So, how'd you boys like the Mongolian beef?"

"It wasn't that spicy," said John.

"Well, don't let Daddy hear you say that."

"*Daddy,*" he said, slumped over, staring glumly at the ring box. She rewarded his petulance by sitting on his lap.

"Suppose he says no?" John asked her.

"Let's just have a great night tonight, the three of us," she said.

Her ass was perpendicular to his thighs, forming the world's most beguiling pound sign.

"I guess I should get a check," said John.

"Oh, Daddy took care of it. He doesn't let other men pay."

"Right," said John.

"Now you cheer up, John Apple. Here, drape your tuxedo jacket over my shoulders and into the night we'll go. What do you say, Cheese?"

Why can't it be my tuxedo jacket? "Sure," I said.

"Now that's the spirit. Let's do Big Thunder Mountain. I love ending my nights in Tumbleweed."

"Tumbleweed?" I asked.

"Yeah," said John. "The town where they discovered gold, then the greedy bastards ruined everything. Maybe I'll throw your ring into the deserted mine."

"Don't be so dramatic," said Virginia.

In the torchlight, as we made our way out, I saw flecks of gold in her wildly pale eyes. Her fate in her father's viselike hands, all she cared about was a place called Tumbletown.

"Tumbletown?" I asked.

"Tumbleweed, silly," said Virginia, the most buoyant girl in the world. I bet she sees flowers in empty vases.

In Tumbleweed, I'm going to tell her that I'm in love with her and be done with it. "Does Tumbleweed have a bar?" I asked. Unrequited love Wayz.

"In theory," said John. "A dusty saloon. Why did you say no to Dimitri?"

"He wasn't you," said Virginia.

John Apple beamed. They both have such white teeth. In Tumbleweed I'll keep my mouth and its mishmash of crooked teeth shut.

*

There was a pronounced clickety-clack sound that did well to soothe me while on the runaway train. I sat behind them; took the opportunity to reach out and touch her flowing hair. Clickety-clack. What a sound. Somewhere in the fake mesa of Tumbleweed was a dinosaur skeleton. Dinosaurs lived for 150 million years. Humans? As we know them today? I mean Wayzing humans? Maybe six thousand years. I used my BlackBerry calculator. If the time of dinosaurs was reduced to a year, Wayzing humans have been alive for 1.2 seconds of that year. A heartbeat. Two clicks and a clack. No time to even raise a glass.

"Don't you just love Cap?" asked Virginia after the ride. "We tried to get him to captain our boat at home, but no dice."

"You have a boat?" I asked.

"More of a yacht I guess, but yeah."

Earlier, on our way from the Adventure restaurant, the three of us in Cap's charge, I had watched Cap look at Virginia's ringless hand and frown. He took numerous swampy moonlit tributaries to get us lakeside. At some juncture something splashed in the dark water and it startled Virginia who clung to John.

"Alligators," Cap had said.

"But not real alligators, right?" I asked.

"And a single *crocodile* in Lake Buena Vista," said John. "A monster of a reptile who swallowed a clock. If you hear her ticking, your fate is sealed."

"In the early days at the Polynesian," Cap continued, "there was a waterskiing show and a cast member dressed as Donald got snatched up by a gator. Was a terrible thing to see."

"I'd swim the length of the lake and back if your father would say yes," John said to Virginia.

I pictured Virginia and me with binoculars on the shore watching him go while enjoying gator suspense Wayz. Oh, how we'd hug if he went under. Wait, that's not me, that's the Ponder talking. How many Wayz since this morning? Sometimes best not to keep an accurate count. But on Saturday nights we were usually north of twenty.

Twenty-seven, I wrote Florence.

*

They walked slowly, like an old couple. In sync. Now they didn't need to hold hands. She wore his jacket and it sufficed as an intimacy. The night had cooled nicely, and we were aimless in the soft Florida breeze, wandering in the fake Old West of Frontier World, when John stopped.

"Did you know?" asked John. "There's a hidden roller coaster here that can be altered to achieve such intense acceleration as to stop the heart. It's called the Euthanasia Coaster and was dreamed up by Walt himself. He didn't want to suffer a prolonged death. 'Cast Members Only,'" he said, reading a sign. "There's a bar back there. You two stay here. I'll be right back."

Virginia and I watched him disappear into a forbidden entryway in his sleek tux trousers.

"He's obsessed with suicide," I told her.

"All great men are, a little," she said, both of us still looking at the place he used to occupy.

"I'm not obsessed with it, not at all," I said.

She turned to me and grabbed my hands. "That's because you're a *good* man, which is way more important, Cheese. And equally as rare."

John reappeared.

"Come," he said, and we obeyed the command of the great man.

*

The bar was a long piece of plywood supported by four empty beer kegs. Manned by a disgruntled Disney employee who was clearly annoyed by our civilian presence. The Wayz were strictly collegiate, amateurish: Southern Comfort, Mountain Dew, red Solo cups. The Holy Trinity of young vomit. There were two other customers, a man and a woman, both dressed like 1950s space explorers, complete with silver gloves and matching silver bootlets.

"Are these two guests?" the spacewoman asked the bartender. "Yeah, but they're with him," he said, pointing to John.

"I've always wanted to have drinks with a cast member," said Virginia. "Space Mountain?"

"Astro Orbiter," said the spacewoman. "But we hope to be promoted in the new year. The Orbiter has no story. My husband and I tried to come up with one, but only got as far as—"

"Fermi's Paradox," said John. "The Universe is grand enough and our planet old enough that we should have been visited by aliens. It's the Astro Orbiter that keeps them at bay. It simulates a speed faster than that of light. You see, the rockets orbit the solar system at a rate that would make intergalactic space travel a reality. And that would threaten the aliens, so they have their cameras focused on the Orbiter. They are waiting for the exact moment when our species has indeed developed Astro Orbiter technology to come for us. Colonize us. Treat us as we treat ants. But as long as they see that it's a mere ride at Disney World and not an actuality, they will hold off. Allow us to scurry about for a few more centuries."

"Uh, what?" asked the spaceman.

Virginia had latched onto John's arm. The Southern Comfort and Mountain Dew tasted precisely like a handful of yellow gummy bears, and I was contented.

"What's marriage like?" John asked the spaceman. "I might be getting in the game."

"I need to tell you something," said Virginia. She detached herself from him; squared him up.

"God, what?" asked John. He placed his red Solo cup down on the table so very gently, as if to prove to an aggressor that he had parted with his gun.

"I was married once," she said. "I was so young, eighteen and he was much older. It lasted all of eight months and I almost died of heartache. I was blind in love and he turned out to be just awful. A liar. Such a liar. It hospitalized me. He hospitalized me. *I* hospitalized me. To the loony bin I went. By my bed, Daddy made me swear on our good name that all suitors henceforth needed to go through him."

"I'm so sorry that happened to you," said John. She handed him back his tuxedo jacket.

"I think I need to be alone now," she said. "Come on, Cheese, let's go."

Being with me is like being alone? Fuck it, I'll take it.

CHAPTER FIFTEEN

"I'M WAYZED OUT, CHEESE," said Virginia Wells.

We were in her room at the Grand Floridian just before midnight, she in boyish pajamas: baby blue shorts and a button-up top. I marveled at the pallor of her freckly skin despite so many hours under the Disney sun.

"What sort of suntan lotion do you use?" I asked.

"Good old Coppertone. To me it smells like young love."

"I love how old-fashioned you are," I fawned.

What slender thighs. Florence's were skinny while hers came with two oblong, athletic muscles just beneath the surface. A surface blessed with more of that soft blonde fuzz that I associated with her home state's famous peaches.

"Old-fashioned?" she asked. "Heck, yeah. Someone's going to have to be in the year 2000. Forty-one days to go, Cheese. You excited?"

"Nervous, Virginia."

"Better hit the ATM before New Year's Eve."

"I'm not worried about Y2K, just the future in general. I have the sinking feeling that something is coming for us. Well, not you. *Me*."

"I'll protect you," she said.

Now was she lying on the bed, on her tummy, kicking her long legs. She was thirteen reading *Teen Beat* in her childhood bedroom that must still look like a fairy tale.

"You know, Cheese, you're old-fashioned too."

"Both John and I are."

"John, I don't know. I picture him already in the year 2000, maybe even 2020. He's just so . . . *new*. The newest boy I've ever met."

"You're really going to marry him, aren't you?"

"If Daddy says it's okay, I'll definitely consider it. I've never met a boy who was self-assured enough for me. He knows when to lead me and when to follow me. How to kiss me and be kissed by me."

"And if Daddy says no?"

"Oh, Cheese, it's just not this girl's style to think about life that way."

With that she got out of bed, opened the hotel room door, yawned. "I need my beauty rest, darlin'."

"Of course," I said.

She kissed my cheek and closed the door. I could hear her yawn, then make a little feline noise that sounded so contented. This human purrs. I wish I could adopt the style of which she spoke. I guess I have it here, at Disney. But come next week, the Murray Marks clock will strike midnight and like Cinderella the peasantry of my life will be fully restored. My flask will turn into a Filofax, and my Virginia into a Chinese warlord.

The Mizner's Lounge was open till 2:00 a.m. and the musical quartet was still playing. Maybe I'll try to dance. I once watched John waltz by himself. With himself. It was the most impressive and touching thing I'd ever seen. She's right. The newest boy in the world. All alone.

*

Sunday morning and this time I was not spared a hangover. (I was actually too hungover to invest in all the syllables that *Harvey Hanginstein* required. For once you're spared my inner babble. You're welcome.) It was 6:00 a.m. and I felt *liverish*. Some parts of me were purely desiccated, like my head and hands. My lips and fingers were red and raw. They stung. My organs felt inflamed, too large for their spaces; they wanted out. My home cure was iced tea and pita bread, but that was for an amateur hangover. This morning I was in the major leagues. Outside the Magic Kingdom was static, stuck. A full two hours until things would start whirling around. I gave myself its deadline. By eight I would be cured. There were two routes, though, really: Wayz or sleep. The latter struck me as defeatist, while the former involved courage and creativity. It would be suspenseful, for if I made a wrong move, a wrong choice, it could result in spew and the day would be lost. But, *but,* in all of two hours I could be bright as a freshly minted penny. I decided to follow my metaphor's lead and choose a copper-colored Wayz. Long Island iced tea?

Yes, Long Island iced tea. An ingredient-intensive cocktail on a Sunday morning in a blue law state in an all but dry Kingdom was just the challenge I needed. My minibar was too depleted to make the complex drink. But John and I were once in similar straits on a Ponder to St. Louis and we came up with something: empty the entire contents of the minibar as if someone had stolen it all. Call housekeeping and sound outraged.

Mention calling the police. Imply that one of the hotel's staff had stolen it all. Suggest that we were also missing a valuable watch. Finally, say, "But we can avoid a spectacle, if you can just get someone up here right now to replenish the minibar."

"Yes, Mr. Marks. I will send someone right up. Have a magical day."

A tired-looking man restocked the little fridge while I sat on the bed watching. He was consulting a graphic chart about where every item was supposed to go. Clearly this wasn't his usual job.

"New to minibars?" I asked.

"I'm one of the night managers."

"Ever see something like this?" I asked. "I mean who would do this?" It was from the script John and I had perfected in St. Louis.

He turned to face me.

"This is why they're thinking of getting rid of minibars at Disney all together. People take advantage. Everything's going to change."

We locked eyes. His were a cheery blue. They belied his dim-sounding prophesy. "Any chance I could get an extra can of Pringles?" I asked.

He obliged. Handed me the extra. I wanted to ask him what he was going to do after his shift. If he was going to Wayz later at some scrappy Irish bar in downtown Orlando. Or if my Pringles request might become part of his day. Johnny Boy and I had a theory that if you said some-thing just south of innocuous to a stranger, that it could haunt them a little. Resound in their heads for twenty-four uncomfortable hours.

Why did he want another Pringles? Why two Pringles? Fucking Pringles.

"You're all set," said the night manager.

"Wait," I said and reached for my wallet. A ten-dollar bill. "This is for you. Have one on me." Bottoms up, I gestured.

"I don't drink but thanks for the tanner," he said and rolled the minibar service cart out of my room.

The tanner? What the hell's a tanner? Must mean ten bucks. Never heard it before, even though it sounded Irish. It must be revenge for my Pringles request. And why in the name of all things holy would some-one like that not Wayz?

I'm having pringles for breakfast, I wrote Florence. *And tipped the minibar guy a tanner.*

Good morning, she wrote.

Her brain was immune to being wormed with anomalous words.

I made my drink, plated it, surrounded it with a circle of Pringles, and sat outside. Here goes nothing.

*

What a life. Three Long Island iced teas, about twenty Pringles, consumed over two hours, and I was the most optimistic boy in all the world. My organs shrank back into submission, and I was down to my skivvies ironing my Sunday linen trousers listening on my Napster MP3 player to my beloved Backstreet Boys: *I want it that way*.

Before the Ponder to London, at the airport, John had gifted us with the players. What a revelation. He'd been involved in some music-sharing racket. Share songs, but not Virginias? Eh, fuck it all.

I want it that *Wayz*.

The first sip of my Long Island iced tea wasn't pretty. I took a step, lurching from the balcony in the direction of the bathroom; bile had escaped from my stomach into my throat, but I had the good sense to cram a few Pringles into my mouth and the toxic tide receded. Then I took an even healthier sip and the morning and my face began to fill with all the colors of the rainbow. I'd been ashen until that brave sip, color-blind to the Magic Kingdom. Now all the whirlies were beautiful to my eyes. Then my BlackBerry buzzed. Florence.

What time is your flight tomorrow?

What flight?

Regardless of the Ponder, I would have responded similarly. But this Ponder Sunday was the real deal. Tomorrow was the *real* Frontier, but not like Frontier World below with its Davy Crockett-ed scrim.

Westward Ho, I wrote my wife.

Can a buzz be a place? I wondered, in my skivvies, on the balcony. Can it have a latitude and a longitude? I say yes! Then a knock on the door. Must be Johnny Boy.

Nope, it was Mr. Wells. Unfazed by my underwear, he made himself at home. Took notice of the ironing board. "I like a man who irons his own clothes," he said, claiming a seat outside. He smelled my Long Island iced tea. "A little early I'd say, but it is a Sunday after all, damn fine day to forget one's worries."

Berobed, sunglasses, hair slicked back; are all true adults caricatures of themselves?

"How did your evening turn out, Mr. Marks? Some newbies have a long night after Mongolian beef. Spicy, yes?"

"Sure," I lied.

"Spicy as a monkey's ass."

I thought last night he said the devil's ass?

"Yes sir," I said.

"We're very fond of you, Cheese. Tell me again why they call you *Cheese*."

"My middle name is Camembert. My parents met over cheese. John coined it."

"Ah, Mr. Apple. Complex fellow, I'd say. Agree?"

"John? I don't know. I mean, there's something famous about him, if you like that type of stuff."

To me he'd always been sort of famous.

"I suppose," said Mr. Wells.

He took a Pringle but did not eat it. Odd bird.

"Ah, Disney World," I said, holding on to the railing. A silence was threatening my buzz. His heavy presence.

"At first, we came here purely for Ginny, but the place has grown on Constance and me."

"It's grown on me too," I said admiring the Space Mountain's reticulated top. An arabesque seashell topped by a spiny horn. Way more nautical than spacey, but beautiful nonetheless. I'd never walked on the beach with a girl who wore a bikini. Florence wore one-pieces. I wanted to ask Mr. Wells how his daughter looked in a two-piece, but he would most certainly impale me atop Space Mountain's razor-sharp finial.

"Constance and I have a notion about you and our daughter."

"A notion?"

"Have any children?"

"Not a one."

"Good to know. I started a little late as well."

He replaced the Pringle exactly where it had been, preserving what remained of my circular design. About small objects the very wealthy can be particular.

"Virginia's beautiful inside and out, this we know," he said.

"I happen to agree, sir."

"Good, good. You know there's a second home on Fairvue, that's our estate in Savannah. A second structure built by Colonel Alton P. Wells, my grandfather. He built it as a marriage cottage for his son, my father. Seven bedrooms. Modest compared to the main house."

I needed a drink.

"Will you excuse me, Mr. Wells?"

"Of course, Murray. Mind if I call you Murray?"

I didn't answer. Shut the curtain so that he couldn't see my Wayz making.

"*M-I-C*," he sang in a weird deep voice. "*K-E-Y*," he sang while I fixed myself a vodka and grapefruit. I needed something sharp, a little bitter. A slap in the face. Wake up, Cheese. Fairvue is not your clubhouse. Back to the terrace.

"I do have to tell you, sir, that I am, um, in fact presently married," I said.

Now there was a Pringle in each of his hands. He was weighing them like the scales of justice.

"You see, Murray, we have a tradition in our family, dating back to our Scottish ancestors, that Wells girls should be married at the age of twenty-four. It's the perfect age and the formula has never failed us. You see, Virginia turns twenty-four next March. Constance and I have our hearts set on celebrating both the new millennium and her matrimony in a once-in-a-lifetime event at Fairvue. Ushering in the future of our family and time itself. Our ballroom facilitates twelve hundred."

"Twelve hundred *people*?"

"My family have always been great matchmakers," he said, then once again expertly replaced the Pringles. "Well, I've said what I came to say. Have a good day, Murray."

He stood, cleared his throat and then a crescendo: "*M-O-U-S-E*,"
he roared.

*

John Apple was back in his stringy denim shorts but had held fast to
his tuxedo shirt. Untucked, sleeves rolled up. And then the ring box
bulging once again, this time from his shorts pocket. We met at the
Grand Floridian bar by the pool that opened at eleven on Sundays.

"Close enough," said the bartender, checking his watch.

"He's agreed to meet me at Club 33," said John.

"Who?" I asked.

"Mr. Wells, of course."

I decided to spare him the details of my encounter with the man.
An encounter I hadn't yet wrapped my head around. The Wellses were
impractical people. It was a language in which I had little fluency. I'd
always held a job since my first year of high school. Work, then the
weekend. Work, then the weekend. I needed my life's scaffolding. The
Wellses though, and Johnny Boy too, they were born scaffold-free. Like
the top of the Chrysler building, glistening and glorious on its opening
day in 1930.

"Thirty grand just to join," said John. "Fucking Washington Wells."

"Join what?" I asked.

"Club 33. An exclusive club inside New Orleans Square. Full bar.
Walt built the first one in Disneyland just so he could drink inside the
park. My hope is that Mr. Wells will be a few deep by this afternoon
and take pity on my bursting heart."

Would John occupy the marriage cottage that Great-Grandpa
built? Would *Cheese*? Would it remain empty? Poor Virginia inside,
alone, growing old and batty at age twenty-four?

"What time are you meeting the old man?" I asked.

"I requested 6:00 p.m. and he countered with 4:00. Seems he's
taking his family cruise with Cap."

I was continuing with the greyhounds, still in need of a drink with a bite; grapefruit and vodka had a grounding effect on me. Well, usually, but not today, not here; some significant part of me was in Savannah, Georgia, in tails in front of twelve hundred.

"I'll have what he's drinking," said John to the bartender

He only ever followed my Wayz lead when he was feeling vulnerable. Rudderless. I could count the times on one hand. Then he'd become childlike. Generous with his words. Inquisitive even.

"What's it like having green eyes?" he'd asked me at Shun Lee after deciding to divorce Kathy.

He had that same look today, a parentless boy lost at the fair.

"Can you stay here with me?" he asked.

"I am here with you."

"No, I mean, I've extended our rooms. Indefinitely."

*

We rode the Pirates ride and John brought an empty drinking glass to collect water. For good luck, he wanted to soak the ring in the ride's dank river. To my nose it smelled of gasoline and yeast.

"The Imagineers used actual Caribbean seawater," said John. "Rumor has it that reefs thrived in there despite the permanence of night. Were the lights ever flipped on, it would be pure turquoise."

He wanted ice cream for lunch; it was the last sit-down meal he remembered having with his parents. At the space hotel. Make-it-yourself sundaes.

"There's nothing really contemporary about it," I remarked about the hotel while we ate our sundaes amid a human puppet-filled buffet called Chef Mickey's.

"I'm going to charm Washington Wells like he's never been charmed before," said John before our toast. We'd ordered a bottle of Sancerre, but then when our stemware met with our signatory force, they shattered. He'd taken it too far and we were asked to leave the restaurant so they could clean the table. John held the glass full of pirate water which held the ring, as if it was a goldfish he'd salvaged from a fire.

Removed from Chef Mickey's, I wrote Florence. *But just so they can clean the table.*

We sat in the seriously generic lobby that connoted outer space through a hollow sounding soundtrack: whales chatting underwater? Dolphins in space? Whatever it was, it sounded like the tediousness of infinity.

"So how long again did you book our rooms for?" I asked John.

"Through to the new year," he said. "They only allow fifty days at a time, but then you can simply extend with a phone call to the front desk."

"I have to go back to work. And Florence and I need to talk. And I sorely need Airport Mama's soup. I just don't know—"

"Listen, Cheese, I need you. At least let's not leave tomorrow, okay?"

"No Monday Bloodies party?"

He sat staring at the ring. People are so fucking needy. A man with a crew cut stopped before us.

"Ah, the portly gentleman from It's a Small World who hails from New York. Only two things hail from New York, steers and queers. I don't see any horns on your head, so you must be a queer. Say would you mind watching after my son while I use the latrine?"

"Um," I stammered.

"It would be our pleasure," said John.

The man had been holding the boy's hand, a hand he delivered to me.

"Did you like It's a Small World?" the boy asked.

"Not particularly," I said, and then he began singing the damn song.

I'd never held a child's hand before, just John's during takeoffs. They were both similarly . . . unctuous.

I might need to stay an extra day, I wrote Florence.

Murray, we need to talk.

Let's talk now!

The cloying layer of grease on the boy's hand. I suspected that the source was the mouse-shaped pretzels I'd seen that glowed with unsaturated fat. Mental note to try two.

I am thinking of adopting a child, wrote Florence. *From China.*

I couldn't let go of the boy's hand fast enough. I threw it back out into the world.

CHAPTER SIXTEEN

WE SAT IN JUNGLE Land near the private club where John was to meet with Mr. Wells.

"You should definitely adopt a kid," said John.

"First of all, if we were to have a kid it would be through procreation. Second of all, that's unlikely because I'm under the impression that I have a low sperm count."

"Go to China in EPCOT. Immerse yourself in the culture. Buy something for Cheese Junior."

"Is it legal for lesbians to adopt babies?"

It occurred to me that Florence did not write that it was indeed with *me* that she wanted to adopt a Chinese baby.

"Why not. Everyone should be happy. Well, it's showtime. Wish me luck, Cheese."

"I would but you probably don't need it."

"Usually not, but times are a-changing."

He found sunglasses in his back pocket and donned them. I'd never seen him wear shades. Clearly an homage to Washington Wells's gold-rimmed Ray Ban aviators.

If he says "no" you still get to be a handsome multimillionaire.

Life isn't fair, I wrote Florence.

"You know what?" asked John. "You should come with me to Club 33. I don't think I can do it alone. Plus you can vouch for me. He clearly doesn't like me, but of course he trusts you."

Of course. Good old Cheese. Well it would be something to bear witness to history. Ponder history. Our history. My history.

"You can be my second," said John.

"What? What's that?"

"Second? It's from dueling. My right-hand man, you make sure our pistols are about the same. You negotiate on my behalf. Step in if my opponent cheats."

"You're weaponless. Defenseless. And I'm not sure I can recommend you to Mr. Wells."

"What? Why the hell not?"

"Come on, you're not husband and father material."

He sat back down, slowly removed his sunglasses. I'd stung him.

"I mean for Virginia. I mean . . . I'll go with you to Club 33." No response. "And I'll vouch for you. I will."

"Really?"

"Of course. On second thought, I'm sure you'll be a good husband."

For some lucky girl, just not mine, you manipulative bastard.

*

Of all the places he'd taken me, this club was my favorite. Grand wooden Art Nouveau bar that looked hand carved. And a serious barkeep measuring out the Wayz with great care and precision. In fact, lots of Wayz accoutrements that Walt Disney himself had owned or used. Aside from a talking vulture that greeted us at the entrance, the club was elegant. A central dining salon surrounded by alcoves and lounges, and a four-top inside an old elevator car. Tiffany lamps and gleaming brass. Oh, and truly inspiring air-conditioning.

"Walt set the indoor temperature to 59 degrees," said John. "And it's never varied all these years."

We were early for John's meeting with Washington Wells. I was not on the guest list, but they permitted me to sit at the bar.

"Look around. They don't afford membership to Biggunz," said John. "Everyone, including us, including *you*, is under 300 pounds."

He didn't seem as nervous as I might have expected, but he tended to turn calm before big moments. A real skill. He would have made a good soldier. A good commander. Someone who would have survived Omaha Beach. Without a scratch. Me? Dead in the water. Wouldn't have made it onto the sand. But people like me have to die in order for wars to be won.

I might enlist in the army, I wrote Florence. *Collateral damage.*

"Sir, I am in love with your daughter," John practiced. "My greatest and only desire is to make her happy and I have the means so that she can live in the style to which she's accustomed. While it's only been a few days . . . *whilst* it's only been a few days?"

"While."

"While it's only been a few days, I can assure you that I have never felt this way nor have I ever done anything like this. I am asking for her hand in marriage." Then he opened the ring box and showed it to a pretend Mr. Wells.

"I wouldn't show him the ring," I said.

"Why not? It's beautiful."

"One, you're not proposing to *him*, and two—"

My BlackBerry buzzed.

I miss you, wrote Florence.

Highly unusual. I smelled a guilty conscience. Fucking Kathy Apple. A bowl of hot salted peanuts was set before us.

"I hate the way you eat peanuts," said John. "You clutch at them and they go flying. And it's not hygienic; by clutching at them your meaty fingers make contact with the innocent ones."

When he felt less godlike he'd critique my manners in order to bolster his status.

"Screw it," he said. "I'm showing him the ring. Where the hell is he anyway? Thirty late. Aren't WASPs supposed to be punctual, always consulting their golden watch?"

"How would I know?"

I helped myself to another clutch of peanuts and John shook his head.

"It's how you're supposed to eat them," I said.

"I'll threaten to elope."

"He'd just laugh at you. She's wrapped around his finger."

Two bowls of hot salted peanuts or ninety minutes passed before a waiter appeared at the bar and handed John a folded note. We'd speculated, at least John had, that Mr. Wells was testing him.

"He wants to know my staying power. That I don't fold. And I don't," he'd said. But the note indicated that Mr. Wells would not be making an appearance.

Mr. Wells is unable to host you. At your leisure please finish your drink. There is no tab and it's been a pleasure welcoming you to Club 33.

"Beautiful stationery," I said. "Definite Ponder souvenir. Look at that handwriting. I wish I had good handwriting. Florence says I write like a child."

"I should BlackBerry Virginia."

"We both should," I said.

And we did, but there was no response. Into the Disney dusk we went. Listless. Monday was bearing down hard.

"Maybe this was all some sort of Disney fakery? A theatrical play starring us," I said. "Maybe we're supposed to brush it off, live to see another day and just bring all these incredible Ponder memories and souvenirs back home with us into the real world."

"Real world? Home? There is no home for me. Not anymore. I am a dandelion's floating white seed."

*

Daddy's suffered a stroke. We're at the hospital. He's alive but non-responsive. In a coma. Pray for him.

We were in John's suite when we got the news.

"That's just awful. Poor guy," said John.

He was trying to seem concerned, sympathetic, humane, but I could tell he was unburdened by the turn of events. Washington Wells was his nemesis, and a damn formidable one. A nemesis in a coma is a victory.

We both BlackBerry'd Virginia with our prayers. Mine were genuine. I *liked* that odd man and couldn't imagine what would happen beneath Virginia's rib cage should he succumb.

Our little blue machines buzzed again.

You should both know that Daddy's last words to me before he blacked out were "marry Cheese."

*

Mine was a knowing smile as John was reduced to a pacing, muttering, ring-box-juggling wreck. A beautiful girl wants to marry me. Or a beautiful girl's comatose father wants to marry me. Into the family. I, Cheese, was a man's dying wish.

"I've never felt this way," I said.

"Me neither," said John. "And stop grinning."

More like beaming. Now I understood the power behind John Apple's victorious dimples after some young thing would buy him a drink or slip him her number. He felt as I did: wanted, qualified, sexually relevant, *male*, dammit. True, the wanting came from a fifty-something stroke victim, but because of his last two words Virginia had been made to imagine a life with me. Maybe even made to wonder what I would be like in bed? Enough. Her life just got turned upside down at Disney World. Her beloved Daddy on the brink. A princely multimillionaire and a rotund Wayz machine battling for possession of her soul. What a fucking Ponder.

They want me, I wrote Florence.

"Should we go to the hospital?" asked John.

"We don't know which hospital, and she would have asked for us, or me."

Let me know if there's anything I can do, I wrote Virginia.

John was also clicking away at the little dark blue keys. So agile on his RIM BlackBerry 857 with those little fingers. Little hands. I was more of a clunker, jabbing at the keyboard, but I rarely misspelled. Unlike John who cared only for speed, his messages riddled with typos. Virginia had exquisite handwriting. I saw her sign her name at breakfast. Those loops and lines. Soft and strong at once. Can penmanship cause arousal? Yes. Yes it can.

"Why don't we go on a ride?" I suggested. "Clear our minds."

But he just sat there typing. It was dinner time now and we hadn't had a Wayz since the wonderfully fancy private club whose name I'd forgotten. Leafing through John's *1999 Birnbaum's Walt Disney World*, I came upon an article about a restaurant in the hotel called Victoria & Albert's, apparently the only AAA five-diamond nominee in all of Florida. Twelve courses? Wine pairings? $150 per person? This is just what the doctor ordered. A gourmet experience where I could luxuriate over my upper hand: the Wells family had chosen me.

"Let's have dinner at Victoria and Albert's."

"BlackBerry me so I know it's working," said John.

"She just wrote us. It's working."

"That was twenty-five minutes ago and she usually gets back to me immediately."

"Fine."

His machine buzzed. Relief.

"What did you say about dinner?" he asked.

"Victoria and Albert's. Over dinner we could make plans for tomorrow. We're not leaving tomorrow, right? I mean, we should see her before we go."

"I'm never leaving, not without her."

Me neither.

*

Every server at Victoria & Albert's wore a name tag that read Victoria or Albert.

"What an awesome coincidence," I said over the fifth course, a white porcelain tasting spoon that was filled with Wakame sea urchin and Alba white truffles. Paired with a 1988 Piper-Heidsieck. For me, some actual divinity at Disney, aside from the girl and maybe, *maybe,* the revelations that are the prehistoric poultry legs.

"Isn't this amazing?" I asked John.

He shrugged. The very wealthy affect little interest in all the kingdoms they can afford, instead feigning appreciation for life's simple pleasures. Eating a hotdog in Central Park underneath a blue and yellow Sabrett umbrella? Fine, but doing so while wearing a $55,000 Patek Phillipe watch and babbling about becoming a Sabrett vendor?

"Imagine living beneath this royal blue and golden yellow umbrella handing children rainbow pops," he'd said.

After his mustard-smeared Sabrett's napkin failed to connect with the trash can, it was Cheese who had picked it up and threw it out.

"Maybe you should go back after all," said John. "To your wife."

"The current one or my future one who hails from Savannah?"

"Very funny."

"I'm serious," I said. "There is you know, a chance she might ask for my hand."

"That's not the way it works."

"Florence proposed to me, in essence. I mean she bought the ring and put it in my jacket pocket. I guess she sort of proposed to herself. Holy shit, is that steak tartare?"

"Yes, sir," said Albert. "The chef uses highly prized beef from Japan. We're the only restaurant to import it."

"Amazing."

"They force-feed the cows," said John. "I'll pass."

"I'll have his, Albert. Wow, paired with a Chablis? Interesting."

"Ironic your being served by a king and queen," said John. "The generosity to open their dining room to a commoner."

A commoner. Asshole. Our Victoria was handsome. A young Katharine Hepburn. Strict shoulders and light eyes that twinkled when she smiled at John.

"You should date Victoria."

At that he scowled and repossessed his steak tartare.

I'm back at Disney, wrote Virginia.

She'd only written me.

Outside the Carousel of Progress. It's Daddy's favorite.

"What's Carousel of Progress?"

"Why?"

"Just curious."

"It's a tremendously uplifting stage show about technological advances in the household starting at the turn of the—"

Care to join me? She asked.

"If you'll excuse me," I said to Johnny Boy.

Oh, the louche manner with which I tossed my napkin onto the table. Then I patted his shoulder in the same loving if patronizing way he'd patted mine over the years. He rose as I left, so confused by my superior gestures.

"Where are you going?" he asked.

"I have a date with Virginia Wells."

You should have seen his face: all the furrows in that famously knitted brow which usually signified mischievous genius, and which he usually employed to attract women. Tonight it signified utter panic, if not horror.

*

I waited outside the carousel, arguably the only truly classy ride in the Magical Kingdom. Old school and artful. Freshly painted antique horses but no Virginia. And no progress.

"Why is this called the Carousel of Progress?" I asked an employee.

"Oh, this is Prince Charming's Regal Carousel. The Carousel of Progress is over in Tomorrowland. I'd be happy to take you."

His job was trash collection, and he wielded his clawed trash-grabber with such dexterity, it was as if the trash, upon seeing the man, flew on its own wings into the cans.

"I used to pick up hot dog trash for my best friend," I said to the man.

"Walt didn't like anything to be untidy."

"But those days are numbered."

"And if you happened to look inside one of the cans, you'd be hard pressed to see or smell anything. Walt imported a vacuum system all the way from Sweden. Sucks the trash down below the park where it flies through tubes just under your feet at thirty-five miles per hour. There's a tour of it all, you know, the behind-the-scenes stuff if you're interested."

Florence would be. It would be the only thing she'd be interested in. She'd take notes too. Pangs of guilt followed while the man spoke of garbage. I'd deserted my best friend and, in theory, my wife, and felt unclean. Perhaps I should throw myself into one of the trash receptacles and be cleansed by Walt's powerful suction?

Are you okay? I wrote John.

How are you? I wrote Florence.

Then I spotted Virginia by the Carousel of Progress sign eating popcorn one piece at a time. When she saw me, she dropped the bag, and my guide flew into action while she ran to me.

"Oh Cheese," she said from inside our hug. "I've prayed and prayed and still nothing. Prayer is arrogant, isn't it? Everyone thinks they have a direct line to God. The best thing about God is his indifference. He doesn't play favorites."

"He did with you. He made you beautiful inside and out," I said, and she hugged me tighter.

The garbage man gave me a little nod and smile. I wasn't sure if it was because my body was pressed against the most beautiful girl in all of Tomorrow World or if he was admiring his own handiwork; the spilled popcorn and its bag were nowhere in sight, no trash can that I could see. I could not figure out how he disposed of it. Perhaps he ate it, bag and all? Perhaps Walt bred employees whose digestive systems could break down paper? Enough, Cheese. During the most passionate hug of your life, clear your mind. What did Oasis entitle their album? *Be Here Now*? Be here now. And I was. But the immediacy of the moment had a side effect: utter arousal. We both backed away from the embrace to observe my bulge.

"Um," I said. "I'm sorry that's—"

"Let's just go on the ride," said Virginia, sounding exhausted by adults, their rings and plans, their strokes and boners.

*

The preshow was flickering images of the 1964 World's Fair, where apparently this progress ride first appeared. New York City looked drab and wintry; faceless men in trench coats with their faceless wives moved hurriedly through the fairgrounds in search of "A Great Big Beautiful Tomorrow," the ride's relentless theme song. There were also transplanted human puppets rollicking about. I felt for them; they were accustomed to warmer climes, coconut patties, and fake friendliness, not New York City nights in the early '60s when Wayzing was a dark and dangerous sport. Expense account alcoholics abounded; this was no place for Pinocchio. I wondered how many of the people who flickered before me in technicolor were still alive. None, I decided. Well, maybe Pinocchio, who met a stunning girl one November night in 1964 at an automat. At Horn & Hardart's on Forty-Second Street. They fell in love Wayzlessly, purely. Pinocchio convinced her to become a puppet too, but she was just too good-looking and got swept away by some rake in a trench coat at the 1964 World's Fair. Heartbroken, Pinocchio booked a one-way ticket to Paris, never to return. That's where he is this very moment, wiping down a zinc bar and remembering his one true love. Maybe I'll suggest that John fly away to Paris, but not forever, just for a couple of weeks. He'll buy a new pair of old jeans that will flaunt his ass, and unwittingly drink at Pinocchio's bar. Despite his melancholy, Pinocchio, now old and gray, will smile, and the smile will reassure Johnny Boy. The message being: unlike me, you will love again. Leave Virginia to Monsieur Marks.

Accepting this fate, John Apple will return to New York City where we'll meet one fine day at Shun . . . shit, the ride is starting and there's the damn song again. I transmuted "There's a Great Big Beautiful Tomorrow" to "There's a Great Big Beautiful Erection." Fortunately that erection subsided in the first scene, Edison's America, where the fake puppets on stage were gossiping about the Wright Brothers. Virginia leaned forward to take in the Americana, her face in her palms.

"Uncle Orville," she whispered.

"Who?"

"You'll see."

Uncle Orville was an ornery heard-but-never-seen puppet who apparently lived in the family's bathtub.

"Is he drunk?" I asked. "He sounds Wayzed out. Bathtub Wayzing is so fucking amazing."

"Gentlemen shouldn't cuss."

"Yeah, you're right. I mean just 'so amazing,' the bathtub Wayzing that is."

"Shh."

Did we just have our first fight?

The ride ended oddly in a futuristic scene that seemed to take place in the garish heart of the 1980s; it depressed the hell out of me. A grandmother playing a highly pixelated video game. A burnt turkey. Virginia watched with such admiration; the girl human puppet could be her cousin. "Sally" who ends up growing breasts after a hundred years of *progress*. Long auburn hair, just like Virginia's.

"Oh Daddy," Virginia sighed as we exited. "Hey Cheese, let's do the ride again?"

"Again?"

"It was his favorite. It *is* his favorite."

My flask was empty. The damn show was long; twenty-five minutes until I'd get to see teenaged Sally and her burgeoning chest.

Sally, I wrote Florence as we entered the nearly empty theater. Sunday night, late November in Disney. Only the diehards seemed to be out. Puppet-lusty freaks just like me.

"What do you think of Sally?" I asked.

"Oh, I just adore her. There's just something about an American girl."

There sure sure sure is.

"Did your father really say that? You know, about me."

"He did," she said, then took my hand, squeezed it gravely, suggesting a predicament. One that we were in together. Then she gave me my hand back as the cloyingly buoyant music picked up. A great big beautiful tomorrow. For Sally's family, yes. Again Virginia leaned forward in deepest admiration of the puppet family and the perfection of their middling existence. Holidays, appliances, and sobriety, aside of course from the bathtub Wayzing uncle. Uncle Wilbur? I forget. Regardless, I could only relate to him. And Sally's tits. Christ, I needed a Wayz.

*

"I'm bushed," she yawned outside of the ride.

Employees with glow sticks were directing traffic out of the land. They wanted us out. According to John, their party started the moment ours ended.

"When the last guest has cleared the gates, you'll hear a roar from the cast members because their time has come. Then a fireworks display, one even more magnificent than the one us guests enjoy, explodes over Cinderella's Castle. What appears to be mere scenery during the light of day transforms into candlelit bars, bistros, jazz clubs. It goes on for only a few hours, but it's necessary relief for the cast members whose lives are more complicated than even I can fathom. By day they shoulder the burden of dispensing magic, and by night the soap opera of their lives unfolds in real time. Broken hearts. Lust. Forbidden love. Even murder," he'd explained.

We walked in silence, Virginia checking her BlackBerry every now and again. John? Word about her father?

"How's your mom holding up?" I asked.

"As well as can be expected. I made her go back to the Grand Flo even though she wanted to stay at the hospital."

Grand Flo. Clearly defeated by the day, still she made the words sound adorable.

That drawl. That Southern drawl.

"What do the doctors say?"

She hunched her freckled shoulders.

"So how's John?" she asked, so matter-of-factly. Or had the question come from the most tender place in her heart?

"He's at Victoria and Albert's. I mean, he was. I guess he's confused like all of us."

"Oh, I'm not confused. Welp, I should go be with Mama. Think I'm going to walk back. Bye-bye now."

I'm so confused, I wrote Florence.

In a few hours it will turn Monday, the Ponder unresolved, still alive. Stephen King's *Pet Sematary*: "Sometimes dead is better."

CHAPTER SEVENTEEN

VICTORIA & ALBERT'S WAS empty but accessible. Hotels can be generous with their night-fallow spaces. Ballrooms and catering halls. There's something peaceful if ghostly about stacked banquet chairs; that they let guests roam among the ghosts must be purposeful. *Book us now before you join the eternal party.* Now I sound like Johnny Boy and his beloved haunted ride. Speaking of the devil, he hadn't responded to my many messages. I wondered if, after all, we'd just assemble for the Monday, Ponder-ending Bloody Mary party at 11:00 a.m. in one of our rooms, bags packed, with scant details about what had preceded. Only the generalized. We'd say: "Jesus, that was something."

"Was that girl even real?"

"We should come back here in a couple of years!"

"Fuck it, make mine a double."

But now I sat where John had (the white linens already impeccable for tomorrow night) in full view of the maître d's podium and Cheese's big back trundling out for his big date; how he must have pushed aside his plate of steak tartare and pouted like a child. But he's still my best friend and still, to me, a hero.

Bloodies party tomorrow? I wrote John.

You make it home okay? I wrote Virginia.

How are you? I wrote Florence.

Covering all bases eroded my viscera. I needed a Wayz to cauterize the salts and acids associated with moral torpor. But it was 11:17 on a Sunday and I'd exhausted the useful bottles in my minibar and hadn't the heart to reprise our deceitful minibar gambit. I double-checked the flask for contents; sometimes one mis-guesses the weight of the vessel and presto, a last Wayz. Not this time. "Disney *Word*" the flask read. What now, at 11:18, what *was* the word? For me, a rhetorical question. *Despair.* It usually happened tomorrow on that desperate last Ponder morning when everything was anesthetic except the loins. Good old pussy stomach. I'd never experienced it alone. Always with John or Florence. So many firsts on this Ponder. Another? There was an Orlando Yellow Pages in the room. Forgive me, Minnie, but I need the company of the feminine even if it means taking a shortcut. Heroic Johnny Boy frequented call girls; why not demi-heroic Cheese?

*

"Classy Ladies" caught my eye. I wanted a tie-in with Disney, and their full-page ad included the graphic of a prince helping a princess from a royal chariot.

Personal Assistant by the Hour. Don't go Stag to the Big event. Companions for the Day or Night. Romantic dinners.

Discretion Guaranteed.

I salvaged a Myers's Rum and OJ from the minibar, which I consumed before I called 1–800-CLASSIC.

Getting classy over here, I wrote Florence.

So smart to be the only one with a full-page ad; smarter still to have a young bright voice answer the phone.

"Classy Ladies, Joanie speaking."

"Well, yes, hello there." I was trying to sound British, imperious even. A constable who doesn't respect the enterprise but grudgingly accepts kickbacks.

"How can I help you tonight?"

"Well you see there, I might, *might* be in the market for a late-evening companion for an important business meeting with Asians from overseas who are jet-lagged and have breakfast at the oddest—"

"We'd be happy to help. You mentioned Asia. Do you like Asian women?"

"Um, well, yes as a matter of fact, but for the sake of this meeting . . . you see Asian businessmen like reddish-headed girls. I mean during meetings they like looking at auburn-y hair."

"Of course. Do you have a fax number?"

"Um, no, but the hotel does, I think. Why?"

"We'll need to fax you the bios and photos of our girls and also a contract for you to sign along with your credit card information."

"Hm."

I couldn't allow those images to sully the magically fragrant lobby of the Grand Floridian. So many children close by. So many puppets.

"Is there any other way?" I asked.

"I'm afraid not."

"It's just that I have become close with the night managers here and wouldn't want them to get the wrong—"

"You could explain that you are a producer who is casting a show and that you need to go through various headshots."

"I've always wanted to be a producer. They have the best desks. And they don't really do anything except have lunch. Which is a form of work in its own right if you fucking do it at all correctly. Oh excuse my cussing. Gentlemen shouldn't cuss."

I showered, then chose my most produceresque outfit: an ironic T-shirt I'd ordinarily wear to bed (Snoopy and Woodstock, Florence's favorites), ironed khakis, and my blue blazer, but with a red pocket square. As well, I wore no socks with my loafers. Nothing grants second acts like showering close to midnight.

"You should have received a fax for me from my colleagues in Hollywood," I told the lady behind the front desk.

"For Mr. Marks?"

"Yes."

Producers sound stern, then flash a toothy smile, signifying nothing.

"It just came through."

She handed me an envelope thick with thrice-folded sex workers. I sat on a couch feigning disgust that my colleagues in Hollywood would make me work at such an hour. There were fifteen girls and a credit card authorization form. The girls were represented by grainy full-body photos (bathing suit and evening wear), beneath which were their bios:

Age:

Height/Weight:

Skills:

Favorite Food:

Favorite Movie:

Favorite Artist:

I kept on coming back to Tanya Tucker, who was one year older than Virginia:

Age: 24

Height/Weight: 5'5/110

Skills: Typing, Dictation, Jazz Ballet, Microsoft Excel, Tie cherry stem into a knot with my tongue.

Favorite Food: Classic French

Favorite Movie: *Pretty Woman*

Favorite Artist: Lou Reed

Two hundred dollars for the first hour, a one-hundred-dollar transportation fee, then fifty dollars per hour. And a thousand-dollar deposit "fully refundable upon the termination of the contract with the person(s) employed by Xanadu Orange County LLC."

Shit, Florence will see this on our Amex statement. John warned me about having my own separate charge card. Fuck it. As per instructions I faxed back Tanya Tucker's page and the signed form. As for the rest of the girls, I asked the lady behind the front desk to shred the pages, if possible.

"It's a tough business," I told her. "Breaks my heart every time. Listen sweetheart, my secretary is coming up to my room soon, so you can just send her up."

I looked deeply into her eyes and shook my head with such resignation. "It's not an easy life," I said.

"Aw, can we possibly send up some warm cookies?"

"Sure, why the hell not."

I'm going to hell.

*

Tanya Tucker was not her real name. Her eyes were brown. Hair metallic red. Quite possibly a wig. But what a presence.

"Shall we get to know one another out on the terrace?" she suggested.

The first thing she did upon entering was check the bathroom and the closets.

"I just want to make certain it's just us," she'd said.

Her face wore the slightest smile. Always. Something otherly. Bemused. The gods love working girls; they whisper in their ears.

"Care for a drink?" I asked. "I've never done this before."

That's what everyone must say. So odd, fill out a form and flesh appears. Flesh in a miniskirt that walks and talks and has a young tight body with glitter on the arms and legs. I made myself a sambuca neat. There were enough Pringles remaining for a semicircle.

"Want a Pringle?"

"No thanks."

"Ever been to Disney?" I asked.

"Once, when I was really little. One day I'll go again. Are you here on business?"

"No."

"That's nice," she said. "Most of my clients are here at a convention. I'm not sure why, but conventions must not be good for a man's spirit."

This woman shouldn't have to do this job. My insatiable horniness was gone, in its place empathy. A wonderful if flaccid-making emotion.

"What's your favorite ride?" she asked, motioning over the lands below. She could work for Disney. As an ambassador. She's detached from things; she's her own land. Inner life land?

"I like the monorail," I said. "People-watching and I bring a flask. Is Tanya your real name?"

"No."

"You're an incredibly calm person."

"It's Maggie. I hardly ever tell clients but you seem nice enough."

She turned to face me, tilted her head. It rattled me. I tried to offset it by tilting mine the opposite angle.

"I might get some more sambuca," I said.

"Okay." So serene, so accepting. No Wayz judgment at all.

She wore her dark insides on the outside. Bach and *Nosferatu* indeed. What do you do with a girl like that? This girl was *free*.

We're not free, I wrote Florence.

"So, if you don't mind my asking, what's your day job? Not to suggest that this isn't an—"

"I don't have a day job. I'm not putting myself through nursing school or beauty school. Cooking school or law school. Veterinary school. Or charm school. I'm saving up," she continued. "And I'm almost there."

"For what?"

"I'm going to travel the world alone. Ideally indefinitely. But I'm going to run out of money in March of 2003, in Australia. It's the fall for them. Sweater weather."

Another head tilt.

"You're not going to want me tonight."

Jesus. No, not in that way.

"Well, ordinarily of course I'd want—"

"It's okay."

"If you don't mind my asking, how will you afford this trip? I mean, I love the idea but can imagine that to do it well, I mean to avoid hostels and other shitty—"

"My last night of work will be next month on New Year's Eve. That's the best night of the year for a girl."

I made quick calculations. One hundred dollars a day times three years. A hundred grand at least. No, more. Then there's transportation, new clothes. And what about Wayz? She probably knows how to mend clothing with a sewing kit. Then again, so does Florence. And probably Virginia.

"Come," she said and led me back from the balcony into the hotel room.

"How the hell do you pack for a trip like that?"

"My grandmother's yellow Samsonite. Passport, credit card, camera. Me."

"I've always appreciated ancient yellow luggage. Still bright and always humble."

Why are you talking about luggage to a prostitute?

"My grandmother was both," she said.

She raised a finger in the air indicating *stay*. I did. Now she surveyed the room, walked its parts, but not in search of third parties. But for what?

She stopped near the closets closest to the bathroom where the lighting was off, the shadows complex.

"Come," she said.

Here she kissed me. Her hands on my cheeks applying a little pressure here and there so that my mouth would open just so, just when. What a delicate sponge bath. Can a kiss best intercourse? *This*, this was my first French kiss. It ended with a flourish of the tongue and then a whisper.

"See you in Sydney. In a few years. In March. I'll be in a sweater because there it will be the fall."

She left and I collapsed fully clothed on the bed. Then a lights out of the mind. It wasn't the hour for which I'd paid, but sometimes in this life, in this *place*, fifteen minutes can best sixty like how a French kiss can best a fuck.

*

Kathy is going to help out at work today. Have fun!

Florence never uses exclamation points. Sarcasm. Shit. Sarcasm on a Monday morning should be illegal. I sat up in bed. All hangovers begin to dissipate when you sit up in bed. It is the first step. Then there's the slow stretching of whatever is left of my muscles. Slow hip rotations. Ankle rotations. Floppy arm exercises. Movement of the head from side to side. And finally the tremendously brave sidling up to the edge of the bed and throwing the legs over. At home there would be my black slippers. Here there are hotel-issued white cotton slipper shoes, ones that do not fit. They fit Virginia and John, naturally, but not big old Cheese and his size 14s. Sometimes 15s pending bloat-ball. Sorry, I mean blotation. I ordered a Bloody Mary with three times the vodka, and a toasted blueberry muffin with butter. My Ponder Monday tradition. Then I turned on the shower. Hot hot water. I'll get the bathroom blindingly steamy, but no shave today.

"You boys need a shave," Airport Mama will say tonight. Or will she?

"What time is checkout?" I'd called the front desk.

"Eleven is our standard checkout so that we can have the room ready for new guests, but I don't have you checking out until, let's see, on the first."

"Of December?"

"January. Have a magical day!"

Today was November 22. He'd extended the Ponder for six, excuse my cussing, fucking weeks. He said he would but I didn't believe him.

January 1st? I wrote John.

Bloody party in my suite. 10:30. She's coming, he wrote back.

Your Kathy is sitting in my desk at work.

10:30, he wrote.

Are you shaving today? I asked.

He looked even better unshaven. Not that Virginia is the type of girl who falls for disorder about the face. Or is she? Southern girls fancy beards, I'd read or heard somewhere. Florence encouraged me to grow one but it didn't suit my orb. I resembled the well-fed homeless. It's not so easy being a man. Girls think it is, but it's not. We're bad at love and then there's the matter of the last shave. The last time we shave. Ever. On the planet. There will be a last shave. Our face will know but our eyes will not.

No shave for me, John wrote. *Virginia likes scruff. But you should shave. Scruff looks dirty on your apple cheeks.*

Such a dick. But he's right. I will be the clean shaven of the two. The magical land was open. From my balcony I could see whirling things and it filled my heart. Terminally ill kids wish for a last hurrah here. How awful it must be for them to leave. From Dumbo to chemotherapy. Not fair. Worse: from the Haunted Manse to death. (Or is it the Haunted Mansion?) I saw a bald girl in a wheelchair entering the ghost house. Fuck this life. Actually no: they sliced my blueberry muffin in half so that the butter could melt on either surface. And the three mini bottles of vodka were Stolichnaya. And the three mini Tabasco sauces. The bald girl will not forecast herself into a ghost. She'll forget she has cancer and giggle in the dark. Life comes with solutions. Beneficent trap doors that lead you from disaster. For some it's Disney World. For some it's Wayz. For some it's both. I'd opened the window and a cool morning breeze found my clean cheeks. I could see the faintest steam from the butter melting against the muffin. My Bloody was strong and spicy. Like me. I touched my face as Tanya Tucker had some nine hours before, then found my United plane ticket for today's flight home. The inside pocket of my navy-blue blazer. Force of habit, I'd placed it there at some point last night. It's what you do; you prepare for the end. I ripped it in half, then ripped it again.

Fuck the end, I wrote John.

Yes, he wrote. *Fuck it.*

CHAPTER EIGHTEEN

JOHN'S SUITE WAS BEAUTIFUL. Flowers everywhere and the dining room table transformed into a breakfast buffet. There was even a piano player at the baby grand playing Disney songs in a soft morning-appropriate manner. There's something so innocent and nostalgic about the smell of breakfast. Bacon, toast, syrup and we are nine years old again. And then there was Sandeep, his uniform transformed to colonial jungle: khaki shorts and high socks. Such smooth brown knees. The period suited him to a tee.

"I did something last night that I've never done before," I told John.

"Stopped drinking?"

"Escort."

You can say anything around your butler. Much like a psychiatrist or a priest, they are bound by higher laws not to divulge.

"Jesus, Cheese. Really?"

"We didn't do anything. She was marvelous. Really serious and deep. She kissed me goodnight. Really *really* kissed me. It knocked me out."

"Kissed what?"

"My face. And she let me know her real name."

"They all do that and it wasn't her real name."

"How would you know?"

"I dated one."

"For free?"

"Sort of."

Sandeep held forth with two gleaming brass pitchers: orange juice and Bloodies.

"Where's Virginia?" I asked.

"I told her to come at eleven so that we could have some time."

He looked tired. Wan. Usually on Ponder Mondays we'd be red-faced and running on fumes. Running exceptionally well on those fumes. Fumes like amphetamines that would take our chatter all the way to the Airport Mama's bar. But now he sat, hands on knees. He hadn't even gone for a run; I could tell. That annoying Ponder habit granted him a brightness that could not be found about the face this morning. No healthful gin blossoms.

"Our fate is in another's hands," he said. "Like ringworm."

"Huh?"

"That's what love is. A monster inside. An unwelcome growing thing with eyes and teeth that fits so snugly inside your contours. Eats your dinner. Breakfast too."

With Sandeep's help I fixed him an extra strong Bloody. For me, the same and a prune Danish (for regularity's sake). His terrace where we sat was three times mine. It also had a small refrigerator packed with glass Evian. I don't mind Wayzless minibars as long as they are unwavering like this Evian minibar. Nothing says *wealth* like unwavering minibars.

"Virginia's not a monster, Johnny Boy." I was buzzed.

Buzzed, I wrote Florence.

Buzzed at 10:40 a.m. which is great but requires great care. Like keeping a jarred firefly alive indefinitely.

"I can't believe we're not going home today," I said. "It feels criminal. But liberating as hell. I even ripped up my United ticket. Cheers!"

"I think you should go home this afternoon. I think I need to be alone with her."

And with that the light in the firefly's belly pulses once, then dies.

"Oh" was my only reaction after moments of chilling silence. We'd had our share of squabbles over the years, but none serious. Not remotely. There was a depth and darkness to this moment. He'd never not wanted me around. In fact there was the famous incident on the Upper East Side at the good old salty JG Mellon's bar. He'd been staring at a pretty young thing who had been staring back for a good two hours. Well finished with my burger and cottage fries, I was bored. And frankly slightly disgusted with the display of nonverbal flirtation. He was ignoring me, which was fine, but I wanted a change of scenery. So I up and left. And out he came running after me, hollering: "Where are you going? Where are you going? You can't leave me! Please don't leave me."

I tried to explain that his staring contest wasn't fun to be around but he couldn't hear me.

"Don't go, Cheese. Promise me you'll come back. Promise that you'll never leave me. How can I be admirable if there's no one to admire me?" he'd asked, clinging to my suit jacket with the might of the truly desperate. So of course I returned to the bar. For him. He even turned his back on the girl he'd been flirting with. How he clung to me that night. Clung to my life and now, this morning, he wants to banish me.

"I don't think that Virginia wants me to go," I told him.

"Do what you must," he said before rising and leaving me on the terrace.

"Hey listen, this is Frank's party," Dean Martin was fond of saying. Meaning it's Frank's world; we just live in it. No two ways about it. Then again, Dean-O hadn't a shot in hell with Ava Gardner. And if he did, Sinatra would have sent him on a one-way ticket to Newark. Or the morgue. I hadn't minded living in John Apple's world until just now, when I found myself outside of its borders on an unseasonably frigid Florida morning.

Forty-eight degrees, I wrote Florence. *I'm staying.*

Do what you must.

Again? Jesus.

*

Virginia was accompanied by her mother. They locked arms as they entered the suite.

"I'm so, so sorry, Mrs. Wells," I said.

"How is he?" asked John.

"He's stubborn," said Mrs. Wells. "And it suits him right now, Mr. Apple. It suits him."

"Daddy's holding on," said Virginia. "I want to come with you today, Mama."

"You should have fun with your new friends. It's what he'd want. There's nothing for us to do but wait, darling. I'll go read him his Flann O'Connor."

Southerners are good at death. Not that he's dead. But they are brave in the face of it. Chins high, swagger intact, pragmatism leading the way and that undying twang in the voice. Some accents can flout death. But not Northeastern American.

"To Mr. Wells," said John. All assembled raised their red cocktails, then sipped.

Nothing like a collective Tabasco-born *ahh* in the morning.

"Oh how I love Monday mornings," said Virginia. "A fresh start and the skies are so limpid on this chilly day."

She wore a cashmere sweater. A purple cashmere sweater and despite the chill what looked like a white tennis skirt. Pom poms on the back of her socks. What a girl.

"It'll warm up," said Mrs. Wells. "It always does. Well, y'all have a nice day. If there's any news, Ginny"—she found her BlackBerry in her purse—"I'll zap it to you. We'll get through anything."

Before leaving, Constance Wells patted my cheek.

"What a nice boy."

"Isn't he, though," said Virginia after the door had closed behind her mother.

"John wants me to go home."

John Apple was now in a bathrobe. Odd for a younger man to wear a bathrobe over one's wardrobe. A white flag? Or perhaps to elicit sympathy. An homage to Washington Wells? In any event it aged him, the collar flipped up, his hands in the pockets. And of course a bulging ring box. Proustian, he'd become. All prisoners in luxury hotel rooms are Marcel Proust. Old men making sense of their youth. I do really think Proust would have liked Disney World.

"Why do you want him to go, John?"

"No, I mean I don't want him to go, just thought he might miss Florence."

Bullshit. He wants to kill the competition.

"Do you miss her, Cheese?" asked Virginia.

"Sometimes."

So easy to be honest with her. That's what a great woman can do for you. Honesty. As a rule. With no downside for you. No repercussions. Just a sigh or a nod. And in this case a sleepy little smile.

"I guess sometimes is better than no times," she said. "I wish I had someone to miss."

"You don't miss me?" asked the berobed man.

"You're right over there."

After today's closing I am pressing pause on Marks and Marks in order to make structural changes, wrote Florence.

Pause? Changes?

I have arranged to outsource all remaining deals of 1999 to our office neighbors.

This required a phone call.

"Marks and Marks," the receptionist sang.

"It's Murray, is—"

"Please hold."

"Well I miss *you* even though *you're* just *there*," said John.

"No sulking allowed at Disney, Mr. Apple," said Virginia. "You should have another Bloody and get out of that robe."

"Marks and Marks?"

"It's Murray."

"Oh, hi Murray, she's really busy."

"Just tell her to call me."

"Bloody Marys are like a woman's boobs," said Virginia. "One is too few and three too many."

Were I a woman, I'd now have six boobs and quite possibly require a seventh. And then from Florence:

Murray I'm going to fax your hotel with some things for you to sign.

*

After law school I'd considered family law. Divorces! I liked the idea of helping people during a crisis. Part shrink, part anger manager, and part windfall maker, but it was all too dramatic for Florence and she was also of the mind that people should marry once and marry right. Two people together for life, working at one private practice for life, helping people secure the right home, ideally for life. I used to love these principles. So solid, these pillars. So safe inside this temple; her strict eternal ancestors nodding approval from above. But now on an unprecedented fourth day of this broken Ponder, the pillars had crumbled. Drunk in the wreckage, I stared at Virginia's palest green eyes.

"Let's hop on the monorail and get on Mr. Toad's Wild Ride," she said.

So carefree. I mean, what a capacity to be happy. To be healthy. It just radiated from her. That sweet-smelling skin. And how she used a finger and moved her lips when she read. She was always reading, those lips moving. *Harry Potter*. And she employed a hippie-ish bookmark which looked homemade, stringy. I used the cleanliness of her spirit to remove myself from the wrecked temple of the ancient Chinese eternals. Screw Florence's faxes and trysts and adoptions and *changes*. Screw John's morose robe-wearing. Even screw Sandeep's shorts. Well, no. His shorts were swell.

"You see this prune Danish?" I asked. "Someone had to apply icing to it. Probably in the dark of morning. Cheerily handling a piping bag."

"What's your point?" asked John.

"His point," began Virginia, circling the room, drawing a finger across the back of my chair, then John's chair. "Cheese's point is that nothing will ever be more important than at 4:00 a.m. this morning in the Grand Floridian kitchen when white icing crisscrossed a prune Danish."

I didn't really have a point, but now I did. That was it. "Life!" I blurted.

"For the record, John," said Virginia. "The man I spend the rest of my years with will be an optimist. Now, who would like to accompany me on Mr. Toad's Wild Ride? They say it will soon no longer exist, making way for the Many Adventures of Winnie the Pooh, but I can't imagine a world without it. I simply refuse to."

Some people can will things.

*

But not everything. The frog ride was nowhere to be found. In its place was Winnie the Pooh. Incredulous, John demanded to know its whereabouts.

"What happened to Mr. Toad? What happened to Mr. Toad?" he called out to anyone who might know the answer.

Virginia, weak from the news, needed to sit down. I'd heard about Southern girls and their propensity to faint. To swoon. Dramatically did she occupy an entire bench; I expected there to materialize suitors with hand fans. I wished I had a hand fan. Florence kept one in her purse.

Do you still have that hand fan? No more Mr. Toad, I wrote Florence.

"Winnie's been here since June," an employee told John in passing.

"Dammit," he said.

"Dear, dear Mr. Toad," said Virginia, her forearm shielding her eyes from the turn of events.

I knew enough not to say, *But it's just a fucking ride.*

John sat with her, consoling her. Disney geeks abhor change; they rely on their memories to have permanent antecedents here lest they question reality. People can come and go from our lives but God forbid Mr. Frog is no longer among the puppets.

Because of how I structured the LLC it's more complicated than I expected, wrote Florence. *Will need many signatures notarized ASAP. Stay tuned.*

Well, it was her firm. She'd put every penny of the inheritance from her father into Marks & Marks. More than a quarter of a million, I think. High finance is not my wheelhouse. But get me to a closing, and I will seal the deal. Should Florence fire me, I really will miss calculating the mortgage recording tax and the CEMA costs. Fuck it, maybe I'll become a real estate attorney here in Disney. I bet there are countless geeks who need to live close to the Castle. Imagine going on a ride after closing? Or even after escrow!

"Mr. Toad is apparently now in the Haunted Mansion's pet cemetery," said John. "A cast member just told me. We're going to go and pay our respects."

They'd bonded over fake amphibian grief.

"Wanna join us, Cheese?" asked Virginia.

It was already lunch time and my stomach was growling. I wasn't worried about leaving them together; it would give her a chance to miss me. John did that with girls; he was immune to any jealous behavior and it won them over: *No, of course I don't care if you see your ex for dinner. Have a great time with him.*

"You two go have fun," I said. "We'll catch up later."

Fish 'n' Chips with Shay Hitchcock? Spectacular idea!

*

When in love with one girl it is so effortless to flirt with another.

"Why hello, Miss Shay Hitchcock," I said, dripping with the optimism that Virginia needed from her future man.

In Canada land, I'd purchased a miniature bottle of maple syrup and presented it to her. "May your mornings always be sweet."

I'd also downed two pints of Canadian beer at a buzz-making pace that had reddened my usually pig-pink cheeks.

"So very kind," said Shay.

The bar was scarcely attended; it was the Monday before Thanksgiving, an irrelevant weekday lunch hour. Some times of the day have no personality. Who in their right minds would be here, would still be here? And what about the parents who forgo their kids' schooling for Disney, I wondered, watching a family of five, glum at the bar, their faces hidden by menus. Perhaps menu reading is part of a young Biggunz core curriculum?

"The fish 'n chips are actually really good," I said to the family. "Add some malt vinegar and wash it down with a black and tan and a Jameson's neat, and you will be transported."

They did not look up from their menu reading.

"Is that what you'd like, sir?" asked Shay.

Shit, she didn't know my name. Had I ever told her my name? Wait: she might think I'm insane.

"I'm Murray, by the way."

"I'm Shay."

"Oh I know, Shay."

She smiled nervously and checked on the family and their bangers and mash scholarship. How long does it take to read a fucking menu? A bible was peeking out of the wife's handbag; I pictured them at church with bibles replacing the menus, the five of them equally frozen on a psalm.

"Yes I would like the fish 'n' chips, Shay. And a double Jameson's neat, Shay."

I saw the bible thumper check her watch, then shake her head at my order.

"It's one-twenty-seven somewhere," I said.

"We'll have five of the chicken fingers and fries," said the dad, collecting the menus.

Unbelievable.

Johnny Boy thinks that I'm too judgmental, that Florence and I are. We do tend to have high standards for bar and restaurant behavior and are not shy to gossip about the misgivings of our fellow consumers.

"The poor manners of strangers are all you guys talk about," John had said.

It's true we rarely speak of current events, or matters of the world. We hadn't even acknowledged the year 2000 was on its way. At least not to one another. For us, CNN was just a TV show. We didn't speak of its content, like we didn't speak of "Who Wants to be a Millionaire?"

"What do couples talk about, Shay?"

"Couples?"

"Yes, like husbands and wives."

"Oh, I don't know, my parents spoke about what they did that day. How work went. Stuff like that."

The miniature maple syrup was still on the bar. In fact it seemed to have moved closer to me.

Isn't it poor manners not to accept a gift? I wrote Florence.

Heading to the airport, she wrote. *We're coming to Orlando. I've arranged for a notary to meet us at your hotel tonight. As Mama always says, never put off important business.*

You're coming to Disney?

We're only staying the one night.

You and Mama?

Kathy.

CHAPTER NINETEEN

THE BALL. IMPOSSIBLE TO scrutinize on a Monday afternoon; I squint at the awfully shiny thing and a headache ensues. I'm in line; for what, I do not know. But people in droves leave the outside world, methodically enter the ball's mouth, and then disappear. I am hoping that the ball contains the afterlife. I had asked Shay for another double Jameson's, then paid my check.

"They're coming," I told Shay.

"They're coming," I told the chicken finger family.

And then for the first time in eons, I lost my appetite. I had only enough room for a clutch of chips. I didn't even bother to sprinkle them with malt vinegar. So I left fake England and headed toward that huge shiny thing. And now here I was about to get ball-balled. (Sorry, but I could not resist *balling* in front of what John said was the most famous *ball* in the world.) Perhaps a wizard was inside the ball, a false god, Oz. A deranged king of EPCOT and all its wide-open spaces dotted with enormous and unknowable geometric structures while techno jingles somehow coaxed the masses toward the mouth of the ball. Perhaps inside we would be ground up and re-formed into turkey legs?

"Want to ride with me?" a stranger asked of me.

"Sorry?"

"I hate riding alone."

I was standing in front of a teenaged girl; half her head was shaved. Skinny, her wrists full of bangles. I liked that she was un-embarrassed to wear Minnie ears. Her lesser peers would probably snicker.

"What's inside this?" I asked.

"Spaceship Earth. Oh my god, you have to smell Rome burning. Come on, let's go."

A smell. That I could relate to.

"Where are your parents?"

"They're with my baby brother. I'm Sammy."

My Wayz flask was nearly full. Was Wayzing in front of an und-eraged girl a crime? Probably, but I needed it, especially for Rome burning. Good old Nero destroying his own city just to rebuild it to his liking without the red tape of the Senate or the annoying opinions of the people. That's what I needed: rebirth with impunity. I took a swig.

"Just so you know," I told my ride partner, "There's just cranberry juice in this, um, drinking vessel."

"It's okay if you drink wine. My dad sneaks it in at night. He has a flask just like yours."

What a smart girl. The best children are reared by Wayzers. And the sweet innocence to assume that all Wayz are soft Wayz.

"Well, if you must know, I'm going through odd times with my wife and the, um, wine seems to help."

"My parents got divorced, but I really love my stepmom. She got my dad into Disney and now we go every year."

So well-adjusted. I just wish she liked Wayz. "How old are you?" I asked.

"Sixtcen."

Why would a sixteen-year-old want to ride with me? Does Disney make people braver? Am I more appealing here? I hope she lives in a state where she's only two years removed from the promised land of Wayz. If she moved to France, she'd be all set. I took a healthy swallow.

"Divorce is a great invention," she said. "Like my dad says, life is too short to be anything but happy."

Jeremy Irons, the unmistakable voice of the ride, agreed. He warned me that I was a passenger on the planet for such a brief time, implying that Wayz, divorce, and Virginia were all most definitely prescribed.

"You're very wise for your years, Sammy. Just remember to enjoy *wine* and never settle for an ordinary man. You deserve the best. In fact, find someone who enjoys *wine* and Disney just like your father. Just like me!"

"Can you smell Rome?" she asked.

I could. It was a tremendously appealing scent. Almost religious, really. That fire could smell nutritious rather than merely be hot.

Rome is burning, I wrote Florence.

"God I love this smell."

"Told ya," said Sammy and poked me in the ribs. Well, poked me in the flesh that covered my ribs.

The ride underwhelmed after Nero's glorious campfire. Although Jeremy Irons essentially predicted the very BlackBerry that was in my pocket. He also stressed how important communication was.

Jeremy Irons, I wrote Florence.

At ride's end Sammy and I were photographed, our faces super-imposed on to Jetsons-like flying car people from the future. I bought Sammy a copy.

"Hold onto this forever. When you look at it, remember what I told you about Wayz and not settling for just any husband."

"See ya," she said, the photo crammed into her pocket. "By the way, I think I like girls."

"That seems to be going around. Well, enjoy . . . whoever."

"You too."

What an unsentimental girl. She didn't even ask my name. Nor look at the photograph. Shit, I needed a copy of it too. Through it, I'll access Sammy's equanimity. Her advice about divorce. The smell of Rome. Jeremy Irons's voice. I'll need all of them tonight. Poor Biggunz heeding Disney's unwavering suggestion that the future is the happiest place on earth. It's not. It's a pitch-black room. A huge dark corridor with something dangerous inside. A nothingness that is becoming conscious, building up its dark steam. (I must admit I adored the fake Mark Twain boat I saw in the Kingdom. Its steam ran Papal white.)

*

We should get to the hotel around six, wrote Florence. *Let's meet in the lobby at seven.*

Florence and Kathy are coming here tonight, I wrote John. *I need to take a Theresa shower.*

They're really coming? Wow.

Theresa shower: Kathy's sister was a gloriously uninhibited Wayzer. John put Kathy's family up at the Waldorf for the wedding where, legend has it, Theresa showered with a tumbler of hard Wayz by the soap dish. The water screamingly hot. I always did like that Theresa and her showers.

"Oh Theresa shower take me away," I'd exclaim to my wife, who would shake her head.

"Murray, the shower is not a place for alcohol and very hot water is bad for your skin."

Theresa shower, I wrote Florence.

Enjoy!

So unlike her.

You're going to take a shower now? asked John. *Take it later. Let's meet at the Wilderness Lodge. Have lots to tell you. Late lunch at Whispering Canyon on me.*

Where is it?

You travel by boat to the national parks of the early 1900s. Deer, geysers, totem poles. Skillets of meats.

I'll ask one of the actors.

Cast members.

EPCOT's wide-open spaces were bringing me down. Somehow they denoted all those hollow zeros in the year 2000. A cozy lodge would do me right, so I asked a rustic-looking Biggunz who wore a cowboy hat while riding his electric steed for directions to the canyon of whispers.

"Boy are you in for a treat. Okay, so you gotta take the monorail to the TTC then TTC to Magic Kingdom then catch yourself a boat over to the lodge. If you get Wandering Wendy as your server, tell her that Brisket Barry said howdy. And don't fill up on the cornbread and maple butter!"

A carb-conscious Biggunz.

"Appreciate that there cornbread tip, partner," I told the happy man.

Maybe tonight I'll affect the vaguely gold prospector lingo of the Biggunz when confronting Florence and her official documents. Kathy and her fake blondness and real chest. They won't know what hit them. Fuck, so many moving parts just getting to the whispering canteen. I think that you can accurately estimate the tenure of a Disney person based on their monorail enthusiasm; it wanes as the trip draws to a close. And then there's that final monorail back to the hotels to sleep, pack, set an alarm. I get it now: the tragedy. I, on the other hand, was still open-ended; I supposed that Johnny Boy could rescind my room extension, forcing me out. Although I did have enough money of my own to last probably into the new year.

After the monorail, the boat ride to the lodge was pleasant enough: a breeze through whatever was left of my hair, a real captain who shouted "all aboard" to great effect, natural sounds muting the chatter of families. Even some flamingos, pink from their brine shrimp diet. Biggunz should be the color of turkey legs.

Hi, wrote Virginia.

Hi! I wrote back.

I'm back at the hospital with Daddy. Thinking about you.

Whenever she sees him, asleep in the hospital, she'll be guilted into loving me.

"Hey," said John. He was waiting for me in the lobby. And what a lobby: a post and beam Notre Dame. Were Abraham Lincoln in heaven, this would be his reward. Biggunz in rockers in front of fireplaces that emitted no real heat. The smell in the air? Buffet chafers and their Sterno. *Conestoga* echoing off the wooden rafters.

"Virginia went to be with her dad," said John.

"I know. She wrote me."

"She's wearing my ring."

"No she's not."

"Just to see how it feels."

Was she examining the bauble while she was thinking about me?

"We were creating a churros shrine around Mr. Toad's grave, and I'd placed the ring box on the ground for just a second and that's when she snatched it up and put it on her finger. I almost fainted. 'Does this mean what I think it means?' I asked. And then she said, 'Don't get too excited, Mr. Apple, I just want to see what it's like.'"

"Did it fit?"

"Like Cinderella's slipper."

*

While he babbled about the hand that wore his ring, I feasted on the skillets. He somehow figured out how to source a bottle of Louis Roederer Cristal vintage 1988 in this chuckwagon circus.

"Hope you tethered your stallion nice and tight," said our server. "He might start when he hears the cork pop. He'll think he's back at the O.K. Corral."

The Carnivore's Skillet was all you can eat, which they euphemized *all you care to enjoy.*

"I'll take one more Carnivore's Skillet," I told the server.

"Yee Haw!" he shouted.

"Yee Haw!" The dining room, in chorus, approved.

"How does everyone know what to do here?" I asked.

"They just do," John said. "They have well honed Disney instincts so that when they hear a cast member bellow 'Yee Haw' they know it means a second skillet which is cause for great life affirmation."

I wish I always knew what to do or say, but I usually don't unless I'm buzzed and with Virginia.

"In fact," John continued, "Yee Haw Bob is an actual entertainer here who sells out every night. We should see him tonight; I'll ask Sandeep to set us up. Yee Haw Bob will cheer you up, Cheese. He plays on a piano that once belonged to Billy the Kid. You can see the bullet holes."

"Tonight I have this stupid fucking business meeting with Florence and your ex."

He just hunched his shoulders and stabbed a sausage from skillet number two but didn't bother to eat it. I don't get skinny people.

"It'll be closure," he said. "Me seeing Kathy here, tonight at Disney World. The expression on her face when she sees Virginia's ring. She sold our engagement ring, you know. I mean, sold it while we were still married." He snickered.

I knew and couldn't believe how easily John had brushed that off. Fuck, I'm so skillet-balled.

"Maybe I'll skip the meeting. Just hide somewhere in EPCOT."

"You should attend. Virginia and I will have your back. Also could be a big pay day for you if she buys you out."

I hadn't thought of that. My great fear was a separation agreement which, should Virginia decide to accept John's proposal, would leave me squarely alone in the world. Disney World.

"Listen, Cheese, everything will be fine. Have a third skillet, then we'll tour the lobby together in search of hidden Mickeys. Finding them is like bird-watching: its rewards are subtle, almost mystical."

I remembered the time I came home from a Ponder. It was Philly, and Florence was in the living room staring at a bonsai tree she'd bought. Tears streaming down her face. I asked her what was wrong, but she had no words for me, not that night and not the next morning. I knew not to pursue post-Ponder intercourse. I knew from how gently she shut the bedroom door to sleep on the couch. I don't know what happened to that little tree, nor did we ever speak of it again. When my wife feels the world, it's stunning; I'm stunned. And also quite afraid. My instinct is to hide until it's over.

Hidden Mickeys, I wrote Florence.

Hidden Murrays, I wrote myself.

*

My Theresa shower was of the single malt whiskey variety. I ordered a bottle of twenty-five-year-old Macallan from Sandeep's stash; regular rooms were restricted to newish Glenlivet. Details matter, it's why I'm a good attorney and a very good Wayzer. Details. Like Sandeep's black bowtie patterned with black Mickey Mouse faces befitting the cocktail hour.

"Any rides today, Mr. Marks?" he'd asked while delivering my bottle.

"I did the EPCOT ball, then after getting stuffed at the Yellowstone lodge I needed an aperitif-type experience so went solo to the Magic Kingdom and did the log flume again."

"Splash Mountain. Most excellent."

"Sandeep, I'm looking at the two crystal rocks glasses you so tactfully placed beside my Macallan 25 and I'm feeling lonely. Do you ever feel lonely, Sandeep?"

"Lonely? Well I miss my family in India but have made many friends here."

"I wish I missed my parents more but they go to a vegetarian Korean restaurant in Boston for Thanksgiving. We speak once a week though. I actually called them from outside the fake fire house in the fake town. They said I sounded down. I was, due to Jeremy Irons's declaration that life is infinitesimally short, but then I daydreamt of Virginia and me in Savannah. Only love can stop time's advance. That's why it's the only miracle in this short life. Cheers!"

"Disney World can be overwhelming the first time. We are here to help."

With that he smiled, then left. I believe he'd said the exact same thing to me on Friday. Charming self-plagiarist, that Sandeep.

Oh Theresa shower, take me away. And it did. Being buzzed in almost scalding water presses reset on current events.

I love you, I wrote Florence.

I love you, I wrote John.

I love you, I wrote Virginia.

All three statements were true. *That's* what a Theresa shower can do for you: deliver unfiltered, heart-pounding truths and the courage to express them.

Let the Pringles fall where they may.

CHAPTER TWENTY

IN THE LOBBY OF the Grand Floridian there are no places to hide. No place to be sly on an unexpected couch, ideally one shrouded by palm fronds where I, who bought khaki cargo shorts for the occasion, would embody the louche backside of Disney World. I also bought red knee-high Mickey socks, flip-flops, and a T-shirt I'd seen on a Biggunz: I'M JUST HERE FOR THE TURKEY LEGS. My goal was to disarm Florence; shock her with this new Disneyfied Cheese. A man who couldn't care less about legal papers and a cold fate. I was part of Disney World; I'd bought in, been to war, become a veteran. Into a fat vein, I'd injected *the magic*; don't fuck with the magic.

I'd invested in a thirty-two-ounce frozen margarita topped with three shots of Don Julio 1942. Nothing signals freedom from sense like adding $150 of rarest liquor to a ten-dollar drink.

"You sure?" the bartender had asked.

"Absotively."

"Love the turkey leg shirt."

Watching us was a head-shaking little person; that was apparently the polite term for *dwarf*. I was a fan of the little fellows and I do not mean that in a condescending vein. They struggled, for sure. Were stared at. Humans cannot help but stare at human difference. We are hardwired to acknowledge anomalies. Amputees have it bad too. And three-legged dogs. And Biggunz, except in Disney World. Smallunz might get a pass here too. I probably wouldn't have noticed him if not for the fact that he looked pissed off. Really pissed off, and he was staring at me:

"What did you just say?"

"Huh?" I asked.

I'd ordered a drink in a rocks glass and had absentmindedly told myself that I loved short Wayz. Had I said it aloud?

"Short Wayne?" asked the perturbed man.

"No, no, I said Wayz. *Wayz*."

"Wayz?" He scowled.

"It's my word for drinks."

Fuck, his name tag read WAYNE.

"You people. In high school they called me *Short Wayne* and the other Wayne they called *Normal Wayne*. They called me *Short Wayne* or *Hummingbird*. A barrel of laughs, right?"

Now he was up off his barstool (no easy task for him) and coming my way. "You people come here. Ride our rides. Eat our food. Fornicate in our freshly made beds. Beds that I had to make. You know what I've found in those beds? Do you?"

"Well—"

"You poop in our toilets. And what again is a Wayz?"

"A drink?"

"Maybe ask *Short Wayne* to go fetch you a *short Wayz*??"

The bartender was monitoring the situation, closely, nervously, "Hey, come on, Wayne," he said to the man.

"No," said Wayne. "We mix the batter. We pour the batter. We bake the batter. You eat the cookies. You poop the cookies. Then Little old Hummingbird cleans the toilets with his tiny little hands just the perfect size for scraping off all the poop."

The bartender brought his name tag to his mouth and spoke into it. Walkie-talkie?

I *had* used the toilets here rather liberally and well. What a forceful flush; a small pig's head would go down with ease. Soon a suited man, presumably some sort of manager, appeared.

"Come on, Wayne, this isn't like you," said the suited man. "Sorry for the interruption," he told me, then handed me a piece of currency good for fifteen Disney dollars. I must say US currency is drab by comparison.

Wayne stopped before leaving the bar to turn around. "Watch out," he told me sing-songedly.

What did he mean? I felt small (no pun intended) in the wake of his warning.

"Sorry about that," said the bartender. "Wayne's a lifer. He was here on opening day. Retired now but likes to visit and speak with the guests."

"What did he mean by *watch out*?" I asked.

"Have a magical day," said the bartender. Damn, that little person did not take kindly to *Wayz*. John is probably right about curbing our stupid little language. These cast members were starting to make me feel insecure. Maybe I did need to start *watching out*, whatever that meant. Did hummingbirds have deceptive weapons? Poisonous beaks? I meant no harm, *Hummingbird*. After all they call me, I call me, *Cheese*. Not nearly as poetic as your nickname. Watch out for what? Hummingbird.

*

Me and my $195 drink (with tax and tip) stood in the lobby by a marble shelf that was the perfect height for vertical Wayzing. A configuration we first used on a Ponder to Chicago when we couldn't get a barstool at the original Pizzeria Uno. We spent hours standing at the bar over a couple of deep dish pies in the dead of a brutal Chicago winter. It was there that we determined that the future hadn't happened to us yet.

"We're in life's pre-season. A dress rehearsal or something," John had said.

This was five years earlier, when we were still shy of twenty-five.

"Such a youthful indulgence to bide time," he'd said.

"When do you think the future will happen to us?" I'd asked, genuinely curious because I felt he was correct, that what we were experiencing at the Uno's stand-up bar jammed in amid wintery strangers was purely prelude. A vacation from our own histories.

"We'll know when it happens, Cheese. When the clock really starts ticking. It'll take our breath away."

"Or kick our asses."

"Quite possibly."

Tick. They each held a handle of a carry-on bag. A stately leather satchel that must have belonged to Kathy. Tick tock. Kathy's bottle blondness was replaced by a brunette bob. Florence in shorts? Tock, yes, Florence in shorts. They were smiling. At each other. Tick tock tick tock. And Florence had also gotten her long dark hair cut and colored light brown. Both sockless in sneakers, so spirited was their jaunt towards the check-in desk. Even for a Disney hotel lobby, their happiness drew people's attention; it was as if they were in on a secret. The secret of self-generated bliss. The envy of we who needed ironically topped tequila Wayz or the Space Mountain to even come close. What else was clear was that these two were not mere friends. Friends do not gaze admiringly at one another while waiting in line. A prolonged smiling silence is the stuff of new love. I wonder whose credit card they'll use; God knows they didn't book two rooms. After they'd finished checking in, I tried to hide in my margarita but when I looked up, there they were.

"Well, hello," said Kathy.

Florence gave me a kiss on the cheek, which was the norm for her.

"We're going up to our room," said Florence.

"You cut your hair."

"I did," she said. "And you're wearing shorts and a . . . turkey leg shirt?"

"You're wearing shorts too," I said.

"Yep, I changed in the airport. We are in Florida after all."

"What an interesting place," said Kathy, looking around the fake Victorian lobby.

"Lots of places for Murray to *Wayz*," said Florence.

"What's that?" asked Kathy.

"Oh, I'll explain it upstairs," she told her chesty friend, then turned to me. "Can we meet you in an hour to go over some things? It shouldn't take too long. A notary public is meeting us down here."

"I like your hair natural," I told Kathy.

"Me too. I don't know what was wrong with me, trying to be something I'm not. Well, it's really nice to see you again. Brings back memories, some really pleasant and some, well, you know."

I tried to hide in my drink again but when I looked up, they'd moved on, holding hands via the satchel's handles.

They're here, I wrote John. *Kathy's different. So fucking weird to see them here together.*

She was indeed vastly different than the acquisitive bitch I'd remembered. There was a lightness to her now. Something was flowing from her that hadn't before. As for Florence, despite the new hairdo and the casual attire, she seemed about the same? How much can a person change in four days anyway? Who am I kidding, she was altered as well. Free-spirited, newly minted lesbians. Tick. Tock.

*

Almost seven o'clock and the lobby of the Grand Floridian is tranquil, settled. A piano plays jazzified Disney tunes from the lounge above. The lighting has been subdued and the candelabras are lit. Mornings here, everyone is a wild mustang fueled by maple syrup and the horribly irksome knowledge that someone not them is already on a ride they covet. But now it is evening and the wild horses have been broken in; they stand stationary, chewing hay. In a daze of sorts, unaware of the day or the date. Deep inside their trip, so many days gone by without seeing a newspaper headline or to where the scale's needle points. There are neither scales nor newspapers at Disney World, and I wouldn't have it any other way. Obliviousness shields us. In the event of a global thermonuclear war, the obliviousness will turn fallout into confetti; only water bugs and Disney people will survive. And the former and the latter never shall meet, for there are also no bugs here. A mosquito-less miracle. (John said it had something to do with an army of bats and the smell of garlic, but, then again, he also said that there was a morgue somewhere along the monorail loop.)

"Excuse me, but are you Murray Marks?"

I'd been in a daze of my own, observing a divan where a young European-looking couple (they were thin and wore tangerine-colored watchbands) sat trying in vain to restore a huge Magic Kingdom map back to its natty rectangle.

"I am," I said to an over-perfumed woman with a New York accent. Lightning bolts of white curls atop her head.

"I figured as much. Your wife said you'd be down here with a drink and here you are. I'm Frannie, by the way. Frannie Higginbotham, the notary. Fancy place, huh?"

The young couple would not be deterred; a Biggunz couple would probably crumple the map into a ball, hunch their shoulders, and laugh at their failure.

"Life is too short for an improperly furled map," I said.

"This is one of the real perks of the job, seeing new places. You should see all the matchbooks I've collected from hotels and restaurants. They say I should retire but I don't think so."

There had been another notary. It was the Vegas Ponder after Johnny Boy wagered the entire cost of the trip on a single hand of blackjack an hour or so before we were to leave for the airport. And he won, naturally. I think it was a $10,000 bet, which counted as well for casino losses incurred. The casino host offered to comp us each another night in a suite if only we'd stay, but we declined. It was some sort of a tax form he needed to sign, witnessed by an official. I remember liking, if not loving, the notary's stamp, which made a box and inside the box a line for his signature. It was as if he were creating a little world for himself, a world that would then be validated by an official stamp. If only life were so self-regulating.

"I love your little black notary case," I told the woman.

"I take it everywhere," she said.

"I wish to exist inside a stamp, warmed by a raised seal. My sun."

"I just got to make sure you have your ID. Without it I'm going home empty-handed. You should see all the people who don't know to bring their ID."

"I will receive the light of the sun; I will receive its approval."

I stared deeply into my margarita while she yapped away about carrying extra pens, and rubbing alcohol and cotton balls in the event of ink stains.

"Hi, so sorry we're late," said Florence.

It was three minutes past seven. She needed both hands to hold the thick stack of legal documents. Kathy passed her palm over the many yellow SIGN HERE stickers, making them flutter for a moment.

"Some species of butterflies are lethal to humans," I said.

"Murray, why don't you leave the drink for now and let's find a place to sit," said Florence.

We chose the couch where I'd first sat with Virginia after she'd been dumped by John. The good old days. Friday.

"Now I know this is all very sudden," said Florence.

"Everything is sudden these days. I do really like your hair, Kathy. Brings something virtuous out in your eyes."

"Why, thank you."

"So, this first contract . . ."

I couldn't concentrate on her words. How the hell did she whip up a twelve-inch-thick LLC dissolution agreement over the weekend? I'd left my margarita where I'd been standing and missed it. There was only a little left, but due to my Don Julio 1942 toppers and aggressive tip I had been promised a free refill. Which I needed. She'd just said something about six month's salary and a sweat equity buyout. The word *sweat* from her lips brought me back to our sex. During which I sweated. Those nights now felt finished, as did I.

"It should last you a good year, so you can get back on your feet and we can figure out what's next for us, Murray."

She owned our apartment; my name was not on the lease. No kids, no pets, no plants. No car. We shared so little. We shared nothing. Not even a photo album. If I heard her correctly my pay-out would be $125,000, more than enough to add three Don Julio 1942 shots to my refill.

". . . and we'll get through this together, the three of us," said Florence.

"See, people don't understand that there's more going on than just a signature," said the notary. "There can be real drama. Let me see your driver's license, hon."

John didn't drive. The very rich are horrid drivers anyway: they start too late and assume everyone on the road has their very best interests in mind.

"I must say, Murray, you're taking this all so very well," said Kathy. "And I just want to apologize for being such a jerk to John and by extension to you."

"So you two are together," I said.

"We've decided not to classify it," said Florence. "That's when people get into trouble."

"What about us?"

"We're still here. The sun will come up tomorrow, Murray."

It might, but it will never again be warm enough to melt Cheese. And now, on this couch, with these women, one of whom is to be my ex-wife, I pined for melted cheese. Warm, comforting, reliable. The welcome unction of melted Brie. Like Florence and me in bed on a weekday night, silently reading our respective books by the lights of our respective lamps. No danger in the air. In the summer, the whir of air-conditioning; in the winter, the pipes knocking with heat. A week-day night. No sex, no midnight snacks, no memorable dreams. Just wonderful if not wondrous consistency. A quilt from her youth spread over the base of the bed, protecting our feet. I knew now that this scene would never repeat for me, and it slayed me. Just how had we traveled so far from 115 West Seventy-Third Street, Apartment 2B, 9:15 p.m., every weekday night ever? (On the weekends we were drunk and as mentioned sweaty, and the quilt slept on the floor).

Florence went on to explain that she'd had an epiphany that started in the women's locker room of the Reebok Club where Kathy was a member. She watched Kathy get undressed for a shower; at the time she thought little of it. A young woman's body, but that after-noon after a stroll in Central Park she spied two birds building a nest. Improbable in November. Even more improbable, they were both females of the species. Florence had taken a bird-watching course with her mother and knew her shit. It was a revelation. The breasts in the locker room and then the birds (yellow-throated warblers, she'd said) and their nest.

"Nothing would ever be the same," she said. "I started to cry. Tears of happiness though. And we hugged for hours, Murray. You and I never hugged. Which is okay. Everything will be okay. Better than okay!"

I wondered what the record for Don Julio 1942 toppers was.

"You two are really inspiring to me," said the notary.

Her business here was done yet there she sat, chin on fist.

"I moved here from Jersey because I was sick and tired of all the drama," she continued, "but you need drama, God darn it. Am I right or am I right?"

"Well," said Kathy, "without it changes are impossible, and God knows I needed to change."

Florence took Kathy's hand and kissed it lovingly, tenderly, as if it were a mouth. I don't think the notary realized the true nature of their relationship until then. Until the back of Kathy's hand glistened. She straightened up, stood, and placed three business cards on the coffee table.

"Okay then, I should check the answering service to see if I'm needed in the vicinity. Best of luck."

An answering service and homophobia *in 1999*? Frannie Higginbotham will never change.

*

"Did you meet someone here?" asked Florence. "It was hard to tell from your many BlackBerry messages, but if you did . . . I just want you to be happy, Murray."

We were at Mizner's on the second floor, an upscale lounge named after the famous Palm Beach architect. Addison Mizner designed the world-famous Breakers Hotel but it was made of wood and burned down one night in 1925. He witnessed the blaze; in fact, in the flickering light, he came out of the closet for one and all to see, hugging his once secret lover, but no one paid them any mind as the onlookers were transfixed by the crumbling palace. Two flames that evening during the roaring twenties. Many ironies in the Floridian night.

"I suppose we both fell in love this weekend," I said. "Cheers."

"Who is she?" asked Kathy, smiling, surprised.

"Just a well-mannered Southern girl who loves Disney, loves John, and whose parents love me. And she might, just might, love Cheese too."

"That sounds complicated," said Florence.

"Oh, John," said Kathy. "That boy sure can get himself into trouble."

"We both can," I said.

"Hold on," said Florence. "Is this Southern girl the girl he proposed to?"

"Like you said, it's complicated."

"Oh, I wanted you to know, Murray, in case you were counting on Thanksgiving at our place, that we're going on a cruise the day after tomorrow and won't be back until early next month."

"What about Mama? And her duck?"

"Mama. Well, I told her the truth about Kathy and me and she was less than accepting. Women of her generation and upbringing are intolerant to say the least. I'm afraid that Mama does not wish to acknowledge me as her daughter any longer."

"I'm so sorry. That—"

"Sucks," said Florence.

It occurred to me to check Florence's ring finger.

"No rings," I said.

"I'm sorry, not right now."

"No, of course," I said.

Why the fuck is everyone so in-the-moment, um, balled?

"When will we get to meet . . . what's her name?" asked Kathy.

"Virginia. Virginia Wells."

I wasn't sure I wanted them to meet her. If it was just Virginia, then Florence would be jealous but she would almost certainly be with John, and then she'd pity Cheese and his unrequited love. She'd think all my messages about love were just the Wayz talking. Which they were, but there's nothing wrong with that; being buzzed accesses truths more efficiently than sobriety, albeit strictly promising truths. I'll write Virginia and ask her to come alone to meet my—

"What the hell should I call you two?" I asked the two . . . lovers.

"Whatever you want," said Kathy. "Maybe . . . 'special friends'?"

Yuck. Gross.

"I like it," said Florence.

Before I could BlackBerry Virginia, Kathy stood from her seat. "Well, hello there," she said to John Apple, who was alone.

I used to find her *slight* way of speaking annoying, but now it came across as humility or poise rather than gossamer bitchery. John extended his hand to his ex-wife, who went for a tight hug.

"Can I have a moment with you?" she asked, then led him away to the bar. He seemed shell-shocked, but then again he was often that way around her, muted and arrhythmic. Some women sap you of your rhythm while with others, like Virginia, you happily join their more advanced timbre.

"*Virginia*, Virginia Wells," said Florence. "A noble name."

Perhaps it was the margarita sugars' retreat but all of the sudden I missed Florence and my old reliable if predictable life. I wanted to rest my head in her lap and cry, *Please just take me home.*

There was a reason that Ponders didn't exceed three nights and four days, a damn important reason: the sanctity of our souls.

"I miss you," I said.

"What about Virginia?"

"She's . . . sort of like this place."

I didn't mean that she was fake, maybe just ephemeral. I gestured around the lounge and Florence's eyes followed my hands but she couldn't see what I saw.

"No, not like Mizner's, I mean like Disney. Maybe just a brief visit with magic is all a human can take."

John and Kathy were back.

"The four of us," said Kathy. "Just like old times. Here's to new times."

John had gotten a drink at the bar and imported it to our four-top; it looked like a mai tai. A little umbrella goes a long way. He twirled the tiny thing: his rhythm was back and so was his winning smile. This allowed me to pivot from my Florence wistfulness and rejoin the spirit of Ponder.

"Drinks are on me," said John, placing his terrifying Key to the World card on the table. "And thank you for what you said," he told Kathy.

"What did she say?" I asked.

"*Murray*," Florence scolded.

"No, it's fine," said Kathy. "I just apologized for being such a little bitch. Cheers."

She'd gotten seven figures in the divorce settlement. Not bad for eighteen months of marriage. I bet she's paying for the cruise.

We should do a Ponder on a cruise ship! That is, if there will ever be another Ponder.

"Do you guys still go to that Chinese place with the cute little bartender?" asked Kathy. "What was his name?"

"Jack," said John. "God, that place seems . . . from another time."

He flicked a bar nap expertly so that it landed where it needed to; mine was missing. Such supple wrists. Well, he did own a dartboard. Advantages are unfair. Christ, I sound like my parents. Socialists. Socialists who go to church. Is that even allowed? I desire to go to church with Virginia Wells. God is in the details. I mean kneecaps. What a pew mate she would be, my short-skirted Virginia.

"Where's Virginia?" I asked.

"Yes," said Kathy. "We're all so curious to meet this woman."

"She's at the hospital."

"Oh no," said Florence.

"Long story," said John. "She's fine; it's her dad."

"So you really proposed to her?" asked Kathy.

"Sort of."

"What a weird trip, you two," said Florence.

"It's called a Ponder," I said.

During their marriage we went on two Ponders. John wore his wedding ring; it was a weird sight. My fingers are way too plump for a ring. Despite the adornment or perhaps because of it, girls still hit on him. But he remained faithful. *Girls* is such an underused word. Kathy called Virginia a *woman*. No, Virginia Wells is a *girl*; she calls herself a girl, like while in line at the Haunted Palace when she said to someone she'd met, "Us Disney girls have to stick together."

"Look at that woman," said Kathy. "She has such beautiful skin."

I didn't have to look up to know. I could smell her shampoo. Smell the Ivory soap. Soap powerless to desiccate that *girl*'s beautiful skin.

John stood and I sniffed.

CHAPTER TWENTY-ONE

"CAN I TALK TO you for a minute," said Virginia Wells to John Apple.

She looked distraught. I'd never seen any worry wrinkles in her brow. It was sort of adorable.

"Sure," said John and to the bar he returned.

"Everyone seems to want to have their special time with Johnny," said Kathy.

"She's stunning," said Florence.

"Thank you," I said, unsure of why I co-owned the compliment.

She was wearing a long flowing yellow dress. She owned many yellow dresses. What a yellow rose of a girl: I could faintly hear her drawl.

"I wish you had more of a Chinese accent," I told Florence.

"That's sort of rude, Murray."

"Sorry."

I did wish, though. All girls should have accents that bring you back to their home soil; through summer errands their pubescent arms and legs becoming lithe, advanced. I had a view of the bar and could see Virginia reach into her handbag and produce the red Cartier ring box. She took John's hand, turned it palm up, deposited the box, and touched his face. Then he touched where she had, bowed his head.

Come to the bar, wrote John.

I passed Virginia, who was on her way to our table.

"Good, go be with him. He'll need you now," she said. "I'll have a drink with your ladies after which we should talk, Cheese. Tomorrow. Luncheon at noon? Good." She held me by my shoulders. "Substantial," she said with a smile.

"What is?"

"Your shoulders. But I need for you to work on your posture, Murray. And also maybe don't drink so much."

I heard her introduce herself to Florence and Kathy. Brightly did she ask: "Y'all like mint juleps? I'm in that mood."

*

"She was wearing the ring when her daddy came to," said John. "She said he looked so disappointed to see it on her finger, like he might burst out in tears. So she quickly took it off right in front of him and put it back it in the box. This made him smile but then he slipped right back into the coma, the smile still on his face. The doctors told Virginia that it can happen."

God bless that Washington Wells. I looked back at the table and my alpha female who, just like her father, had taken the liberty of ordering for her new friends. Three mint juleps. As for Johnny Boy, he didn't look so good. That glorious Cartier ring and its thick red box had become his kryptonite; he sneered at it.

"It's cursed. I'm cursed," he said. "Am I cursed?" he asked me.

"Of course not. You're John . . . fucking . . . fucking-A Apple."

I'd never called him stuff like that before. I was grasping for straws because I was indeed starting to think that today was the beginning of the end for him. That the 1990s had been an unthinkably glorious decade for John, one in which he generally grabbed what he wanted, did what he wanted; had his way with people, things, me, and time itself. It's sad for me when stuff ends. For some reason, looking at John, I was brought back to the end of the last decade and those sledgehammers that slammed against the Berlin Wall and the statue of Stalin. I was perhaps alone in ruing that moment in history, especially for a nineteen-year-old, but children of bookstore owners read their way to an early old-fashioned-ness. So I guess I'm a fan of those old ways, no pun intended. Just what history was I now witnessing at the Mizner's Bar? I could hear Reagan's voice: "Mr. Gorbachev, tear down that man."

That man, John Apple, whose superpowers were unable to secure the love of his life, was crumbling before my eyes.

*

What would turn out to be our last ride together was on a slow-moving but well air-conditioned thing fascistically named the Transit Authority that rode through the Space Mountain. I'd convinced him to leave the bar for the Kingdom hoping it would lift his spirits. We shared my flask, Wayzing mechanically. Him for numbness and me because I could not wrap my head around the new order. *John fucking fucking-A Apple* had been reduced to a pile of graffiti-ridden rubble (my parents had bought a block of the Berlin Wall and displayed it under glass at the bookstore). As well, in about fourteen hours I was to have lunch, or *luncheon*, with Virginia Wells, who, I could tell, in her astonishing pale green cat eyes, had serious plans for me. And then there was Florence: that hadn't really sunk in yet. A cruise? A cruise to where? Plus I was unemployed.

"No!" John wailed.

The ride had snaked its way into Space Mountain but the damn thing was lit up with floodlights. John shielded his eyes. He might as well have been screaming about his fortune; protecting his eyes from a painfully illuminated turn of events.

"Jesus, it looks so paltry in the light," I said.

Of course I could have been speaking about him, poor Johnny Boy. After the ride we sat on a bench where a talking garbage receptacle that moved robotically mocked us with its squeaky voice.

"Hello friends," it squealed.

"Push," said John. "It's called Push the talking trashcan."

"Why the long face?" asked the garbage can.

John opened the ring box to show Push that it was still populated with a ring.

"She said no," he told the thing.

The robot turned to me.

"What's in the flask?"

At this late hour on a Monday night, having crossed the Ponder Rubicon, honesty with the trash robot was necessary.

"Wayz," I said.

"Wayz, wayz," it shrieked.

"What's the *word*, Push?" John asked it, reading the inscription on the flask.

"No," it said.

"She said no," it said.

"Wayz, wayz," it said.

"Cheer up," it said. "We're in the happiest place on earth," it said, then rolled away into the night.

*

We were set up where I'd first had lunch with the Wellses in the courtyard back outside the Grand Floridian. And again we were the only table prepped for lunch. The skies were clear, the day bright, the white tablecloth admirably starched. Virginia wore a dramatically floppy hat; the brim cut across her chiseled jaw. A cubist beauty at noon on a Tuesday. The table was set for two, catercorner. I'd passed out the night before, again in my clothes, but slept the sleep of the dead and woke somewhat refreshed. John had stayed behind in the Magic Kingdom; he wasn't so coherent when we parted.

"I'm going to hide," he'd said, then bolted deeper into Tomorrow World.

I'd decided to wear my trip-home outfit: blazer, slacks, dress shirt. It was barely seventy degrees and pleasant. Not sweaty thighs weather, which is always optimal. *Trip-home outfit*: but I hadn't come close to packing my suitcase, nor had I booked a ticket home.

"Hello, Cheese," said Virginia, smiling.

There was only one menu, and it was placed in front of me. I watched the sun on her arms, then took control.

"Two Lobster Clubs and a bottle of rosé," I told the waiter.

"So how is Mr. Apple holding up?"

"Not too well. I think he tried to become a stowaway last night in the Kingdom."

I'd of course taken a Theresa shower this morning, a truly long one that had pasted a permanent little smile on my face. Wayz can really transform life's absurdities into little smiles.

"I liked meeting your wife . . . is that what we should still call her?"

"I don't know," said my queer little smile.

"Well, I found her elegant, but I must say, *reserved*. You know I tried to convince her and Kathy to ride Tower of Terror with me after our mint juleps, but she wouldn't have it. Not that she was rude about Disney, she just politely declined. So the two of them are . . . ?"

"I think," said the silly little smile.

"Your eyes look so pretty in this light," she said, then leaned in to kiss the excited little smile.

"I'm sorry," she said. "I just had a moment."

It was a singular kiss but a fine one. So soft and barely moist, but moist nonetheless. It occurred to me that I had kissed three girls in my life, two-thirds on this trip: the escort (What the hell was her name? Wayz can really fuck with your memory). And now Virginia.

She spoke of Savannah while I drank rosé.

"It's nice and mild this time of year. Cashmere weather. I bet you look very handsome in cashmere. Ooh, and next month there's Christmas Eve at the country club. It's so beautiful and the dessert buffet is indescribable. And you should see the old oak trees that line the driveway leading up to Fairvue. Some are a thousand years old and they're all covered in moss. When you drive under them it's like they're soldiers touching swords. The country club driveway has the same old trees too. In fact we're just about neighbors of the Club. I'm more of a tennis girl than a golf girl but I can play both, just so you know."

In the Backstreet Boys' brilliant album *Millennium* that took the world, and Cheese, by storm this past summer, they sing of love and loss. Specifically of taking great human risks to achieve that pinnacle of human experience: requited love. I believe that should the Backstreet Boys bear witness to this luncheon, they'd be inspired to write a song about us. "The Indescribable Dessert Buffet" or "Soldiers Touching Swords" or "I Want it Savannah's Way."

We strolled after lunch, locking arms, stately. We strolled to the porte-cochère where the elaborate grilles of turn-of-the-century Cadillacs gleamed. There, helping a bellman pack their car's trunk, were Florence and Kathy. They'd rented a car. John and I never had; he didn't drive and I was always way too drunk.

"It's a nice day for a drive," said Kathy.

The car keys were in her little hands. I always did the driving for us and took some pride in that, getting Florence somewhere safely, sacrificing Wayz. I suppose it bothered me that I'd been replaced.

Well," said Florence, "I guess this is so long."

She looked troubled and the trouble leapt from her to me.

"Don't look so sad, Murray. Things always seem to work out for you and why shouldn't they? You're a white young male heterosexual and have a law degree."

"You have a law degree too," I said.

"My road's going to be bumpier, sweetheart."

It was the only word she could say so effectively softly. Was this the last time she'd ever call me that?

"Maybe we could be bumpy togeth—"

She hugged me tightly. Why didn't we hug like this before?

"The funds should hit your checking over the next few days," she said.

"What funds?"

"The buyout. Marks & Marks. It's substantial. Like I said, things always work out for Murray Marks. And now with a cherry on top."

"Huh?"

She motioned to Virginia.

"It was so nice to meet y'all," said Virginia.

"Likewise," said Kathy.

Florence, however, did not respond. Instead she looked at me, bit her lower lip, then gave Virginia a rather intense twice over, head to toes, then toes to head. Florence was wearing sunglasses, a rarity for her, and I feared that she'd begun crying. In fact, now I felt like crying as Florence secured herself in the passenger side.

"Well, take care of yourself, Cheese," said Kathy.

"I'll try. I'll try very hard."

For most if not all my of my adult life Florence had taken care of me.

That's the thing about being insufficiently Wayz'd: true emotions sneak in and it fucking hurts.

"So what shall we do with this fine afternoon?" asked Virginia as they pulled away. "I suppose we should get to know one another a little better?"

"Okay," said the anguished little smile.

CHAPTER TWENTY-TWO

THE SMELL OF SAVANNAH: the night-blooming jasmine slave-labors in the dark so that a fine floral powder permeates the day. It smells complete. As if everything works . . . everything must, or else. Fairvue smells like the Club; the Club smells like Fairvue. A vanilla-almond in which Virginia Wells grew up. I wanted to shake her, tell her that the smell wasn't *fair*, for I knew that beneath the white flowers was an historical stench waiting to ascend, but it wouldn't happen today nor tomorrow. On that the Wellses could always count. And so could I as I shut my eyes and feasted on it from the comfort of a rattan recliner upholstered in white with green piping (the family colors) in the back yard, over-looking 852 acres of marsh and farmland. Cotton, naturally. And sweet onions, watermelon, blueberries. And of course peaches. I toured it all with Mrs. Wells and Virginia narrating from one of their fleet of golf carts. Horse stable. Shooting range. Cemetery. They'd converted the jail into a candy store. They have a jail. They have a candy store. How did you get here, Cheese?

*

The Tuesday afternoon after Florence and Kathy drove off to Miami for their cruise (I never did find out where the hell they were going), some serious ennui had set in. John was MIA: no BlackBerry correspondences and no answer from his room. I did however confirm with the front desk that he hadn't checked out. So he was here, somewhere. As for Virginia and me, we couch surfed the lobby of the Grand Floridian.

"No rides today," she said. "It doesn't feel like a rides-y type of day, does it?"

Nope. It felt like a nuclear winter-y type of day. Muted, dangerously white. She read her Harry Potter book while I tried to compose a BlackBerry love letter to Florence and something close to a love letter to John. Both unsent; they sounded desperate, contrite. Although I hadn't really done anything wrong. I just wanted my old life back, the one from Friday. The last moment of normalcy that I could remember was from that first day when I'd bought Florence her Ponder gift. That expensive pendant necklace of Minnie Mouse. The shopkeeper's tired eyes as she looked on so lovingly at the piece. She wore a pin that celebrated her twenty-fifth year as an employee at the Sandy Cove. Her name tag read HEDY.

"Do you mind modeling it for me, Hedy?" my amazing late-morning buzz had said.

It brought her such joy; she told me that she'd never worn it but had always wanted to. She told me they were only allowed to try on the jewelry if a guest requested it of them and they really only asked the younger girls.

"Not us lifers," she'd said.

I'd made a stranger happy. My room was waiting for me. My wife was waiting for my return home and Monday night's lovemaking. Monday night. *Gone.*

"I have to go up to my room and get something," I told Virginia.

"Okay darlin'," she drawled.

I couldn't get to the Sandy Cove fast enough to give Hedy the necklace, a sacrificial offering that would surely realign my life, but Hedy was no longer there, I was told.

"She decided to retire over the weekend."

I imagined that she'd told herself one morning, dusting the jewelry case for the seven thousandth time, that she'd know it was time to go when someone finally asked her to model the ruby-eyed mouse. I skulked out of the store.

"Here," I said to Virginia and handed her the gift.

I needed to surrender to the new alignment, and this was a start. *My* girl should wear *my* necklace.

"Oh my word, I just love it," she said, putting it on. Yeah, yeah. Let's Wayz.

"Time for a Wayz," I said.

"I'm definitely going to show the bartender my new necklace." Her left hand clutched Minnie, her right hand clutched mine. How do people become couples? Witchcraft. "But let's just have club sodas, sweetheart."

*

I checked out of the Grand Floridian on Wednesday morning, footing the bill for my room charges, a Ponder first. Seemingly I'd gotten the girl; how could I make John pay, as well, for the room? Johnny Boy: I asked him if we could have a goodbye drink by the pool.

Okay, he wrote. That word can be deceptively cutting. Indifference is a sharpest arrow.

The bar was called the St. John's Pool Bar. I wondered if losing her would sanctify him? Martyr him? Render him even more powerful? And why name a Disney bar after an apostle of Jesus?

"No, mon," said the bartender. "It's named after the Caribbean Island of St. John, my hometown, mon."

The plan was that I'd go back to New York and collect my things, pack clean clothes, sort out my office desk, and then fly to Savannah to stay with the Wellses through the holidays.

"Get to know one another a little more," she kept on saying, and she also kept on insisting on non-Wayz during the daytime. And telling me to watch my posture. Nicely, of course. Oh, and she didn't care for men cursing. Fuck.

Tomorrow, Thanksgiving, I was on my own. A solo Thanksgiving. Another first in my life. I'm awful at being alone, a real weakness. John's good at it, great at it in fact. And Virginia is as well. I guess I'm decent at being alone if there are Wayz involved. Is Wayz a person? Sadly it's not, Cheese.

"What you drinking, mon?" asked the St. John's bartender. "How 'bout a mocha piña colada?"

"Perfect. But can you topper-ball it?"

"Ya mon!"

I love it when civilians instinctively pick up on Ponder parlance. Unlike that little fellow who sneered at *Wayz*.

"*Ball*," said John. He'd been standing behind me; I turned to see his wildly disheveled person. "I told you not to advertise our idiosyncrasies but I guess it's too late."

"Jesus, are you okay?"

Had Harvey Hanginstein, I mean Harvey Harstein, beheld this lost boy, the mythical Harvey, devoutly Jewish, would have crossed himself. John's tux shirt had been torn and all the studs missing. His hair was a mess, his pupils huge, lightless and looming, a lunar eclipse, and his face . . . sticky?

"What the hell's on your face?"

"Dark rum, neat," he told the bartender. "Dark rum is on my face," he told me.

"Where were you yesterday? We were worried."

"*We*," he said, then downed the rum. "I'll take another."

"Ya mon," said the bartender, unenthused. Rapid consumption of straight Wayz before 11:00 a.m. can dim the *Ya Mon* spirit.

"I'm really sorry—" I began.

"Don't."

He ordered a third drink, downed it; the bartender frowned. While I prefer devilish bartenders who encourage bottomlessness, certain more admirable ones actually worry about their customers' health.

"How 'bout a Swiss cheese omelet and some fresh pineapple, mon?" the bartender asked John.

"No," he told the bartender, then turned to me. "Charlemagne was surrounded by the Twelve Paladins. All dressed in white. Beacons in this dark world."

"Huh?"

"They didn't need alcohol. Nor women. They aspired to white cloth. They became their garment's color and were the only Christ-like mortals on this earth. They could walk on water and actually glowed from within. A silver phosphorescence. At night they shone under white sheets spun by white spiders. The silk of the just. My father told me of them. The happiest men in the history of time. Only twelve, with the promise of a thirteenth. My father came close but died too soon. He wore white suits. And a white hat. Cheers."

He's cracked. Fuck.

"See you around, Cheese." He patted my back and walked away. Woozily.

I'd never seen him so literally wasted. I wanted to explain about Virginia, how I couldn't really grasp the exact nature of our relationship. How I was going to Savannah to sort of heal my own wounds. I wanted to break things to him easily and softly. He'd probably already figured it all out, the smart bastard. Hell, I wish he'd explain it all to me then. How it would all play out down south, the auguring genius and his obsession with . . . white suits?

"Excuse me, *I'd* actually like the cheese omelet and fresh pineapple you'd mentioned before."

"Ya mon!" he said.

His inner Ya Mon light had returned. Then and there I prayed for my best friend's light to return as well. That he should gain the brightness to which he aspired. While the silent prayer began *Dear Lord* it ended with *Bless you, Walt*.

"Are friends more important than girls?" I asked the bartender.

"No mon."

*

Thanksgiving at the Shun Lee bar.

The red-eyed monkeys forever frozen swinging above the bar, waiting for the dark place to close so that they might come alive and throw duck sauce and hot mustard at one another in ritualistic anger.

"I don't understand," said Jack.

"He's still in Disney World. A girl broke his heart."

"Terrible," he said.

I had slept poorly last night, trying to bridge both sides of the bed. I thought that somehow part of my body on Florence's side could become Florence. As well, the Airport Mama didn't work Wednesdays and her chicken soup was nowhere to be found. Without it, Ponder poison runs amok. However, I was able to deposit my Dali tarot card with an unfamiliar woman behind the airport bar.

"I always wondered what those things in the register were," said the Airport Mama's replacement. "Creepy pictures if you ask me."

"Are you sure Mama didn't leave any soup?" I asked.

"Knowing Mama, she probably took it home. She hates to waste, y'know."

"You can tell her that the deck of tarot cards is missing one. The Prince of Cups."

"We got no business knowing the future. Want a hot dog?"

"Sure."

Virginia BlackBerry'd me that her father was being transported by a medical helicopter from Orlando to Fairvue, where he'd be watched around the clock by a team of nurses.

They're going to set him up in the ballroom, she'd written. What the fuck did that even mean?

Shun Lee was packed with families.

"We do five hundred Peking ducks on this day," said Jack. "Banquet style! You should be with your family, Murray Marks, banquet style!"

I'd called my parents from the Shun Lee pay phone to wish them a happy Thanksgiving and hadn't intended to get into everything that had transpired this past week but they said I sounded *fragile* and then it all came out: that Florence and I were taking a break as she was in love with Kathy Apple; that John was still at Disney World because a girl broke his heart; and that this very same girl had invited me to spend some time with her and her family down south. Oh, and that I'd met a relative of Alfred Hitchcock named Shay. Not sure why I'd added that, but I was buzzed and missed my times with her at the fake pub.

"May you live in interesting times," my father had said. "I mean, Murray, may you *not* live in interesting times."

"You should reread *A Brave New World*, sweetie," my mother had said. "The character John hangs himself at the end because of a broken heart, not that your John would ever do that."

Bookstore owners are weird. My parents are weird. And deeply in love, still.

Shoot, I was supposed to get a souvenir for the Airport Mama's grandchild.

"You're a good person, Murray," my mother had said. "And for that we're most thankful today."

Am I a good person?

"Am I a good person, Jack?"

"No." He wagged his finger. "Too many drinks and you left your friend in a horrible place. A Harvard man at Disney. It doesn't make any sense."

*

John's BlackBerry messages. Frequent, dark, and confusing. He was still at Disney World. Figuring stuff out, I surmised.

A nightmare born of rum, Cheese.

He wrote me shit like that. There was no room for nightmares at Fairvue. Here, dreams were sweet. Grandfather clocks ticked loud and clear. Flowers were freshly cut. The laundry was always folded and warm. And the trees. Virginia was right about the trees: ancient, kingly, dressed in robes of moss. Fierce creatures, these oaks. It must affect a man like Washington Wells growing up under their canopies; it must make him feel kingly just like them. As part of my daily routine at Fairvue I'd visit with Mr. Wells, who was lying in state in the enormous ballroom, the centerpiece of the mansion. In the middle of the ballroom in a hospital bed flanked by IVs, monitors, and nurses under a crystal chandelier the size of a Volkswagen Beetle. The Wellses had a wine cellar that would put many a four-star restaurant to shame, and I was given full access to its bottles, including cases of nineteenth-century bourbons and whiskies. With a vintage brown Wayz in hand I'd toast Mr. Wells (still handsome even in a coma), this usually after dinner, which was either at the Club or at Fairvue. The man who had built Fairvue had also built the main clubhouse, and certain nights, meandering one patio or another, I couldn't discern to which grande dame I owed the pleasure. Luncheon was always at the Club; I'd wear golfing outfits and the Wells girls would wear tennis outfits, but they never seemed to actually play despite toting racket bags and cans of tennis balls. I took golf lessons on the weekdays from an amazing Wayzing Scotsman who taught me from a chair, flask in hand. I once brought my Ponder flask but he told me in a thick accent, "There's no *cairry oots* allowed on the driving range. I'm the only one *oot of his tree* here."

The Scots have their own annoying little language. I thought of the Disney dwarf and his disgust with me. *Wayz.* Perhaps it's time to retire that silliness. Nah, not until the new year.

"Rotate those apish hips of yours, willya," the Scotsman would growl.

I sucked at golf but the bright-colored shirts and pants, and the sound the spiffy golf spats' spikes made on marble, became me. And Virginia's skimpy tennis skirt . . . well, it might have been the most appealing item of clothing I'd ever seen on a human being. It covered just enough of her thighs that the eyes could not help but take the journey from quadricep to crotch, only to be stopped, every time, by the pleated hem.

"Are you looking at my skirt?" she once teased. "Don't worry, beaus are permitted."

Beaus. We slept in separate bedrooms and would usually kiss goodnight on the cheek unless she was drunk, in which case she'd land on the lips. While I missed Florence, from whom I had not heard a word nor BlackBerry buzz, things like Virginia's thighs, how she wore pink sweat bands on her delicate wrists, the little peaceful smile on her breakfast face . . . nothing on earth emits more raw femininity than a princess in her castle. Virginia Wells at Fairvue was, quite simply, awe-making. Those legs cascading down one grand staircase or another. When I first arrived I had wondered how those muscles were maintained; carrying tennis rackets between the pro shop and the clubhouse, or twirling in the ballroom around her sleeping daddy, were not sufficient workouts. However, on my second day at Fairvue I figured out the secret to her fitness, not to mention her mother's admirably youthful figure: they helped clean the damn place. Twice a week they donned aprons, gloves, buckets of soapy water, kerchiefs in their hair and joined the all-Black staff for six hours of backbreaking work. Six till noon. Apparently it was a family tradition that dated back five generations.

"It's how we show love for Fairvue and the magical people who help keep her grand," Mrs. Wells had said.

"Oh, the magical people," swooned Virginia.

"Did Mr. Wells help clean also with the, um, magical people?" I asked.

"Of course not," said Mrs. Wells.

"Only us girls and the magical people can handle such a tough job," said Virginia. "No offense to your manhood, Cheese."

None taken. I feared they'd recruit me into the magic, and I was in no shape for the stair climbing and broom work that the job required. I'd gained weight here: Dutch apple pancakes, reuben sandwiches, roast beef and Yorkshire pudding, lamb chops with mint jelly. Rich people eat in preexisting decades from roast beef trolleys with burnished domes. Nope, no room for nightmares at Fairvue.

CHAPTER TWENTY-THREE

IN EARLY DECEMBER A doctor from France and his team arrived at Fairvue. The little man in his lab coat specialized in radical therapies that aimed at awakening the comatose. A syringe the size of my arm filled with newfangled steroids was to be injected into a vein just below Washington Wells's ear. Virginia and Constance Wells held bibles. I held, well, a *drink*. (Inner language is proscribed during medical miracles.) And holy shit how he came to.

"Voila," said the doctor. Are the French the most smug little bastards on earth? Yep. Why? Because they invented Napoleon. A five-foot man should not be able to conquer the planet. Nor become a custard-filled dessert. But he did, and this doctor stirred the dead.

The Wells girls? Tears of joy. He shot up.

"Virginia."

"Daddy!"

"Oh, Washington," said Mrs. Wells.

"Virginia, what matters in this life is virtue," he said, his voice miraculously unstrained. Then he looked at me as if he didn't know

me. Was he confused or bothered by my presence? Something cold.
Back to Virginia.

"Virtue," he said. "As you know, honey, it's on the family crest.
Virtus."

Then he looked queerly at me again. I was unsure why the possible
change of heart regarding his chosen son-in-law. Perhaps he'd had a
revelatory dream about a fat atheistic Wayzer who, like most people in
the world, didn't actively think about being virtuous.

"Vir—"

With that he went back to sleep. Permanently. He was dead. The
Wells girls? Tears of sorrow.

"I am sorry," said the doctor. "So sorry for your loss."

"Bring him back!" cried Constance.

"Madame, I told you over the phone that this therapy can last a
minute, ideally a lifetime, or be fatal. I am very very sorry."

(I could have sworn he said *Voila* again.)

Selfishly, I wished the shot to the ear hadn't worked at all. From
that moment on, I could tell that Virginia was not as keen on her
future with me. At first I thought it was just the grief, but beneath her
tears and fits of sorrow was a look in her eye. A version of how her
father had looked at me. I was familiar with that look; only once had
I looked at Florence that way, on the first day of our honeymoon, on
a hotel terrace in Paris. Jet-lagged and obligatorily hungover, I felt
trapped. Doomed to be with only one woman forever. A woman whose
stern temperament I hadn't yet unraveled. A sealed fate is an awful
feeling and it comes out in the eyes. Virginia was nice enough to me,
though, as the month trundled on towards Christmas and her grief
began to dissipate. She even spoke on occasion of a wedding in the
ballroom. But to whom? She wasn't specific about that, though I was
the only man in the house and she still, some nights, would kiss me
on the lips. Her Southern strength in the face of death only made me
love her more.

How she cared for her mother. How she stood up straight with

Wellsian pride, her chin pointed at heaven where, she was certain, her daddy stayed. Can death turn a girl into a woman?

"Now my ribs are made of steel," she'd said one night in mid-December when the crying jags had ceased to be. *The strength of the strong*, Florence had written in florid Chinese calligraphy on a sign on the lintel.

They say that women sprang from Adam's rib. Some sort of bony afterthought. Hogwash. *Steel*. Steel ribs.

"Strength matters," said Virginia, echoing my wife's edict.

Then, her palms pressed up against my chest.

"Murray, I need for *you* to be stronger. And smarter. I need for you to drink less and become a better man. Someone whose arm I can cling to with my eyes closed. Someone who I can trust with my truest words. I don't want to be with a drunk, Murray. Drunks cannot have virtue, so tighten that shit up."

She took a beat.

"Or you'll lose me."

Fuck.

*

On Christmas Eve day, the phone rang while the Wells girls were out shopping. They employed a dedicated phone answerer who jotted down messages with an outrageously beautiful and long ostrich feather pen, but she was off for the holiday so I sat where she did, in front of the fluffy white writing implement and her official message pad.

"The Wells residence," I answered.

"Huh, where's Virginia?"

A familiar accent. Russian. "Dimitri?"

"Who is this?"

"It's Murray. Murray Marks. The guy from Disney."

Silence.

"The larger man."

"Oh. Oh yeah. I heard you were staying there. Actually your friend call me last month. He sounded drunk. Laughing like crazy governess of my childhood. My mother thought governess be good training for when I marry crazy person but Virginia said 'no'."

"Virginia's crazy?"

"Of course. Best ones are."

I want to marry that crazy girl and go mad with her. A diet of Wayz and sex. Early graves after an ecstatic if *crazy* life.

"So, the Cheese, Apple ask me what I think of you. I tell him the truth. Am not surprised Mr. Wells choosing the Cheese. I tell Mr. Apple that he is cute guy with nice butt. While you have bubble ass of famous bald basketball player."

"Charles Barkley?" Shit.

"But you see, Cheese, a girl like Virginia listens to her dad. Mr. Wells, he is about control, especially control his daughter. Look, Mr. Apple is man. Man cannot be controlled. No offense to you, Mr. Cheese, but of course you can be. Mr. Wells knows this. It's okay. Most of us need to be controlled. How do you say? Makes world spin around."

"Mr. Wells passed away. And now I'm not sure if he still likes Mr. Cheese. You know, from beyond the grave."

"Yeah, I know he died. John Apple told me this."

"How did he know?"

"Virginia told him."

"I miss John Apple." I said. "I miss his . . . face."

Is it easier to confess when someone has an accent? Yes, it is. Wait: they've been in touch?

"Anyway," said Dimitri, "before I hung up he started laughing just like governess. You love her. I get it. I loved her too, But I think he *really* do. Crazy laughter must mean real love. Hard to figure out. The heart hides behind the eyes until it decides that it cannot hide anymore. Have you ever cut open the belly of a sturgeon?"

"Um, no." (Why is everyone crazy?)

"They look like little eyes, the fish eggs. Some so light. The Golden Ossetra."

"I love Virginia's eyes."

"Impossible to know what's behind the girl's eyes. Impossible to know a woman's heart. But know Disney, and maybe the rest will make sense. At least this is my theory. Will die trying."

"Are you going back there?"

"Of course. Soon will start over. Next month. With one Pan, and then, we see. The job of knowing Disney World is very hard."

"Well, good luck," I said. I wanted to ask him the specifics of his, um, *job*, but decided it was a necessary madness that must pass into silence.

"And luck to you, the Cheese. Greatness for the man who gets to be with Virginia Wells."

"Greatness," I said, momentarily feeling that way. (Me, the Cheese, got to tap her shoulder blade when she'd mislocate her Blackberry, then direct the Golden Ossetra eyes to between the couch cushions. "You're my hero," she'd say and reward me with a one-legged hug.)

"Some women make a man great just by standing next to them," said Dimitri.

"And those who don't get to stand next to her?"

Then he laughed a crazy governess laugh and hung up.

*

Cheese, wrote John.

Hello! I wrote, genuinely enthused. While one cannot sniff out flesh from one word on a blinking screen, he sounded himself again.

We should all be together for the new year. Come to Disney. Bring Virginia. I need you guys now. It will be the last thing I ever ask of you. I've changed. I have much to tell you both. I am on a life wagon, Cheese. No more alcohol. I found my white suit. I found the light. Tell me you'll both come? It would be a life favor.

This during Boxing Day dinner at the Club. The day after Christmas. Roast goose and potato dumplings.

"Pass the cherry sauce, please," said Virginia.

Looking around the dining room, it occurred to me that we were the smallest party, us three. It was always the three of us, every meal. Did they not have friends?

"Who's your best friend?" I asked Virginia.

"My mama."

"Well, mine is John," I said defensively.

"Pass the cherry sauce, please," said Mrs. Wells. "They make it with port wine."

Constance Wells had been medicated since her husband's passing. She spoke infrequently and when she did it was of things like port wine.

"I don't even mind that it's the color of fresh blood," said Virginia. "Daddy loved it too. To Daddy," she said.

We toasted him every night. Virginia seemed, at least recently, to have come to grips with her loss.

"I know I'll see him again in heaven," she'd said. "Meanwhile, *virtue* for this girl. I know he's watching. I love you, Daddy."

Of course we'll come, I wrote John.

I hadn't felt like myself in so long. Of course I'll come for you, Johnny Boy!

"We're going back to Disney to see John for New Year's Eve," I told Virginia. "He needs us now."

"Is he okay?" she asked, clutching my arm.

Such a strong hand for such a slender wrist. Will those long fingers ever have it in their hearts to wrap themselves around my—

"Let's skip dessert and go home and pack," said Virginia, already up from her seat.

CHAPTER TWENTY-FOUR

I AM STARTING TO understand the South. From where I sat at an Atlanta airport bar I had a close-up view of a man standing, wearing a pork-pie hat, suspenders over his prodigious stomach bulge. He grins about nothing, everything. He eats a corn dog, wipes sweat from his brow. Always grinning. He is white and has white hair. I'd put him in his late sixties.

"Wouldn't think the airport's the spot for a corn dog," he tells a Black woman who just bought one for her son.

His accent is deeply Southern and to my ear almost incomprehensible. "You'd think at the country fair," the man continues.

"True 'nuff," says the woman. Her accent matches his.

He tips his hat at her, still grinning. And she shepherds her boy away from that man. That hat. That shit-eating grin.

Nooses were hung over the great mossy branches of Georgia's ancient oak trees. Those trees are façades; what's beneath the summery surfaces?

"I am beginning to understand the South," I told my travel companion, Virginia Wells. We had a one hour twenty-minute layover in

Atlanta on our way back to Orlando. To the mothership of all façades to commune with John Apple.

"How so, Cheese?" asked Virginia, sipping on a White Russian. While she frowned on my excesses, she permitted herself the occasional cocktail.

"Alligators in the waters. And ropes thrown over tree branches."

"Don't be so dramatic. It's 1999, we all get along so well these days and it will only get better."

It was December 30. I'd confirmed that John had not checked out of the Grand Floridian. With all his talk of white suits, you'd think he'd found a convent. Although Sandeep did volunteer that he hadn't remembered seeing Mr. Apple in recent days.

"But that's rather common here, Mr. Marks. Especially on the verge of New Year's Eve. Our suite guests are busy getting ready for the party of, well, the century."

The only accommodation available given the late date was a smallish room that was apparently crammed into one of the hotel's cupolas.

Sandeep had been kind enough to make the reservation. "Architecture buffs really enjoy the dormer rooms," he'd said.

"How so?"

"The dormer rooms reflect the hotel's façade."

Façade.

"What size beds though?"

"One queen-sized bed."

"Just one?"

Butlers don't respond to stupid questions.

Shit. Not that I didn't want to sleep with her—it was practically all I'd thought about the past forty-one days—but a queen bed forces the issue. Our bodies would touch. And how the hell do I make love to a non-Florence girl? Especially this one, whose every lightest brown freckle demands masculine expertise.

"Is there a couch?" I'd asked Sandeep.

"Not in the dormer rooms, no. But there is a view of the Seven Seas Lagoon."

Alligators.

"I can't believe that tomorrow we're going to spend the last night of the millennium together," said Virginia.

Watching the grinning man had white-guilted me (I would have said *guilt-balled* but it sounds like a symptom of testicular cancer), so I'd ordered a Black Russian to offset Virginia's Caucasian drink.

"Okay, but just one," she'd said. She hadn't really mentioned John these last few weeks at Fairvue except for one night.

"I consider Mr. Apple to be a dear friend too, and you might need my help. Girls are good at rescuing men. We know just what to say to talk them down off the roof."

"I don't think he needs rescuing."

"All men do, trust me."

She'd surmised that her returned ring combined with being stuck in Disney World had brought him over the line. In fact she said the *Kurtz* line. Being compared to Brando's Colonel Kurtz would appeal to John Apple, even though in that film the mad man was more my body type.

"He'll need our familiar faces to remind him," she said.

"Remind him of what?"

"That there's great purpose in this life above and beyond what's underneath my skirt."

Not so sure about that.

I did ask Virginia to let me see him first; I needed to glean his true mental state before letting him set eyes on the girl of our dreams. His shattered dream. Although she insisted that she'd have the exact right touch.

"I've had plenty of experiences with lovesick suitors. I know just how to hold their hand and lead them back into the light."

"According to him he's found the light," I said.

I thought she'd follow with *I am the light*. Which she was. But she held her tongue. That tongue. A pink dexterity that lived inside plump lightly freckled Southern lips. Lips that spoke with ever-increasing authority.

"We'll figure it all out. In the end, everything will happen."

Perhaps my sweet girl but still, something wasn't adding up. The life wagon. The life favor that we spend the new year with him. A white suit? Still, I was secretly thrilled to be going back to Disney. I'd read of Vietnam War vets who wake up at home, in their beds next to their wives, when all they could think of was being back in the jungle. It was really all they wanted: to be back in the jungle. What does that say about human nature? Joseph Conrad wrote *The horror! The horror!* Speaking of which, I hadn't yet done the Jungle Boat.

"Have you ever given to charity?" she'd asked me the night before we were to leave for Disney, as I watched her add to her suitcase. She'd been packed for days. "Or volunteered to help the needy?"

"Charity? Umm, not really, no."

She snickered in disappointment.

"But I could, I guess. If you wanted me to."

"You have to want you to."

Was she adding lingerie to her suitcase? Was it something crotchless. Oh God. Please be charitable with *me*.

We flew first class; it was all she knew. I made the arrangements. It was odd: Virginia didn't ask me to call my travel agent, it was just implicit. In the air at Fairvue: *Cheese will make all the arrangements and pay for the trip.*

And I didn't mind at all. I had Florence's settlement money in my checking account. Virginia wasn't acting spoiled really, just adorably impractical. She didn't know *how* to do things like book travel. When I told my travel agent that Virginia Wells, not Florence Marks, would be traveling, she was not surprised:

"Oh I know, Murray, Florence is still at sea with her friend."

"Still?" I asked.

"Oh, I thought. Oh sorry, I thought you knew—"

"Where are they?"

"Let me see . . . they are, um, switching between Western and Eastern Caribbean itineraries," she'd said brightly, trying to make it all sound so innocent.

"They were supposed to be home by now."

"Yes, well, they keep on extending the cruise. Back to back to back to. . . ."

Back to back. Tonight I'll take Virginia from behind. That'll show 'em. I watched her press her little nose to the window as the plane to Orlando took off. She must have been on a hundred flights like this yet there it was: the wonderment in her eyes.

Florence would always lower the window shade, then turn on the buzz-undoing reading lamp. What an aggressive source of light.

"Please never turn on the reading lamp," I told Virginia.

"I won't. It hurts my eyes."

I wish kissing her would taste like those eyes. Key limes. Key lime juice. I'd yet to cross the threshold of those lips though. Tonight. Key Lime Pie.

*

Ah, the Grand Floridian. How she bounced from the car to the lobby. Home again. "Welcome home," said the bellhop.

Virginia's luggage was leather. Louis Vuitton. A long garment bag for her dresses. A trunk for the rest. I'd never traveled with someone who had world-class luggage. Truly adult luggage. *Killer* luggage. Mine was brandless, nylon, sophomorically blue. Florence had tied a red ribbon to the handle so I could know it from the rest of the shitty bags. Girls who own Louis Vuitton luggage have never touched the handles. I gave the bellhop ten bucks and checked us in.

"You go to the room and unpack," I told Virginia. "I'm going to John's suite." I'd written him since his plea for us. Told him we were coming.

Fantastic news, Cheese, he'd written.

"Well, Mama usually unpacks for me," said Virginia in the lobby, a team of three bellmen standing behind her with her hardware. "It's a Southern thing, I think."

"I'll unpack for you later, okay?"

"Aww," she said.

I'm here, I wrote John. *I'm coming up.*

But first I needed a Wayz. I couldn't really day-drink in front of Virginia and I was sober at Disney World. There, I said it.

"What can I do you for?" asked the bartender, tossing a cocktail shaker into the air and catching it behind his back. The technical mastery of this bartender lightened my mood. Of course John will be as he always was and is. He'll be down here in the lobby with me later, both of us commenting on the man's great skill. Just like old times.

"You and Virginia? Good for you, Cheese," he'll say. "Let's plan our next Ponder right here, right now! And I'm going to get off this life wagon pronto, just for you! Hey, let's play darts for money?"

"Okay!" I'll say. He'll win as always but will then refuse my twenty-dollar bill, the sweetheart.

Only one bed? wrote Virginia. *Ambitious.*

Sorry it was all they had.

"Here for the convention?" asked the bartender.

I suppose I could ask for a cot, she wrote.

Shit.

"What convention?" I asked.

"Something to do with lawyers."

"I'm a lawyer."

Or maybe we could figure out some arrangement, she wrote.

Yes!

I made quick work of two double vodkas, lime. Then, with a third in hand, asked for directions to the convention hall.

I'm too old to have someone else unpack for me, she wrote. What a girl!

The convention was actually a recruitment fair that traveled the country; Florence and I had attended the exact same one when we were fresh out of law school. All the big national firms under one roof in search of grunts. Hundred-hour weeks, low comp, high pressure.

I stood before the Bernstein, Benic & Burke booth, one of the nation's top real estate law firms. Headquartered in New York, they'd always piqued my interest for the simple reason that they were in One World Trade Center only one floor removed from the restaurant Windows on the World and its bar called "The Greatest Bar in the World." One floor. A five-second elevator ride to a bar that opened at the incredibly civilized and particular hour of 10:45 a.m. There had been some very early morning closings, the timing could be perfect. A bright morning on the 106th floor, the city at my feet, happy clients, new keys in hand, on their way to their freshly painted future.

I'm going to take a bath. Yum.

I filled out an application at the firm's booth.

"Marks and Marks," said the recruiter, nodding.

"You've heard of us?"

"Great boutique firm. I think we made your wife an offer a few years back but she didn't bite. I could tell you right now that we'd love to have you and your wife visit us in New York."

There's no balcony, she wrote. *It's cozy though. Thank you, Cheese.*

"It would just be me. My wife is . . . elsewhere."

He gave me his card.

Uh oh the minibar's empty, she wrote.

"Sometimes I miss the law and New York. But I fell in love with a Southern beauty. And Savannah, Georgia. The trees. The peaches. Her skin."

"Well, you know where to find us."

"The 105th floor."

"Yep, on a clear day you can see forever."

I can see forever, I wrote Virginia. My first BlackBerry'd non sequitur, at least to her.

With your pretty green eyes, she wrote. She doesn't miss a beat. *I'm in the bathtub*, she wrote.

"Are you okay, Mr. Marks?" asked the recruiter.

I'd been paralyzed by her nudity; my eyes were shut, their lids trembling. "Oh, sorry," I said. "Just . . . love."

*

Sandeep found me loitering in front of the Roy O. Disney Suite. "I saw him earlier," said Sandeep.

"You did?"

"Yes, we were outfitting him."

"Outfit?"

"How is your dormer room, Mr. Marks?"

"Um, no balcony, but it's cozy. Oh, and the minibar's empty. Sometimes kids steal all the contents, then call for a free replenishment. Clever if shameful."

Kids. We were once kids but were we now men? It was feeling that way. And just in time for the new millennium. The advanced number will have no use for man-children. Or drunks, as Virginia had said. But that can start on New Year's Day.

I'm out of the tub and all unpacked, she wrote. Nor woman-children. (Or drunks.) Not being buzzed at Disney is a huge fucking mistake.

I asked Sandeep to take care of our minibar, then went back to the lobby bar.

"Vodka with a lime please."

I no longer asked for Stoli. I'd been conditioned by the Club, where the hard Wayz were all generic. No brands. Just *gin, vodka, bourbon, scotch*. It was deemed gauche to specify, I suppose. Or maybe more elegant not to? Regardless, the damn WASPs could afford the best but settled for Seagram's, Smirnoff, Gordon's.

I'll be up soon, I wrote Virginia.

Although I decided to take my own sweet time. I had my MP3 player. "Larger than Life" by the incomparable Backstreet Boys. To listen to that triumph while on an ocular Biggunz safari. I love life and its inhabitants who eat jellybeans the size of robin's eggs and wash them down with liters of Dr. Pepper. Seriously, bless you Walt for inventing sugar. Without it the happiness disappears and all that's left is the starkness of the calendar. Fuck December 30, 1999. Amen, Walt. Amen.

Where are you? wrote Virginia.

In heaven.

No hyperbole there: I'd ordered mozzarella sticks and another vodka. I'd conversed with a bar Biggunz about something called the Tiki Birds.

"That Iago is up to no good," said the Biggunz.

"Shakespeare!" I said.

"Huh?"

"Oh, nothing, yep, gotta keep an eye on that Iago."

"There you go."

Iago, I wrote Virginia.

Are you getting drunk?

Yes. I ordered a fifth? No, a sixth vodka lime and made my way out back towards the lagoon. I mean the fake lake. The sun was setting; silvers and golds reflecting off the water, making scrutiny difficult. Or maybe it was the six hard Wayz. Regardless, Cheese, floatingly, strolled through the unreality. There was a fake sand beach, a crescent of sand before the water. Empty loungers. A volleyball net into which I walked, then stumbled into the sand. Nothing brings back childhood like the taste of sand in one's mouth. Between the teeth. That grit. When I opened my eyes, before me was a man in a white suit and a beautiful white hat. Gatsby? No, John Apple, beaming. He helped me to my feet.

"Look at you," he said brushing sand off my person.

"Holy shit. Look at *you*."

He was tan and clean. So clean. Maybe he was on to something with all this white suit talk. To call it a healthy glow; well, the only other human being who emitted brilliance by way of the epidermis was up in my room.

"Is she here?" he asked. "Of course she is. I can sense her. You see, Cheese, goodness is a sixth sense."

Now he's in possession of *the force*?

Crazy non-Wayzing Gatsby Skywalker. (Or Vader.)

"Let me buy you a drink," he said. His hand had not left my shoulder. He was guiding me. Firmly, happily, to the bar overlooking the lagoon, where he ordered an Evian. And a lemon which he squeezed into his glass. He spoke as he squeezed the life out of the lemon.

"I'd read that one needs to throw oneself into the abyss, like a child might a pebble into an endless well."

"An endless well?"

"Yes, but instead of a forever fall, one finds a bottom, then turns into one's best self," he said.

(Or did he say best *Christ*?)

The John Apple I knew and loved wasn't Christ-like. That's for sure. I remembered John's glee about a certain ice cream dessert they served here called, I think, the Kitchen Sink:

"They serve it in an actual sink," he'd said. "Not even a Biggunz can finish it. It has 21,640 calories. I watched one try and he passed out. He left on a stretcher. Tremendous. One of the best things I've ever seen. You should try to finish it, Cheese."

He might have suffered cardiac arrest, you bastard. Should I try to finish it, I might suffer a heart attack as well, you bastard. Ah, well, all's forgiven now, I suppose.

"You see, Cheese, the night after I had gotten off a phone call with Dimitri, I drank a bottle of Myers's rum in the sand right where I found you just now. Beyond drunk, was I. It wasn't pretty, Cheese. I was in a place where I was seen. When you are in a place where you are seen, you must change your life now. So I stripped naked and decided I must swim out into the Seven Seas Lagoon. Alligators be damned. It was a dangerous baptism for sure. You see the buoy?"

"Barely."

"Swam there and back. How did I know it would work? I asked my deceased father for guidance and he populated my mind. I could hear him. Clear as you hear me now. He said that I needed to complete his white-suited dream. I think I told you that he was obsessed with Charlegmegne and his Paladins?"

"Uh, sure."

"So I swam."

I searched his body for missing limbs. His suit for blood. Not a dinosaur bite. Not a scratch.

On the beach a sign read: STAY AWAY FROM THE WATER. DO NOT FEED THE WILDLIFE.

When John excused himself to use the men's room, I asked the bartender, "What would happen if someone swam out there?"

"Out there? No one would do that. Like I always say, if you want to see the gators go on the Jungle Cruise."

Upon John's return: "You should know, Cheese, that I've given a significant portion of my fortune to help the needy."

There's that word again.

"The Make-a-Wish Foundation. It answers the prayers of sick children, many of whom choose to come here. Look, I know you think I'm this arrogant—"

I have a wish. Crotchless lingerie please. Tonight, before this cloyingly excellent version of my best friend steals her back. Mental note to remind Virginia that her father did indeed choose me for her despite the quizzical face on his deathbed.

"Shall we three meet for dinner tonight?" he asked.

"We have plans, so maybe tomorrow," I lied.

"Tomorrow it is. You two sharing a room?"

"They only had one left, so yeah."

"Sharing a bed? Never mind. None of my business, right?"

Something really didn't add up about this new John Apple. (Or maybe I was too jaded to believe in self-cleaning souls?) Virginia should never see this . . . this *man*. Not tonight and not tomorrow.

CHAPTER TWENTY-FIVE

I HID HER BLACKBERRY in case he tried to reach out. I'd instructed the front desk not to allow any strangers to be connected to our room phone. My theory was that if I took her tonight, sexually, she'd be back in my good graces. She'd be mine. One hundred percent. My plan was to tell her I loved her during the act. Then after the act, propose. With an eight-dollar Disney ring I'd bought at the good old Sandy Cove. It was a plastic monorail fashioned into a ring. An endless circle. I would speak to her of our eternity. Tell her: *I may not be handsome or that rich but I'm a good guy and would never cheat on you. That's my virtue. Reliability. Plus I'm fun at Wayz-y dinners. And I truly love you. Beware of men in white suits. Like my Irish grandfather would say,* beware of a wolf in sheep's clothing. *I am a sheep in sheep's clothing. My wool isn't white. It's dirty with mud. It's real. I'm real.*

Please let the average Joe get the girl this time. Please let the average Cheese into the fairytale. But who was I praying to? I hadn't God's ear, that much I knew. In my life, the only person I'd ever prayed to was Walt Disney and that was today, earlier at the bar. So Walt, if you're listening and magic is real, make her love me as I love her. Or at least like me enough to spend time with me, just us two, and of course her mama. (I'm good with a girl and her mama.) I'm likeable, I really am. Give me a couple of years and she'll grow into Cheese. Well, you know what I mean, Walt.

"Should we go see John?" asked Virginia.

"He's busy with some white getup."

I hadn't told her that I'd seen him. Just that I had amazing plans for us tonight. She was already drinking a glass of champagne, which boded well. Plus it was already dark out and our room's visibility was, for me and my big self, mercifully limited.

Florence had once said that humans are all the same in the dark. I hope she's right.

Have you seen my BlackBerry?

A question she never asked. Adorable that she couldn't care less.

We were both on the bed watching the hotel's Must-Do's loop with the not-as-adorable-as-Virginia host, Stacey. She downed her champagne then turned Stacey off.

"Well," she said. "It's going to be awfully awkward in this bed if we don't just get it over with and do it."

"What?"

"It's just sex."

This was a part of her I never knew. I started sweating.

"Let's get under the covers," she said.

"Okay."

I was ill prepared. I thought there would be room service and pillow talk leading up to *me* making the first move. A move I hadn't yet divined, but here she was with me under the covers, removing her clothes and my voluminous boxers. I am extra of the events under the sheets. What is sex anyway? I ask myself as she does to me what Florence had only ever really done once. Sex is a hijacked mind. Does the body hijack the mind or vice versa? Either way it's a hijack, the cockpit overtaken.

"Don't you like it?" asked Virginia.

The captain and the copilot are resisting the terrorists.

"Why don't you get on top?" she suggested.

I'm not good on top. Too fat. Florence was almost always on top. Cruising altitude. I can't get this stupid airplane analogy out of my head.

"Sure, I'll get on top," I said. "That's my wheelhouse."

No, it isn't. I stayed on the bottom and Florence did all the work, except those Monday nights after a Ponder, then I'd take control. Me on top. But today is Tuesday and as noted she is not Florence. Her touch is gentle and profound. But it is not working on me. And now the flight attendant we frequent the most on United, Ann, the Ann Abler from our trip here to Orlando, she is in the hotel room, wheeling the cocktail cart down the aisle.

"Enjoying the sex, Mr. Marks?"

"Not really. The plane's been hijacked."

"Oh, I know. Just get hard and everything will be fine. Where's Mr. Apple?"

"In a white outfit pretending he's Jesus but I can't stop thinking about him. Does that mean I'm gay, Ann?"

"I don't know, but you sure aren't hard."

"What's wrong with me?"

"Oh well," Virginia said and turned Stacey back on.

"That's never happened to me before," I told Virginia.

"Uh-huh."

All the poor women who have heard that line but I was being honest.

"Maybe we could try again later?" I asked.

"Maybe, if you sober up. I'm going to take my bath. What did you call that bath with the drinks again?"

"It's actually a shower. Theresa shower."

"We should make up our own private words." That was a good sign.

She'd turned on the lights. Her body was even more perfect than I could have possibly imagined. And I'd imagined long and hard. The heart-shaped ass. The wavy hair down her back. The light brown trim between her legs. Bodies are composed of parts, that's how you take them in; your eyes visit places. Not this one: you took it in all at once, then needed to avert your gaze.

She stretched and yawned before slipping into a bathrobe. I couldn't believe she permitted me this view.

"It's just the human body," she said.

I'd once eaten something called a double gold raspberry. It had this blush gold color. A marriage between pink and the sun itself. Her nipples. Just human? No. No way.

"I'm sure I'll do better next time!" I shouted at the bathroom. No response.

"I'm ordering us room service," she shouted back.

"Okay, I need to have a word with Sandeep. I'll be back for room service."

Desperate and ashamed of my performance, I needed to ask another man how to, well, get it up.

"It's really never happened before," I whimpered to myself as I replaced my pants. No proposing tonight. No way, you flaccid fool.

*

"Why hello, Sandeep."

"Good evening, Mr. Marks."

I'd tracked him down in the lobby, where he was organizing what looked to be lavish gift bags for tomorrow night's festivities. For suite guests only, I hoped. That's the way it should be. John would look handsome in one of those Happy New Year's hats. Well, he looks handsome in his current white hat. Too handsome. I flashed back to when I'd been in the very same bed as John and Virginia's lovemaking and the memory made my loins stir. Stirred wildly. Maybe my bedroom malfunction wasn't guilt but something else? Could I only access Virginia through thoughts of John? Through thoughts of their coupling?

"Have you seen Mr. Apple around?" I asked Sandeep.

"I've been working down here on the party favors."

"They're just for the suite guests though, right?"

"Yes, I'm afraid—"

"No, I think that's great. So John will get one, right? He'd look rather handsome in one of those party hats rather than that absurd white hat. How do you know if you're, um, gay?"

"I'm sorry?"

"No, nothing, just girl troubles."

While he was inside of her, my mouth touched their persons if only the soles of their feet. And just like that: massive arousal in front of the butler. God bless butlers.

"Do you mind if I borrow a hat, Sandeep? I promise I'll return it."

"Here, take a bag of party favors. Consider it a New Year's gift."

"No, that wouldn't be right. But I would like to borrow the hat. I have a bit of an issue down here, Sandeep."

Boner balled (well, it's true) at Disney World. I placed the hat over my protuberance. Sandeep, embarrassed for me, feigned searching through a bag so that he could all but put his head inside.

*

We were now in bed and my manhood was functioning.

"Looking good, Mr. Marks," said our flight attendant, the Ann Abler. "Care for a cocktail?"

"Not during physical congress, Ann."

"Of course not. *Well*, she certainly looks happier than before. What's the secret?"

"At first, Ann, it was Mr. Apple. He sort of jump-started my um *cockpit* but then I took it from there."

Now my body was liberated from my mind. I needed no thoughts. I was a tiger. An uninhibited beast who had its way with her. Embarrassed by my fleshy torso, with Florence I kept my shirt on. Tonight I let it all hang out, and now as the sweat cooled from our bodies, she smoked by the open window.

"I didn't know you smoked," I said.

"I only smoke a cigarette after sex."

At one point she'd said *you feel good, Cheese.* It was the highlight of my life. Tomorrow night I will propose to her. After sex, I was empty.

"May I have a puff?" I asked.

On her Parliament filter, to taste the spit that I must own. Tomorrow.

*

"I have a New Year's Eve tradition," she said the next morning. "Ever since I was thirteen, at the stroke of midnight, I kiss whichever boy is nearest me. Is that weird?"

"No. I just hope it's me."

"Maybe it will be. Who knows?"

It'll be me. Wait: will we ever have sex again? She said we'd get it over with. Was it gotten over with?

"Some guys have gotten wasted too early. They pass out and live to regret it." What a lucky stranger to begin the year with that mouth.

"Welp," she said. "I am headed to the spa. Lots for a girl to do on a day like this."

Please don't run into John on your way to the spa.

Where are you? I asked John.

Safari.

Phew. Thank God he still likes the stupid rides. (Sorry, Walt.)

"Have a good spa day," I said.

"Catch you later," she said. "Let's make a plan with John for tonight. I just realized I don't have my BlackBerry. Could you write him?" she asked.

No. "Sure."

"Can't wait to see him," she squealed.

My plan was to actually contrive an evening for us three. To meet at a distant hotel's formal restaurant at 10:00 p.m. and never show. By then she'd be wearing the monorail on her ring finger. I would get it monogrammed in microscopic print.

Please stand clear of the closing doors, it will read. *Por favor manténgase alejado de las puertas*, it will read forever.

*

Forced gaiety is what my grandfather called New Year's Eve. He loathed the night. I recall him telling me in his brogue, "At all costs stay at home, child. Treacherous night, 'tis. 'Tis the devil's night, child."

He was a strange and superstitious man with a long white beard. Born in the old country, he emigrated to Boston when he was a teenager and worked as the superintendent at the Cathedral of the Holy Cross where, on display, was what was widely believed to be a fragment from the actual cross. The relic was under a glass case to which only Grandpa had the key. On holy days it would be taken out and thousands of Bostonians would wait in line to hold it, including the terminally ill and the wheelchair-bound, in hopes of a miracle. I also wanted to hold it when I was younger, and fatter, and ask Jesus for the miracle of weight loss.

"You'd be a fool to touch that piece of wood. That wood is stained with the blood of a young death," he warned. "And besides you'll grow out of the blubber, you will."

I didn't grow out of the blubber and I didn't heed Grandpa's advice so I waited in line for over two hours one Good Friday to have my moment.

Grandpa died on New Year's Eve, 1994; after locking up the church for the night he got run over by a drunken hansom cab driver and its drunken horse.

I'd never told anyone about that Good Friday for fear they might corroborate Grandpa's warning. However, the night before this Ponder

I felt the need to tell Florence. As far as I knew, Disney was a danger-ous place where curses came to pass. I needed to know what I was up against and pack, and Wayz, accordingly:

"I once held the cross of Christ," I told her. She crossed herself.

"Does that mean I'm cursed?"

She crossed herself again and fixed me a Hard Wayz. Not just any Hard Wayz but a water glass filled with Stoli, neat. She patted my head and left me with what I had dubbed *End of the World Wayz*.

*

Hey Cheese. Let's meet at Tambu Lounge. Poly. 5 pm., wrote John. *A girl should never come between us.*

I was actually enjoying a round of miniature golf at Fantasia Gardens near the fake boardwalk when I received that most wel-come message. (Is it weak or wrong to wear a golf glove when put-ting? Will have to ask my Scottish instructor when we return to the Club.) It was only around three o'clock, but I couldn't get myself to the Tambu Lounge quick enough. Was his message a concession? Had I won? Fuck crucifix curses. We'll be the three of us tonight, but with *him* as the third wheel. Handsome in defeat he'll wish us the best and hug us into the future. Every great couple has a third wheel.

Scott and Zelda had Hemingway. Tonight we'll take a famous pic-ture of the trio that we'll refer to time and again. In front of the Castle as the fireworks go off at midnight. But we'll make it black and white. Revenge against the stupid new number. A technicolored four-digit disaster. Thank you, Walt, for the Tambu Lounge, where I waited in delirious expectation for my good ol' best friend with a caffeine Wayz laced with chocolate syrup. The Tambu Lounge, where I chatted up a female Biggunz who wore suspenders covered in Disney pins.

"Some are real collector's items, like this vintage one of the Little Orange Bird," said the female Biggunz.

"I know that little fellow," I said with a twinkle in my eye.

"Isn't he just the best?"

"He's no Dole Whip with a rum topper!"

"Ahahahahahahaha."

Ah, the Tambu Lounge, where everything is funny. The Tambu Lounge, guarded by tiki statues who kill curses with fly-swatting ease. Tambu, where there's gossip in the air about tonight's luau where apple-sucking pigs are roasted in the world's largest fire pit and the poi is candied.

"I love the Tambu Lounge," I told the female Biggunz.

"They should do a pin of it," she said.

"They should do a pin of everything. Of us right now. They should commemorate our amusing bar banter, our sugary drinks, the sesame chicken you're enjoying."

"Hey, I'd trade up for *that* pin in a heartbeat," she said pulling at her suspenders.

"They should do a pin of your sweet beating heart."

"Aw."

"Screw it. I'm going to order a *real* Wayz and some pork dumplings. Ever been to Shun Lee in New York City? It's sort of how I got to this ecstatic moment. It's a long story that I thought might end sadly but I think that everything's going to be okay. Do you believe in curses?"

"Oh, sure," she said then crossed herself.

A familiar face: "I know you," it said.

"Wow, you're the boat guy, right?" I asked.

It was the boat captain who'd sailed us around EPCOT in that shiny wooden boat. His name tag read CAP.

"What a coincidence! I'm about to meet up with John. John Apple who you met that night on the boat. Seems like a million—"

"Oh, I just came from Mr. Apple," said Cap. "He's making all sorts of preparations for tonight."

"Tonight?"

"Yes, we're decking out the *Lealana*. He's being very particular, and I can't blame him. Big night for sure. He showed me that big ring of his again up close."

Fuck.

"I never do ceremonial cruises at night but like they say in that I-talian movie, he made me an offer I couldn't refuse."

"Ceremony?"

"The *Lealana* has seen her share of nuptials. I'd do anything for that old girl and she needs a new four stroke, but the Mouse is cutting back. Apple said he'd cover all the expenses, so I told him *whatever you need*."

Cap got a virgin piña colada to go.

"So romantic, getting married on a boat," said the female Biggunz. "Sorry for eavesdropping."

"Well, happy new year," said Cap and left after a two-fingered salute.

"Have any plans for tonight?" asked the female Biggunz. "Because I'm flying solo and I thought that if you were too, we could ring it in together. Maybe I'm a little tipsy but I think you're cute. I like big guys."

CHAPTER TWENTY-SIX

"What happened to your stupid white hat?" I asked John at the Tambu Lounge.

He was now hatless and in an off-white linen suit. "What hat?"

"Is that a new suit?"

"Nope."

"I thought the one from yesterday was whiter."

"You should cut back on the alcohol, my friend."

Yes, yes, but not tonight. (Wait, there was really no white hat?) I'd decided not to divulge what the boat captain had told me. I'd propose to her first. Remind her of Daddy's wishes. Remind her that she thought I was *good* in bed. A girl such as Virginia Wells will find my plastic monorail ring adorable. Quirky.

"So where are we meeting?" John asked me.

"Ten o'clock, California Grill."

"How the hell did you get a reservation on the big night?"

"I've become resourceful. Being around the Wells family does that to a man."

"Well, it's a perfect choice. You're really getting to know your way around here, Cheese."

You have no idea. I'd even made a fake reservation. Well, a real reservation. A table for three that will be occupied by just one John "Johnny Boy" Apple, while I will be engaged well before the clock strikes twelve. Maybe tomorrow he'll forgive me. Us. And he can graciously take his place as runner-up. An agreeable third wheel and dear friend to Mr. and Mrs. Murray Marks. Handsome, filthy rich, and now philanthropic, there will be more Virginias for him. For me, it's once in a lifetime. No, more than that: once in a hundred thousand lifetimes. And with his newly fashioned white-suited moral superheroism, I am quite sure a very *good* girl will find, then fill his heart.

"You're really done drinking?" I asked. "Like not even tonight?"

"Not even tonight, Cheese."

Another reason Virginia will say yes to me. She likes her champagne. Our two flutes at dinner.

"Well I guess I'm proud of you, John," I lied. Or maybe I was. I hadn't yet the courage to live a sober life. But I theorized that having Virginia would suffice for Wayz. The poets wrote that one could get drunk on love. Cheers to that, poets. (Although you probably wrote that shit when you were drunk, didn't you, poets?)

"What's their place in Savannah like?" he asked.

"Amazing."

He had that look in his dark eyes. He was there beneath the majestic trees. There with her, taking my place in the marriage cottage. Sorry, Johnny Boy, envision someplace else. Someone else. These are my fortune.

"Hey, whatever happened to your tarot card?" I asked.

He patted his chest pocket then did something sexual with his eyebrows, if that's even possible. Virginia's eyebrows are so feathery and his . . . bushy. They should never meet.

"So you still have it?" I asked.

And then came the dimples, cryptic sexy bushy-browed bastard.

*

"Wave goodbye to the people at the dock," said the fake boat captain. "'Cause it's the last time you're ever going to see them."

While I was pretty sure she was in jest, it struck a chord. It was night and I was on the Jungle Tour but was desperately anxious for my life at Fairvue as Virginia's husband to begin.

"I do though need to get back home. Savannah, Georgia," I told the fake boat captain. "Three Fairvue Lane."

(I like saying inexplicable things to strangers, but John's right, I should pare back my secret little world of thoughts and *words*. There be trouble brewin' ahead. Wait: is that from a ride? Hmm. And why not *One* Fairvue Lane? There were no other estates on the lane. Will have to ask Virginia.)

The jungle boat captain had a fresh New England college student way about her. The type of coed who might twirl a lacrosse stick through her four-year adventure up in Maine, always in the same L.L. Bean fleece. Here she wore jungle khakis and a floppy hat. Sturdily built and fast to smile, I liked her. Audrey said her name tag.

"Well, it is a jungle out there," said Audrey.

She spoke through a microphone although I was seated right next to her. "You seem wise for your years, Audrey. Will she say yes?" I asked.

She cupped the microphone. "Don't worry, we'll get you back to Adventureland in about eight minutes." (Strangers translate my nonsense into banality. A promotion).

Closing in on 7:00 p.m. and Virginia was closing in on the end of her beauty appointments that had stretched from the morning until the night. She was now in our room, which she had claimed as her own for final New Year's Eve preparations. I loved it when her girlishness prevailed.

"A girl's beauty secrets are her own," she'd said. "You go do boy stuff."

What could be more boyish than a jungle adventure in the dark of early New Year's Eve wearing a pre-tux elegant safari shirt?

Audrey, oh captain my captain, joked about water's indifference to human perspective. Behind a waterfall, tears of joy ran down my cheeks. A lifetime of sex with my peach. Walt Whitman was gay. I am not. At least not with Virginia Wells.

"The backside of water," said Audrey. Virginia Wells's backside.

"She's going to say yes, Audrey. I just know it. Her backside will say yes too."

Florence didn't permit me that position. The Chinese have a mortal fear of incontinence during physical relations. At least that was John's theory, which I accepted as fact. "Doggy style" is such a revolting name for something so lovely. So natural, that angle. At Fairvue there were countless pets that roamed freely. Beasts with perfect coats of fur. A little army of golden retrievers. A dog handler lived on property with his wife, who was also the baker. How that place smelled on Sunday mornings. Cinnamon rolls. The dogs huddled by the fireplace. It is work, observing perfection. It brings me to the brink of a headache. But I love this work. This job of mine at Fairvue, watching Virginia Wells's limbs silhouetted against the rising sun. How she stretches her arms and makes a little noise. In the distance, a horse whinnies. There's a glass of blood orange juice in my hand. Its hue is . . . *crazy*. I am smiling. The insides of blood oranges are beautiful and not of this planet. The weather here is also not of this planet: it is almost always perfect, even when it's not. At Fairvue storms aren't half-assed. Thunder is rich, louder than in New York. Much louder. The crash of God's cymbals. But you don't cover your ears nor do you rush inside. You lock arms with Virginia and stroll to the main house; the rain will wait for you. Yes, it is a job observing this way of life. In a way, observing means assuring it remains as it is. Timeless. And to use an un-classy word: *classy*. Real estate law in New York will have to wait. Forever. She will say yes. When Constance Wells passes we will move from the marriage cottage to the main house. John will visit us every summer. Dear friends sipping cocktails at dusk by the carp-filled pond where tadpoles compete with waterlilies for our silent adoration.

Uh oh, on the shore of the Nile I see a headhunter. "Say hello to Trader Sam," said Audrey.

"Hi Sam," said the passengers.

I said it too. What a queer smile on the headhunter's face. A haunted cast? Ideally more of a knowing grin.

That's right, Sam, we know the secret. Waking, then taking your young wife from behind while downstairs cinnamon rolls rise in the oven and dogs have no reason to bark.

"Y'all have a nice day," I told Audrey. That's how people spoke at the Club.

"Have a good one," she said.

I do.

*

An homage to yellow fruit. I was at something called Citricos. on the second floor of the Grand Flo. (Oh, how I love knowing Disney abbreviations. Although I took umbrage with some lout who called the Space Mountain merely *Space.* Invest in syllables during this short life.) Virginia still occupied our room. She'd apparently sniffed out her hidden BlackBerry and written me asking for a curling iron, which I'd sourced from Sandeep, the world's most resourceful man. It didn't hurt that for all of his putting up with me I'd greased his palm with two hundred-dollar bills. Butlers know how to make their palms subsume cash; by the time he thanked me the bills had disappeared. Or maybe I was seeing things again, like John's white hat. Twelve-thirty-one-nineteen-ninety-nine, and who the fuck cares if I am a little cracked? If any night is for apparitions, 'tis this.

"Fucking al Qaeda," said a man next to me reading *USA Today.* Such a fuss when that rag went full color; I for one detested the switch, just as I will detest writing 2000 on checks. Who the heck is Al Kayda?

I should know more about the world. I do pay my taxes but I don't vote. Not even for president. I am quite sure that my vote, Murray Marks's vote, does not count. I like being invisible. Uselessness is a luxury.

"Want the paper?" asked the man, who had settled his bill.

"I do," I said. "I should know more about the world."

"You should read this story. World's going to shit," he said.

"Not tonight, it's not," I answered.

"Especially tonight. They didn't program the computers right. Guess they thought we'd already be nuked by now. The machines are going to think it's 1900. Walt wasn't even born yet."

"To Walt," I said holding forth the whiskey sour I'd ordered. What a pretty color yellow.

"Yeah, well, this vacation is costing me a fortune."

This morning Virginia and I had had an odd exchange. When I awoke she was sitting up, sheets in her fists.

"Hi," I'd said.

"The man I marry I want to watch storming up the hill, the men behind him willing to die for him. Do you know a man like that, Cheese?"

I could not respond. She did kiss me softly on my lips before disappearing into the bathroom, though. Virginia had said that many of her past beaus did not make it to midnight. They started too early and were unaccustomed to poison. So she kisses lucky strangers when the year turns. Tonight she shall kiss her fiancé.

In *USA Today* on the page with the photo of the Arabic-looking guy was an advertisement.

New York's Legendary Windows on the World restaurant wishes everyone a safe and happy New Year's Eve. We'll see you next year!

Heard the food wasn't that great. People go for the view, but the halfway house at the Club after the ninth hole is on a tall hill and below you can see for acres upon acres of marshland below, untouched since its Indian inhabitants hunted black panthers with their bare hands. Plus the food is great, if you like hot dogs and Gatorade. Which I do.

All yours, wrote Virginia.

You?

The room.

Can't blame a Cheese for trying. Come with me upstairs, magical monorail plastic engagement ring. Round and round. Like a serpent who eats its own tail.

"Want the newspaper?" I asked the guy next to me.

"I don't read the news at Disney," he said.

"Well there is Al Kayda out there," I said. "It's apparently quite the story."

"Gotta get five kids and the wife to Liberty Tree Tavern before they run out of stuffing and gravy. That's the only story that matters to me."

How did this country ever win a fucking war?

Tux time!

*

Our hotel room smelled especially of her; when the wake of a girl-shower achieves the essence of freshly cut flowers, my nose is elated, there is a God, and somehow my tuxedo still fits. Oh, and it's still 1999, God damnit. (Sorry, God.) Who am I kidding, that throne room has been empty for eons. If I want holiness, my lips brush against the grain of her golden arm hair. Heaven is where it should be, on Earth.

As I fussed with my bow tie (where's dear Sandeep when you need him?), I wondered what Florence was doing tonight. I wanted to see her one last time. Perhaps apologize to her for having been a lesser version of my current sexually robust self. Over a Wayz, finish the last page and close our book. Bravely hug one another goodbye. Maybe even cry. Maybe even reveal that we are both having improved sex. Facts that will surely put an end to the sentimentality. Maybe even have one another one last time? No, too much.

These were my thoughts as I sat in our room in my tuxedo smoking one of Virginia's post-coital Parliaments. I decided to slow down on my Wayz consumption, lest I not make it to midnight.

Please do not kiss any other boy ever. Love, Cheese, I wrote. My first admission of love sealed with a Send button.

I must say there is something so incredibly satisfying about my BlackBerry's little scroll wheel. Nothing bad will befall Cheese with so much control at his fingertip. Scroll until you hit on what you want, then press and it's yours. Every time. Just like Virginia is yours. Well, mine. The walls of this oddly shaped room closing in on me, it was time to enter this famous night. I placed my recently replenished Disney Word flask in my inside breast pocket. Wasn't there a president whose flask stopped an assassin's bullet? I'm certain of it. Maybe Teddy Roosevelt? Reason number five-million-thirty-seven why Wayz are miraculous. Fear not, superstitious Grandpa from the old country, the bullet will merely make a dent, the Wayz safe inside its vessel, and the last night of the last two thousand years, bloodless.

I was back at Citrico's, the green and yellow paean to bright drinks. Earlier I'd enjoyed one of the best whiskey sours of my life. And there sat Tanya Tucker, the escort I'd kissed.

Well, she kissed me. What was her real name again? She'd told me. Something Irish. There she was, metallic red wig, miniskirt. I'd forgotten how petite she was. A tight little package. She was with a man. An old guy who wore lots of Southwestern hand jewelry. Turquoise rings and bracelets. Liver spots against that color equals the end of the line. He was puffing away on a cigar. Annoyed by life, he made quick little motions with his hand, indicating that an invisible fly that was nearby should go away.

"Hey," I said to Tanya. "Do you, um, remember me?"

"Hi there," she said.

The man, her *date* I presumed, shook his head, mumbled something, flicked his wrist again, shooing away the fly.

"You're Tanya, right?"

"I am," she said.

"We—"

"This is my boyfriend, Fred. Fred Astaire."

Wow, even the Johns have fake names. I should have affected one. Fred Flinstone would have suited me. I remember she said that New Year's Eve was the biggest night for an escort and that after tonight she was off on a Ponder around the world that would end in . . . Australia?

"Are you still going to Australia?"

"That will be my final stop. In 2003, March. It's their fall. I packed my little red sweater this morning."

"I'll miss you, babe," said Fred Astaire. "I really will."

"Well, we have tonight," she said.

"You carrying a piece?" he asked me.

"What?"

"In your pocket there, it bulges out like a piece. You know, a gun."

"Fred used to work for the government," said Tanya.

This will be her last *trick*; thank God for her and her little red sweater.

"No it's actually my flask," I said and showed it to the wrist flicker. "Did you know it saved Teddy Roosevelt's life?"

"It wasn't a flask that saved Roosevelt. It was his speech. It was thick. The bullet couldn't go through."

"Really? I could have sworn it was a flask."

"You swore wrong, okay?"

He was getting agitated. Tanya had to hold his liver-spotted fidgety hand.

"Kids don't know their history," he said. "It was his speech and eyeglasses case that stopped the bullet. Instead of messing around with ghosts and pirates, visit the Hall of Presidents. Only ride worth a god-damn in this place. Do you even know the dates of the Civil War?"

"Now, Fred—"

"No, Tanya. I'm putting my foot down. Do you know the dates of the most important event in the history of our country, son?"

Shit, I didn't know the answer. And he was right, I should know. I wondered if John knew, if even Virginia knew. My parents surely knew. That's just it: our generation can sleep at night knowing our parents are in possession of the important dates. The *moral* knowledge. But this laziness will surely come to bite us on our Gen X asses, for our parents are not eternal.

"I don't know the dates of the Civil War," I said. "And frankly, I'm ashamed."

"Come here," said Fred.

Now he stood before me, arms outstretched. I rose and he hugged me.

"You're an honest man, and I respect that. April 12, 1861 to April 9, 1865. You'll never forget it. Okay Tanya, now let's go to the room and fuck."

CHAPTER TWENTY-SEVEN

STILL AT CITRICO'S. (WHO doesn't love the chroma of Floridian fruits? Colors that combine to equal my future wife's eyes), a turn of events.

We're meeting John at California Grill at 10, wrote Virginia.

I know, I made a reservation, I lied.

He double-checked and there was no res, so he made one for us. Then to Cinderella's Castle to get a good spot.

He probably canceled mine and replaced it with his own. John Apple was nothing if not thorough. Still, I had time to get to her first. Propose my heart out, monorail ring snug and safe on the tip of my pink pinkie.

I'll be right up. I want to talk with you! I wrote. *Really exciting news for us!*

Okay!

I love her exclamation marks. More ebullient than most. At least her handwritten ones. Screw it, her BlackBerry ones too. Girls such as Virginia can grant machines a romantic soul.

"Oh, hey!" said a little person when I was just about to order a final pre-proposal whiskey sour. (Damn you Cítricos, but this will be my last until midnight. Deal? Deal.)

"Hi," I said. "Oh, it's you, um—"

"Yeah, Wayne," he said, cheerily. "Rhymes with Wayz. *Short Wayz*."

"No, I never said—"

"I know, I know. It *was* Wayz, right? Ha! *Wayz*. Kind of catchy. Look, I'm sorry about what happened, just caught me on a bad day. How about if I buy you a *Wayz*? What do you say?"

"Really not necessary."

"You'd be helping a little guy out. I have a guilty conscience. So what are you going to have?"

Then it hit me. In order to be the man, Virginia's man, who could lead men in battle, up the hill, I needed to change. To, well, de-Cheeseball myself. Sub out Wayz for bravery. Become an abstemious hero. Grow the fuck up before midnight. Pick myself up by the boot straps, perform a miraculous somersault right here on this barstool, and land as a virtuous man. A man who would order: "You know what, Wayne? I'll have a club soda lime."

Did you know John donated substantial money to the Make-A-Wish Foundation? wrote Virginia.

Distracted by this bit of unwelcome Virginia knowledge, I almost didn't notice Wayne handling my drink, his little hand over my non-Wayz, his fingers a spider scurrying in place.

Something granular in the air? Nah, all the crazy people who used to work here are still supposed to seem like they are applying pixie dust, and my club soda appeared wonderfully pure.

"Well, have a magical day," he said. "Hi ho, hi ho, it's off to work we go."

Being a dwarf here (the eighth one?) mustn't be easy. Well, bottoms up. To you, Hummingbird. I'm sorry about the poop with which you had to contend. I hope that your size elicited great sympathy and then great housekeeping gratuities. You can use the extra savings to woo, well, taller women. You weren't at all a bad-looking guy. Your eyes were two different colors, like David Bowie's. Hey, Wayne: why are you wearing Johnny Boy's silly white hat? There was no hat, John had said. And with that vision, blackness. Only David Bowie's spaceman persona ascending into a starless night sky, his blue and green eyes both growing yellow. Vomitous yellow. Hey David Bowie, there is no life on Mars. It too has turned yellow, for the universe is lit only by bile. A hummingbird flies into my ear; its razor sharp beak spears my brain tissue.

*

I was on a hospital bed, metal probes attached to my naked chest and an IV in my arm. Where the needle had stuck was discolored all shades of periwinkle. In the movies when a patient wakes from blackness, they rip off the wires and tubes, as there is no time to waste and urgent work to be done. Then a nurse says: "I'm sorry, sir, we need you to stay where you are."

Which is what this one said.

"What happened?" I asked. She was starting to replace what I'd removed. "Did I drink *that* much? But I'm reformed. I'm a club soda man. I lead men in battle up—"

"Rohypnol," she said. "We had two others today."

Roofied at Disney. That little fucker. And my BlackBerry was all but dead. 1% it said.

"What time is it?"

"It's almost eleven."

"Fuck."

I lurched upright. Unwise. Too fast, then turned to retch yellow into a metal basin that was full of yellow.

"Sir, you should really *really* lie back—"

"That's my last puke. I can tell. Humans know when it's their last puke."

I didn't bother to put on my tux shirt and studs, just gathered my belongings and left. My mind wasn't right. And my inner electricity was hyper, firing. One moment I shivered and the next sweated. What an evil little man to turn me into this. And why do it to two others as well? Did they also utilize an annoying parlance that brought him back to high school bullies? (We all must pay for the bullied childhoods of strangers.) Brought him back to the toilet bowls he was paid to clean? The tarry stools of Biggunz stubborn on the side of the porcelain.

John and I are at Cali Grill. This last and only message was sent at exactly 10:00. Her punctual reminder gave me pause for hope. Before I could write her back, the little machine faded and died.

"Humans know when it's their last puke," I told the taxi driver.

"You need me to pull over?"

"No sir! To the Magical Kingdom! It's where they'll be!"

Weird: I felt oddly powerful. Something akin to 'roid rage, but there was also the torpor that comes with fever. And the one sensation would live above the other for a moment, then they would switch floors. An unsustainable duplex for this body but if I could just get to her in time. Propose then pass out. She'll ride in the ambulance with me back to the ER, engaged. (Please body cursed with mal electricity, please stop jerking this way and that. I will require bodily equanimity when I take a knee.) At the ER Virginia will help the nurse with the probes on my robust Civil War colonel chest; her touch will be my smelling salts. Like after John got knocked out by that Irish boxer. He will get knocked out by another Irishman tonight. Figuratively, of course. (I could never hurt my hero.) Shit, another wave of hot steaming bodily ennui. I wonder if any rides are medicinal? No, only Virginia Wells, the ride of my life. (Although John did say that there were magic carpets on which wishes were granted but only if a camel spat on you? Spit away: I wish to have back control of my central nervous system.)

*

I couldn't shake these shakes. Outwardly, I suppose I looked somewhat normal, the occasional twitch. Then the occasional forehead shiny with sweat. Inside, however, I was rattled. I was on the monorail debating something drastic if not seriously dangerous. Before being poisoned, I'd filled my flask for New Year's Eve with Hawaiian Punch and 100 proof Stolichnaya Blue Label. I decided it could be a Hail Mary antidote to how I'd been snake bit. Did it make any scientific sense? Probably not. But I just needed to somehow be internally settled. *Normal* if only for an hour in order to pop the question. Pop it with confidence and maybe even some optimism. John once said that confidence was a self-generated smell. Girls were drawn to it like sharks to blood. My nose agreed, at least with Johnny Boy's never-say-die pheromones. My pheromones? Who knew, but they probably now smelled more like bloodstream spurned whiskey than *I smell a Yes, darlin'.*

Could my flask contents reverse the curse? No, Cheese. No more drinks. Tighten this shit up, as she had advised.

"Got big plans for tonight?" asked an older gentleman, smiling for a fun answer. I locked eyes with him. I needed his humanity. But what of *my* humanity? Exit the Wayz circus. Become a latter-life *man*. A sober man with steady hands. Fuck you, flask. Fuck you too, roofie dwarf. I took a deep breath and willed myself normal.

"Well, sir," I told the old man, marveling at my suddenly steady hands, "I'm going to ask for my girlfriend's hand. Hers never trembles and neither does mine."

"Congratulations," he said.

He was wearing an interesting shirt. A tuxedo shirt. On board I'd now seen three others wearing the same. Not a formal shirt with a collar such as my white Armani blouse, which was of course back on my person, but of the novelty T-shirt variety with a tuxedo image printed on the front.

"Do *you* have any big plans?" I asked, overjoyed that my electric grid was stabilizing by the moment.

"Meeting up with all the other Masons. Think there might be over a thousand of us tonight. For a second I thought you might be a Freemason but then I realized you were wearing a real tux, not one of our one-pieces. Eyes aren't what they used to be."

Freemasons, shit. Aren't those medieval wannabes only a few degrees removed from Dungeons & Dragons?

"Tell you what," said the man. "Here's a Mason's coin for you. Consider it an engagement gift."

"Thanks," I said. On the coin was all sorts of weird cyclops shit. Were the Masons sinister? This one seemed nice enough but I'd have to be vigilant tonight. Protect Virginia from the cult of the faux tuxes as only I can. Murray Marks, anti-Wayz hero.

Wait: what happens if my new virtue wears off? This place is dominated by Cinderella mythology. Nothing good lasts forever. Balls (I promise I'll never use it as a verb again), balls end and not everyone leaves behind a slipper. I bet Cinderella left it on purpose. Like I always say, girls are smarter, they know precisely how to get their prince.

*

I could tell that the great majority of the hordes were already gathered in and about the Castle from where the fireworks would be launched, but their numbers bled all the way down the main street almost to the entrance. The place was packed and there didn't seem to be a clear conveyance to the Castle's entrance where, just inside, at least according to Virginia, was an arched thruway covered with mosaics telling Cinderella's story.

"I want to huddle in there," Virginia had said. "Hear the fireworks echo and boom in that tunnel and watch the lights reflected off all those pretty stones."

So many damn barricades everywhere. And so many Biggunz, many of them Freemasons. As I made my way, a gentleman wearing knickers was handing out caramel apples. Wasn't that the fruit of John's tragic youth that had helped produce his first mature tear on that first Virginia Wells day?

"Can you believe 1899 is drawing to a close in, well . . . " The apple vendor produced a pocket watch. "All of half an hour? Who knows what the 1900s will bring but I sure think it will be as delicious as your apple."

I wanted to tell this outcast from the Circle of Progress: Two world wars and the Holocaust but Virginia Wells will be born and so will I, technically. How the fuck to get to her. I looked at my apple, blamed it for the human logjam, and bit it like an animal.

"Howdy, young fellow," said an old-timer in a top hat wearing a patriotic sash across his torso that read MAYOR.

"How's that apple treating you?" he asked.

He seemed official enough, perhaps he could hook me up with a flying car. This was Disney, after all.

"I need to get to the Castle but everything's blocked off. If I was granted one wish in life it would be to get there before midnight."

"Yes sir, it is getting close to the witching hour," said the mayor. "And I can see the worry in your face, but don't fret. Mayor Weaver will get you there without a hitch."

"Are you really a mayor? I mean have you the authority?"

"Well, it says so right here, but between you and me I'm seeking reelection so go pull the leaver and vote for Weaver! Ever hear of the Utilidor? Walt's very own idea. In Disneyland, which was of course the original park, he once saw a cast member dressed as a cowboy walking through Tomorrowland and it bothered him like nobody's business, so he built this here park above a vast series of tunnels so that cast members could appear and reappear at the right spots. Follow me young fellow. You're in for a treat."

He hiked up his trousers, revealing sock garters.

"Walt himself inspired me to invest in these. Saggy socks bothered him like nobody's business."

Only once in my life had I removed my socks for sex, and that was last night with Virginia. Actually she removed mine and then her own. How I kissed her polished toes. Then they were red and tonight black, she'd written me. Along with her fingernails. I'd seen them polished black before. Very few girls can pull off wearing black polish. They come across as angry, rebellious, *Goth*. On Virginia they were purely mysterious, somehow capturing the scant light of tonight's crescent moon.

"Well, here we go," said the mayor. "Just no pictures allowed."

We opened a fake door next to a penny arcade and then descended stairs. Many stairs, alighting in a tunnel bustling with activity. Puppets driving golf carts. Over the speakers Sarah McLachlan's gloomy ballad "I Will Remember You." You'd think they'd play happy Disney tunes. Sad songs shouldn't exist. Why flasks should, but mine was forever off limits. Come on, Cheese, believe in earned happiness. Endure the song in silence. Silence can be the new Wayz. No, the new *way*. Overhead were huge pipes full of something whooshing by.

"That's our trash system," said the mayor.

He tipped his hat to one and all. A golf cart would beep and we'd move to the side. We passed a barber shop, a pharmacy, a snack bar. The place smelled so odd: sterile, yet also pungent with a distant meal. Cafeteria smells can sink the spirit. My public school smelled similarly in September. Fresh paint and something over-braised. Odors aside, this place was impressive. I could see myself working here. Getting buzzed on Diet Cokes at the snack bar, then popping out in a land and making some kid happy. I couldn't dress as a puppet because then I'd be sweat-balled. I mean sweaty.

"Do you like working here?" I asked the mayor.

"The privilege of a lifetime."

I could learn to candy apples. Mine shone with perfection. So did the sun in the Savannah morning. The Savannah sun that had birthed the light freckles that dotted my Virginia. Who am I kidding, the work of my life is that girl.

"I love love," I told the mayor.

"That's the spirit! Well, we've made it all the way to Fantasyland. You just need to go through that door and up the stairs and you'll be right where you need to be."

"Thank you," I said.

He tipped his hat, bowed a mayoral bow, and walked back whence he came. In a hero's journey there are characters like the mayor who serve the sole purpose of delivering the hero to his fate. You never hear from the mayor again. But as Sarah woefully sings, "I will remember you."

And I will remember him. Not tonight and not tomorrow but one night at Fairvue in front of that fireplace like a cathedral's bay altar where the dogs don't bark.

"The lovely old man who showed me the way to you. Guided me so gently, his hand on the small of my tuxedoed back. We'll never see him again, but sentimentality is for the lonely and we have each other, Virginia."

CHAPTER TWENTY-EIGHT

NEAR THE CASTLE THEY were dispensing free cookies and hot cocoa. Noisemakers and hats. Year 2000 eyeglasses. And the world's largest confetti ball (it's an actual ball) that was to explode at midnight, raining down paper and candy, smothering the kingdom in glitter, streamers, and chocolate mouse faces. Ten thousand individually wrapped Mickeys. The Biggunz brought buckets.

Virginia had mentioned spending tomorrow by the pool. She was melancholy about it. Rare for her.

"I'll rent a cabana," she'd said. "I'll do nothing."

"We could—"

"There's nothing wrong with doing nothing. There's something honest about it, but it's melancholic for sure. Like being in a prison, I'd imagine. Sometimes it's good to build yourself a prison. Then step right inside. It might be the only thing that makes Father Time smile."

Father Time, the warden of us all. Old, bearded warden with Death's scythe and a rather enormous pocket watch. That smile would be a smug one for sure, if not positively sardonic. Our tickets home were for January 2. I'd mentioned that to her but all she did was hunch her shoulders. January 2: a shoulder-hunching day for sure, but not for the recently engaged.

"What time is it?" I asked the backs of men.

"Getting close," was the chorus.

Shit, the Rohypnol was doubling down and my body felt especially not my own. And then there were the mazes of iron fencing between me and the entrance to the Castle. Plus they'd darkened the place in preparation for the fireworks. I was bumping into iron or flesh.

"How do I get to the mosaics?" I asked faceless men. "How do I get inside the Castle?"

"You won't be able to see anything from inside there," they warned.

"I know."

"Must be gun shy," they said of me.

"Maybe he's a veteran," they surmised. "Seen lots of Desert Storm folks 'round here."

"Uh-huh," they said. "That explains it."

"He should probably head towards the speedway," they said.

"Agreed," they said.

I was being spoken of in the dark, my future being planned by good-natured American strangers.

"Which way?" (Was I yelling? Yes).

"Okay, see that talking garbage can?" they asked.

"What? No!"

"The Castle's right here, but getting inside is a whole other story."

"Then tell me the fucking story. I mean . . . *please*."

"Okay, make your first right towards the speedway, can't miss it cuz of the gasoline smell, then circle round back the Castle, all the way around. Take the first bridge on your left, it'll be the one where all the waterfowl stay beneath. Geese as white as the lord's beard. If you want to make it by midnight, you should probably run. And thank you for your service."

I cannot remember the last time in my life that I ran. Dodgeball in eighth grade? I ran blindly, knocking over popcorn, cookies. Children?

I couldn't focus on faces. I couldn't really see anything. Everything whirring by in the staged darkness. I couldn't tell a Biggunz from a baby stroller from a puppet. No sense of the passing of time but there weren't yet spent fireworks in the air, which boded well. I stopped momentarily, panting in a place that stunk of sweet benzine. Were those fake cars? Good, the racetrack! Despite the acute pain of a side stitch, and my limbs full-on puppeteer'd by the Hummingbird's poison, I continued to run. A beast in black tie. I prayed again to Walt that the Castle's elusive entrance would soon be before me. And that Virginia would still be there. Safe. Single. Unmolested. What had Virginia said about the arrogance of prayer? Florence attended church a few Sundays throughout the year; I never thought of joining her and only asked her why once.

"Because God exists," she'd said.

"I hope so."

"Hope won't suffice; you have to earn His existence, Murray, or else there's evil."

Even for her, she was all business on those Sundays. I never drank in front of her those long afternoons while she sat on the couch contemplating the morning's sermon. I must admit she'd awaken Monday morning radiant and new. While I'd be hungover after meeting up with John at Shun Lee, where we'd laud our atheism and cackle with the bar's red-eyed monkeys above our cocksure heads. Were *we* evil? You know, I *did* give to charity once. Seeing-eye dogs. They touched me. *They* did, but not their owners.

*

White as the lord's beard. I could see the fowl they'd spoken of. Those I could see, and I had the momentary clarity of mind to find them beautiful and pure. The only things truly visible tonight. Darkness didn't stand a chance. That white feathers could overcome darkness. Was this what John was pretending to be? Was this proof of Florence's God?

All these thoughts while racing over the bridge. Acknowledging beauty while in pain. Now that's virtue.

After the bridge, a sea of fake tuxedo T-shirts. Masons. "Please what time is it?" I asked one of them.

"My watch says that we have two minutes, but his says two and a half. He has a Timex and I have Mickey. Mickey's hands don't lie," he said.

I could see where I needed to go, where the entrance was and pre-sumably where she would be. Only twenty feet away. Every inch spoken for. These people do not budge. Still I tried to make my way, apologizing profusely for my person's interactions with their blubber. Progress was slow. Calling out would be fruitless. What a din.

"Sorry. Sorry. Sorry. Sorry," I repeated, fitting into humanity-crevices where my person had no business.

"Sixty seconds," someone called out.

There was a celebrity who started narrating the event via multiple loudspeakers the size of small trucks. The world had never been so loud.

"I'm scared, I'm scared," said Robin Williams, annoyingly stridently. "The end is nigh. Get ye to the ATM machine. Oh look: it's Dick Clark French-kissing Minnie. Always fancied him a goofy man . . ."

A chocolate chip cookie fell into in my hand. What heavens here tonight.

Fifty-five, fifty-four . . .

The feature event of my school's annual spring field day was a volleyball match between the juniors and the seniors. We had a somewhat sadistic gym teacher named Mr. Adams who dictated that the event should be shirts versus skins; the juniors to play shirtless. My junior year I pretended to be sick on that May morning to avoid the embarrassment of revealing my girlish tits. As I cowered in bed that morning, my mother spoke words to me that I will never forget.

"Murray, your greatest life is on the other side of fear."

Tonight, I felt I'd finally made it to that side. John's side. Where protagonists stay. I could smell her. Only her. Masons in their fake tux tees were like football linemen; they were all that stood between us. They were at the last barricade, gawking up at the Castle spires, waiting for them to be lit by the first fake war of the twenty-first century. I appreciated that the backs of the tuxedo shirts depicted vents, just like on mine. Larger people need them; corpulence requires jacket vents. I took a deep breath, then knocked on one of their backs as one might a long-lost family member's front door.

Forty-nine, forty-eight.

"I'm so sorry but I just need to sneak by here."

"We've been lined up for this spot since early in the day, partner," said a thickest Freemason.

"No, I just want to go inside the Castle. I won't take up your space, um, partner."

"Like I said partner, we've been lined up all day so—"

In order to communicate one had to yell or lip-read. "Wait, you haven't seen this!" I yelled in his ear.

I produced the Masonic coin I'd been given on the monorail. It made him smile. He showed it to his fellow linemen.

"You can stand with us, partner!" he yelled.

"No, I just want to go inside!"

"You won't be able to see anything from in there!"

My voice hoarse and my brain having relinquished all control to my liver (an angriest organ hell bent on retribution after ten years of 100-wayz-weeks), all I could manage was a nod. I mouthed, "I know."

"Suit yourself," they said.

Then four of them lifted me up from either arm like a Ziegfeld Folly, placing me down on the other side of the barricade. I turned to thank them but they'd resumed their neck-craning.

Twenty-five, twenty-four.

From where I stood before the corbeled arch I could not see into the dark innards of the Castle. I could not see her. (For that I would need the fireworks.) In the history of time how many men have walked under a corbeled arch to become a future king? I decided that I was going to become part of that great tradition.

But this is not a real corbeled arch, Cheese.

It is because she's in there.

How do you know, Cheese?

Because I can smell her.

It could be *Cinderella's* scent, Cheese.

She doesn't exist.

What's with your fast twitch muscles? You're embarrassing us, Cheese.

No I'm not.

You look as though you're doing the Robot, Cheese.

Stop calling me that.

It's who we are. Cheese.

*

The sound of a flask rattling about trompe l'oeil cobblestones. Painted to be uneven, my flask was in on the effect. How did it get away from me? How did I get away from standing? (I am to be The Falling Man.) But tonight I find myself already on the ground, on my tummy, a sniper in the bush. (Mental note to tell one of the Mouseketeers (wait, Imagineers?) about adding a Tet Offensive scene to the Jungle Boat.) Now the countdown was in single digits. To my ears the voice submarine. A rare comfort. A child beneath bath waters. I had only enough energy to propose marriage.

Four words. Nothing more. Adrenaline was not an option.

Four, three.

Yeah, yeah. Let them run out the clock. I remember Larry Bird in 1984, Game 7 against the Lakers. Seconds left, their lead insurmountable, he dribbled the ball slowly, assuredly, as the clock ran down to zero. All the Lakers could do was put their hands on their hips. How triumphantly did Larry hurl the ball into the rafters. *We won.* That was his proposal. And here comes mine.

Two, one.

*

Disney doesn't fuck around with lumens. The first bomb showed me Virginia's yellow strapless dress. (Everything's yellow.) Hair worn up, curls cascading. Her hands were over her mouth and she was shaking her head. I could only focus on her. In the brief dark before they dropped Nagasaki, I coerced my monorail engagement ring from my all but numb little finger, transferring it expertly into my fist. Propped up on my elbows. Now if I can just stand, brush myself off, get to that dress. I sighed. Oh how I know that canary yellow dress. This must be what it's like to see your wife on TV at the Oscars. They can look, but you know. *You know.* Late that Oscar night, that dress gets stepped out of quicker than you can say *no panty lines* and is discarded bedside, lifeless yellow. And here's a little secret for you, there's also no bra. Sequins are expertly placed so that what is mine can never be yours. Hiroshima was the best bomb. The second one was less bright but it showed me another. Him, kneeling. Oh, *now* I could smell him. My roofie sweat had cooled; my pheromone swagger over. Only his hung in the air. I suppose that for a few moments my spice challenged his, and we were equally alluring. Not any more. For in the jungle of the new millennium he exuded the dominant musk. Why the breatsplates of kings show lions. Time for a Disney ex machina:

An errant firecracker nails him in the head. Dead.

Minnie Mouse herself intercedes with the engagement and slaps him in the face for proposing to another man's girl. White suit, sorry, off-white suit my ass.

In fact Minnie will rip the mask off his Peter Panian face exposing Hook. Chin, nose, warts. She'll gasp in horror, then run to me.

Fireworks turned the couple into stop action. How her head-shaking went from side-to-side to up-and-down. Up and down. How her hands left her mouth and found his hands. She helped him to his feet. Stop action makes it worse. It speeds things up. Makes things seem inevitable, the story written. Diamond ring slipped on finger. Stop. Embrace. Stop. Kiss. Stop. Hand-in-hand they exited, their backs to me. Stop. Over his shoulder, he threw a Chinese Star at me. No, a tarot card. It settled, displacing glitter. From me, it was her body's length. (Five feet nine and one-half inches. Love knows this ruler.) Then they were gone. I missed their movie. Without them it was just flickering light, like the end of a reel, the scratchy nonsense before oblivion.

Maybe one day someone will find my plastic monorail engagement ring and use it for the good of their heart. For now I tossed it towards the Prince of Cups. With some skill, too. (At Fairvue we played lawn games.)

Card and ring. What a fucking time capsule. Oh, and nearby the flask.

"Hello?" someone called out.

"Hi," I whispered as if it were her.

"Hey, partner?"

"Hi," I whispered in her ear. "Hi, my Virginia."

I shall never see either of them again. They will embark on their own history, starting now. Next summer I will be invited to their wedding but will not attend. They will register for a beautiful blue bowl from Tiffany's that I will gift them. They will place it in their foyer. For M&M's. It will always be full of the candy. Someone will replenish it for them. They will never comment about the bowl, just that they never eat the M&M's. They will prioritize health. Dully. And after such long lives, when they pass away, the blue bowl will be snatched up by their granddaughter who will scratch the surface with her change and keys. She will never wonder who paid the $389 for the blue bowl. No one will wonder about anything. No need. For as Virginia noted, eventually everything will happen.

"You gonna be okay, partner?" a generous voice asked of me.

I wanted to respond to the man, I really did, but there was literally no time left in the world to ponder.

ABOUT THE AUTHOR

DANIEL ROBERTS'S DEBUT NOVEL *Bar Maid* was a *USA Today* bestseller. Prior to becoming an author, he wrote plays: *Haunted House*, which the *New York Times* called "Sparklingly original with characters that stick;" and *Brando*, of which *Time Out New York* wrote, "An impressive piece of writing recalling Edward Albee or John Guare." Vocationally, Roberts works as a private investor and venture capitalist in New York City, where he lives with his young daughter, whose first ride was Peter Pan's Flight.